DEADLY RECKONING

A Mining City Mystery

Marian Jensen

www.miningcitymysteries.com

Dedication

To Butte, "the most unplastic place in America,"
and what's left of the Wild West

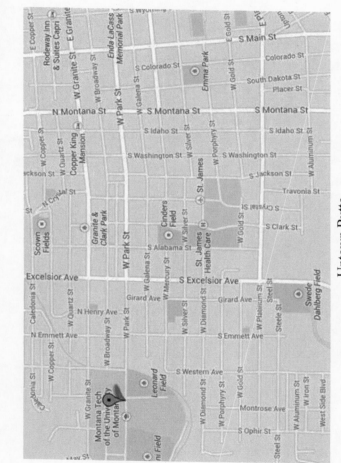

Uptown Butte

Chapter 1

When Chance Dawson saw the Cessna go down, he thought he was hallucinating. Maybe if the street hadn't been empty, he could have asked someone, "Did you see that? That plane disappeared from the horizon."

But it was Labor Day weekend, which in Butte, Montana, translated into the last decent opportunity to get out of town before the cold nights put an end to the short summer. The town was deserted.

He had taken to the road on his aging Bianchi alone as the sun peeked over the East Ridge, the temperature a balmy thirty-eight degrees. Adrienne had snuggled under the covers, and begged off. "You are a handsome rogue," she said when he had tickled her feet. Kissing her all the way up her spine, he declared that her years in California had softened her. Then he ventured out for the twelve-mile ride around the town's perimeter unaccompanied.

His chain busted at the top of Park Street, which was where he had propped his bicycle in front of the Marcus Daly statue, a tribute to the Copper King's long lost mining empire. He had begun to rummage for his chain tool when the drone of a plane in the distance distracted him, a single engine Cessna making a wide circle above Uptown. He recognized most of the local aircraft, but this one he didn't know. Some out-of-towner had stopped to refuel in Butte probably, and then do a little low-level sightseeing before continuing its journey.

Maybe he would go flying later himself, he had thought. For sure, his bike ride was over. The chain tool was missing in action.

Across the skyline, he had caught another glimpse of the Cessna just north of the Mother Lode Theater. The plane had seemed suspended in air— like the miniature models from the numerous bedroom ceilings of his childhood. Then with a sudden dip of the wing, the Cessna had careened downward and disappeared as quickly as a bleep on a radar screen.

The faint wail of a siren interrupted his attempt to order events. He focused his attention on the direction of the unfolding emergency. Then he broke into a trot eastward down Park Street, propelled by a mixture of apprehension and excitement. The anxiety of what every pilot had imagined consciously or in his nightmares—crashing his plane—gripped him. What if someone he knew was in that plane? What if it *had* come down hard?

Another siren joined the first, and Chance looked around to see if anybody could give him a lift. Not a single car went by. Park Street might as well be in a ghost town.

He reached the Islamic Center, an adobe duplex recently acquired by the college's Arabic student group, and boosted the disabled bicycle over the wrought-iron fence that fronted the house, and tossed his helmet down next to it. He grabbed his digital camera from the seat bag and tried not to think of himself as an ambulance chaser as he raced down three long blocks of Park and turned south on Excelsior.

His thoughts were already at the crash scene, not on the best route to get there—or where exactly "there" was. He turned east again onto Mercury, his heart thumping as he tried to figure out where the plane would have come down.

He had heard nothing that sounded like he thought a plane crash should sound. Maybe the pilot had been able to ditch safely after all. He could have steered the plane down onto Washington or maybe Idaho Street. Either would provide a wide enough straightaway for a small plane to land—provided, of course, no unsuspecting traffic got in its way, and the pilot had the skill to maneuver the downward slope and stay under the utility wires.

Mercury Street opened up into Chester Steele Park, and Chance welcomed the flat ball field. A gust of wind cooled his clammy cycling jersey as he ran diagonally across the outfield and then east again up Silver Street. The terrain rose in front of him but he ran easily, the upper floors of St. James Hospital visible to his right. At least if anyone was hurt, the emergency room was nearby.

He crested the block, lined with aging miners' cottages and bungalows, as a fire engine sped by, heading south. Chance turned in the same direction, but didn't have to go far.

A half block beyond, at the corner of Washington and Porphyry, the nightmare became reality. Regal with its red and gold trim, a shiny Cessna 180 rested upright, its nose buried in the splintered siding of a small, square house. The sight of the crash was surreal—like a cow atop a barn roof, or a pickup poking halfway through a billboard.

Chance doubled over with his hands on his knees. His chest heaved as he willed himself to catch his breath after what seemed like a mile-long sprint.

"If a plane crashes into your house, you gotta wonder if the good Lord is trying to tell you something," a man standing nearby muttered. The woman next to him hovered with her hand to her mouth, her eyes tense with fear as she watched the police and other emergency workers moving back and forth around the wreckage.

The Cessna's white fuselage with its high wings jutting out from the clapboard dwelling was a relief to Chance. A small plane's gas tanks rest in the wings which, had they been connected to the underside of the fuselage like some models, might have split open. Spilling fuel across its path, the inevitable explosion could have engulfed half a dozen nearby homes with flames by now.

Chance maneuvered cautiously toward the yellow emergency tape that already circled the house and the adjacent, vacant corner lot. Walking toward the barricade, he shuddered to see the track of the tail dragger—the plane's back wheel—which had snagged a roll of chain-link fencing and pulled it across the lot.

His stomach became queasy thinking about the pilot's reaction in those last few seconds. Had he tried to catch that fencing? Quick thinking if he had. The drag had probably helped to slow the plane and lessen its impact. It was possible, if not slightly miraculous, if no one had gotten hurt after all.

He turned and scanned the skyline to the north, looking back at the dome of the synagogue, the spire of St. Patrick's and the Mother Lode Theater, and shook his head in amazement that the plane had missed all three.

The Cessna probably needed about five or six hundred feet to land on flat ground. With the gentle incline of Washington Street, the plane would have needed twice, three times as much landing distance, depending on the airspeed when it came down. If the pilot lived to tell this one, he might want to contact *Ripley's Believe It or Not.*

Chance tried to imagine what he might have done in his own plane, a smaller Cessna 152. A, if he had sensed even the slightest possible problem, he would have turned the plane toward the sprawling open space that surrounds Butte. Hell, anything west of where they stood now was wide-open along the interstate toward Rocker. Novice fliers always practiced there to avoid potential disasters involving any structures, let alone houses and their occupants.

And B, if he thought he was going down so fast he might have to ditch, he could have at least tried to land on Park Street, the boulevard that ran east to west. Even Granite could have worked. Both had level stretches and were much wider. And on a Sunday morning, the traffic would have been light. Not that it would have been that simple, or that he would actually have been able to pull off such a landing. The utility wires and the traffic lights would have been damn tricky, but at least you would have flat ground.

An older couple stood on the steps of their house across the street, the man with his arm around his wife's shoulders. She hugged herself tightly, as though trying to contain her trembling. "Dear God, it could have been our house," she said.

Chance asked if he could stand on the bumper of the pickup parked in front of their house to get another angle of the scene. Even if the *Mining City Messenger* didn't run gore on the front page, they would be hard-pressed to deny the crash was newsworthy.

Chance lined up a photograph, wondering where the plane had come from. What was it doing flying that low over uptown Butte anyway, especially if it had just taken off from the airport? It had gotten into some kind of trouble that was for sure, but how? He scanned the handful of spectators for possible witnesses.

"Did you see the crash?" Chance asked a trio of kids standing just beyond the wooden horse barriers the cops had set up.

"We were walking home from Mass," a redheaded ten-year-old said, standing on his tiptoes to take in as much of the scene as he could. "You should have heard it—kaboom! Mom says the Lord looks after the ones that look after themselves. Think it's going to explode?" the kid asked, his voice ripe with anticipation as Chance moved away.

Still no sign of who was in the plane, although Chance could see a cluster of uniforms wading through the debris of house siding and twisted pieces of gutter. He could see now that the bottom half of the house was brick, which explained why the whole side of the wall hadn't collapsed.

For once, he wished he had carried his cell phone on his bike ride. He hated talking on the phone, although he had to admit they could be damned handy. He could already be making calls to find out who owned the plane.

Silver Bow Aviation was like a home away from home. Tyler Fitzgerald, who managed the place, might even know the plane's owner, especially if the Cessna had stopped to refuel. If Tyler didn't know, his mechanic, Kev, might have helped them gas up. He usually subbed as lineman on the weekends to accommodate the occasional weekend flyer who might want to fuel up.

Either way, Chance would find out. He took a picture of the tail number, still visible even though the cockpit and most of the fuselage lay hidden in a six-foot hedge of lilac bushes next to the house. He scoped the scene for the best shot of both the house and the wrecked plane so bizarrely joined—like Siamese twins of different species.

He couldn't help feeling the excitement the story would generate, especially if he could get a line on the plane's owner, who hopefully had survived the landing.

"Mom says maybe Mr. Mandic should have been at church too."

Chance smiled at the boy who was now following him. He was most likely a Tutty—a family on the west side who had been supplying

Butte with redheads for generations. He made a mental note of the name "Mandic" and wondered if the guy had the misfortune to be at home when the plane dropped from the sky, and whether he would end up a victim or a witness. "Who's Mr. Mandic?" Chance asked.

The boy shrugged. "He likes motorcycles."

Chance smiled to himself. Boys and their toys, his sister would say.

"I seen it. I seen it all," said a voice from behind, and Chance turned to see Ozzy Fentner.

"Hey, Ozzy," Chance said. A wiry man of indeterminate age, Ozzy had been around Butte for as long as Chance could remember. When Ozzy was sober, he worked as a swamper—a Butte euphemism, or as Chance liked to call it, a Buphemism for one who cleans up the swill left at the end of the night in any one of Butte's countless bars. The rest of the time Ozzy seemed to wander the streets, usually cradling a forty ouncer of Colt 41.

"What you doing up this early?" Chance asked with a wry smile. "It's not even noon."

Ozzy's shabby flannel shirt and dusty, worn jeans could well have been slept in, but he looked distinctly awake. "Cleaning up over at the Hoist House," he said. "I come outside to dump the trash and heard the plane real close, you know. Didn't seem right."

The Hoist House was at the corner of Galena and Montana, only three blocks north. "Engine trouble?" Chance asked, again trying to piece together how the accident might have happened.

"No sputtering or smoke or nothing. One minute it's up in the air and the next minute, the wings are waddling and down she goes. Lost sight of it behind the houses, but I heard it hit. Sounded like a train driving through a lumber yard."

"What else did you see?" Chance asked. He wanted as much detail as he could in case Ozzy's story wasn't so much an eyewitness account as an exaggeration from what he might have overheard.

"Well, I had to lock up, didn't I?" Ozzy said. "Then I high-tailed it over here to see what happened. I knew the plane was headed for them houses, and when I didn't see no smoke or fire, I figured the people in the neighborhood would call the ambulance or the cops. I mean, I figured they would have heard it if I did."

"Okay, okay," Chance said to calm Ozzy, who was rubbing a hand across his stubbly chin as if he were worried someone might think he had shirked his duty. "You did the right thing."

"How many was in it?" Ozzy asked, giving voice to what everyone around them must be wondering. He stood on his tiptoes to try and see into the cabin of the plane.

Nick Philippoussis, an ambulance driver and a deputy coroner, appeared in the doorway of the house. Chance wondered in what capacity Nick had arrived at the scene.

A broad-shouldered guy with the beginnings of a beer gut, Nick motioned to an EMS worker who came toward the front part of the plane carrying a stretcher. "Guess we're about to find out," Chance said, his voice grim.

He jockeyed for a position among the growing crowd of spectators and finally retreated to the bumper of the pickup. He took a deep breath as an evidence technician wedged against the back window of the cockpit, trying to photograph inside the plane. Two clicks later, he watched Nick and an EMS guy, with the help of two police officers, slowly extract a body past the plane's dual controls and through the door on the right side of the plane.

The bystanders stepped back, fighting curiosity, when Nick and the EMS worker reappeared minutes later. A woman gasped when she saw the stretcher loaded with a black-bagged body. Another crossed herself as the stretcher passed by. Neighbors whispered to each other, and then quickly turned back toward the house to see if more victims would be forthcoming.

Chance snapped shots of the corpse being loaded into the coroner's van and then called out quietly to Nick. "Anybody else?"

Nick shook his head. Chance's heart sank. The pilot hadn't made it after all.

"Got a minute?" Chance asked. Nick was a golfing buddy from way back, at least when he had the time. When he wasn't driving an ambulance or subbing for the coroner, he worked at Duggan Dolan mortuary. Like a lot of people in Butte, he worked three jobs to make ends meet.

"I'm headed to Missoula," Nick said. "Crash investigator is coming in from Seattle tomorrow, and he wants the autopsy results ASAP."

National Transportation Safety Board investigators would figure out what went wrong, that was for sure. Might take them months, not that it would matter much to the pilot now. "Any idea about what happened?" Chance asked.

"Gotta book," Nick said, tapping his watch. "The medical examiner is cutting short his weekend in the Bitterroot. He said he'd do the autopsy soon as we can get the body there. Let's have a beer later," Nick said quietly. "Something ain't right about this one." Then he hopped into the van, which sped down the hill toward I-90 and the State Crime Lab.

Chance looked at his own watch. "Oh, crap," he said, a predictable apprehension beginning to rise in him. He raced the two blocks to his Land Rover parked in front of his duplex on Mercury Street and sped away.

Chapter 2

Mesa Dawson hoisted her carry-on bag to her shoulder with a deep sense of gratitude. The landing approach into Butte over the mile-wide Berkeley Pit, filled with 800 feet of toxic mine seepage, seemed to tempt fate in ways her nerves barely tolerated. The largest open-mine pit in the world and the pilot has to fly right over it to land? Give me a break, she thought.

Consolation lay in the fact that within two minutes she had de-planed the Sky West commuter from Salt Lake and stood inside Bert Mooney Airport, known as Bert and Ernie's to some locals. The terminal still looked like a ski chalet from a Doris Day movie, but at least baggage claim was less than twenty yards away. She looked half-heartedly for Chance over the heads of the dozen or so other passengers, unsurprised that her brother was nowhere in sight.

What caught her attention instead was an aging American Legion color guard and a tearful reunion between a returning soldier on crutches and just about everyone else in the airport, including several people in traditional Indian dress. Mesa quickly recognized she was in the middle of someone's tribal welcoming.

She eased her way to the outskirts of the crowd, ducking apologetically in front of a woman in a long, buckskin coat with turquoise-beaded fringe, poised with a camera to her eye ready to record the moment. Once Mesa reached the half-moon shaped baggage carousel, she offered her own silent prayer that her luggage had made the connection.

Just as well, Chance was late. Once the plane had left Cincinnati, she spent most of the eight hours of travel time rehearsing how she would break the news to him. Five weeks before, she had succumbed to his relentless pleas for help with the family newspaper. Circulation had dropped and advertising numbers were down. They needed her. Initially, she had felt a rush of adrenalin thinking about what she could do to turn the paper around. But little did she know how the timing would suck.

Her dream job had finally opened up—arts and entertainment editor for *Pacifica Magazine* in Portland, Oregon—and she had a bona fide inside track. Derek Immelmann, *Pacifica*'s managing editor and her former boss, wanted her badly, and soon. Her interview was scheduled for Friday, and she didn't plan to miss it.

While she waited for her luggage to appear, a ceremony began around the wounded soldier. The crowd parted as an elder in a buffalo hide vest stepped forward to present the soldier with a war bonnet of eagle feathers and intricate beading. One of the greeters lit a smudge pot and began to wave the smoke around the soldier's head. The sweet

smell of sage permeated the lobby. Another of the
Indian elders began a chant. Mesa looked around
half-heartedly, curious to see if some Homeland
Security type might object. Thankfully, no one
appeared. Mesa smiled. Only in Montana.

She watched the tense expressions of the
soldier's family and friends softening as the ritual
came to its conclusion and they swarmed to touch
him. While she understood little of the symbolism
involved, Mesa understood enough about Indian
custom to realize that a ceremony for a returning
soldier, a warrior—modern or otherwise—had
significance, and she also knew enough not to do
anything that would disrespect it.

The luggage carousel droned to life as the chant
ended and half a dozen suitcases, backpacks, and
fly-rod cases circled into the terminal. Relieved
when she saw her three jumbo-sized nylon bags,
Mesa wheeled them behind the color guard and
toward a chair by the revolving exit door.

The airport soon emptied, and Mesa found
herself settling into a more relaxed pace. She sat
near a glass-encased fly-fishing display and stared
out the window at the wide, open space.

It was hard to convey to someone back east the
sheer size of Montana. Butte's Summit Valley could
hold a city four times its size, and once did. To the
south, the Highland Mountains filled the horizon. To
the west beyond the Copper Baron Hotel, open fields
of sagebrush edged rolling foothills that quietly
spread away from city streets.

Uptown Butte, as the locals referred to the oldest
section of the city on the side of the mountain, was

majestic, even if rough around the edges. Its tallest building, the Hotel Finlen, stood a mere seven stories. Moulton and Sheepshead Mountain rested beyond at the edge of the Deerlodge National Forest. Everywhere the skyline was easily visible, and the feeling of vastness lay at the front door of any Butte home.

She was thinking of her grandmother's house when she caught sight of her brother's vintage Land Rover, circling the parking lot. The vehicle represented everything she loved about her brother. He had pulled the World War II relic out of some rancher's field and spent months repairing it. If something had historic value and he could restore it, Chance was smitten.

He came to a screeching halt right in front of the airport's revolving door. With its steering wheel on the right side, Chance deftly stepped out of the car and swept into the airport in three quick strides. She could feel the dampness of his biking shirt when he hugged her with all his might.

"I know, late as usual," he said as he picked up her bags and herded her out the door before she could even say hello. Amidst welcoming chitchat, he started the Rover and made a quick turn into the Silver Bow Aviation's parking lot on the way out.

Before she could ask what they were doing, Chance had jumped from the Rover and run toward the building next to the terminal. "Bet you're tired out," he said over his shoulder. "This will only take a second."

Mesa sighed, took her cell phone out of her purse, and clicked on the speed dial. "This is the

Ducharme residence," she heard her grandmother's clipped but polite British accent on the answering machine. "Kindly leave a message."

"Hi, Nana," Mesa said, feigning nonchalance. "I made it. Chance and I are on our way. See you soon. Bye." With a sudden swell of emotion, she tucked the phone back into her purse. She imagined her grandmother lying in bed listening to the voice on the answering machine.

Mesa thought back to the Fourth of July weekend two months earlier, when Chance had called to say Nana had had a heart attack. She was out of ICU in two days, but Mesa and Chance had remained anxious since. At seventy-three, Nana Rose Ducharme kept as busy as someone half her age, running the *Mining City Messenger*, immersed in local community projects. Slowing down would be difficult.

The thin, aluminum car door clicked shut, and Mesa watched her brother while he cranked the engine. "Sorry about that little side trip. I'm working on this story about a plane crash. Some guy tried to land on a street Uptown, and didn't make it."

"I thought you only took photographs and edited the sports page," Mesa said. Chance's impassioned plea about the fate of the newspaper rested on the fact that he didn't have the know-how, and his concerns about what it would do to their grandmother if the paper folded. Mesa also knew that Chance's real passion was restoring old buildings, of which there were plenty in Butte. Better she should be here to rescue the paper than leave it to him.

"Well, I probably won't write this," he said, his smile implying *hopefully, you will*. "But I took some great shots, and Tyler can give me an inside angle."

Tyler Fitzgerald, one of Chance's longtime buddies, had recently taken over the management of Silver Bow Aviation from his aging father. Mesa could imagine the two of them with their heads together, figuring out how to tell a story. "You sound almost glad the pilot's dead," she said.

"Of course not, but it's not like I knew the poor bastard," her brother answered with another grin. "So how are you? Doesn't look like the flight pushed you over the edge. Nan's gonna be mighty glad to see you."

How *was* she? That was a good question. She looked toward the mountains and considered the question. Not bad, she guessed, for a thirty-year-old woman who had caved into her brother's pleading to return to the wilds of Montana to nurse an ailing grandmother and rescue the family business, right when the career opportunity of a lifetime had been tossed into her lap. At least she hadn't died in a plane crash.

Precious little had changed in Rose Ducharme's neighborhood in the four years since Mesa had last visited—too long away, she knew. Mesa took a long look at her grandmother's storybook house and tried to shake off the feeling that by returning to Butte she had somehow failed to make it in the larger world.

"Open the door," Chance said. He stood next to her on the porch, her luggage balanced precariously in his arms. Mesa knew she should move but found herself paralyzed.

"Go ahead," Chance urged. "She's probably in the parlor, or the sitting room. She's using it for a bedroom these days so she doesn't have to walk up all the stairs. I'm sure she can hear us," he said with a rare show of irritation.

Mesa didn't know what to say. She had talked to her grandmother weekly since her recovery began, but still she had dreaded coming face-to-face with Nan's debilitation. Once she saw her, the illness would be real.

Finally, she pushed open the wide walnut door and took a step inside. To her left the mahogany double doors of the sitting room stood ajar. Muffled voices rose. Chance called out, "Hey, Nan, she's here," and headed up the stairs with Mesa's bags, taking them to the room she always occupied when she stayed with her grandmother.

Mesa looked after him and for a moment considered following him. *Why delay it, you chicken?* "Hello," she called and peeked through the open door.

The sitting room looked stately, as always, dominated by a large, claret-colored Oriental rug, and delicately crocheted ivory curtains. Only the daybed across from the sage green settee signaled anything unusual. Her grandmother sat on the settee, a shawl around her shoulders, hands folded in her lap, talking to a dapper looking gray-haired man in a jacket and tie who sat in the Queen Anne chair next to the lamp table.

"I was beginning to think you weren't coming in," she said with a smile. "Give us a hug, and take that look off your face. I'm not dead yet."

Then, without skipping a beat, she motioned gracefully with an open hand toward her companion. "Perhaps you remember Philip Northey."

Mesa didn't know whether to chuckle or scratch her head. Her grandmother looked just fine. Her eyes were bright and full of the usual liveliness. She certainly didn't look pale and wan. Mesa couldn't help but be relieved.

Mr. Northey was none the worse for wear either, and he did look vaguely familiar. Nana had never been short of companionship since Grandpa Ducharme had died more than a decade ago. Not that she ever thought of remarrying, but an escort was always nice, she would say.

Mesa recovered her manners, nodded to Mr. Northey, and quickly came forward to give her grandmother a hug and join her on the settee. All the pressure about her decision—when she would hear about the Portland job, how she would make Chance and Nana understand—temporarily disappeared with the warm embrace.

"Rose, I should be going and let you help Mesa get settled," Mr. Northey said. "Where is that grandson of mine? Perhaps I should phone again."

"You mustn't fret, Philip. He'll be along. Let's hear about Mesa's trip."

No sooner had Mesa begun to describe her landing over the Pit and the welcome-home party at the airport when the b-r-r-ring of the old-fashioned doorbell reverberated through the hall. Mesa sprang to open the door to a tall, fair-haired, thirty-something man, dressed in a blazer, dress shirt, and jeans. Only the telltale smokejumper boots kept her from thinking she was back east.

"You must be the returning granddaughter," he said with a smile. He reached out his hand and said, "I'm Shane Northey, the footloose grandson."

จ~๕

Midnight approached and Mesa still sat in front of the small maple dressing table with its matching stool where her mother had overseen the nightly brushing of her daughter's hair. Now she could barely get her long legs under the table.

Her grandmother had changed nothing about the room. The poster from *Legends of the Fall* with a shirtless Brad Pitt hung on the opposite wall. She had conned an usher at the mall theater into giving the advertisement to her one summer.

She wondered if the appearance of Shane Northey had been a setup. When he came in for a few moments to exchange pleasantries, Nana and Philip Northey had seemed all too delighted.

After they had gone, Nana had confided, "Philip doesn't drive anymore, bad hip." But wasn't Shane nice, she had continued. He's running for the legislature, you know. Just broke off an engagement this summer. Too bad, really, he has such nice manners.

Mesa picked up her brush and began to stroke her hair, staring into the mirror at the reflected image of the room. So many times Mesa had arrived here and fallen asleep in the bed after some long journey from an Air Force base halfway across the world. Nothing felt more secure than the knowledge that the house never changed. And in it, she had her own room.

The house had its share of sad memories too. Her mother had come home to die here. But Mesa and Chance had faced that horror with their grandparents' steady hand to support them. She would never contemplate leaving her grandmother in a predicament, if in fact that was the case.

A soft knock interrupted her thoughts. Chance stood at the door.

"This is just temporary, you know," he said. "Tara's lined up a bunch of apartments for you to look at. Tomorrow, if you want."

Tara McTeague, Mesa's best friend since childhood, had grown up in the house across the street from Nana's. Now she was a real estate agent when she wasn't having babies. "And here's a key to my place." He put it on the dressing table. "You know, in case you need a little more privacy in the immediate future."

Mesa grinned. Chance tended to approach the potentially intimate details of her life shyly. She picked up the key with a snicker. Like she would have the time or inclination even to strike up an intimate conversation with anybody in the next week.

"This will do for the time I plan to stay," she said. "I'm beginning to think Nan's not going to require as much help as I thought. I'll need to check out the lay of the land at the paper before I decide how long I'm staying."

She could see a small cloud come over her brother's otherwise sinfully cheerful expression. He had a way of making her feel guilty like no one else in the world, not that she wanted to burst his bubble on the first day.

"Tyler called while you were helping Nan get tucked in," he said, using his typical ploy of changing the subject when he didn't like what she had to say. "He told me something curious about that plane crash today. Turns out Kev—you remember Tyler's mechanic?"

Even she knew Kev Murphy, a strapping, down-on-his-luck disabled vet. His reputation as a heavy drinker made keeping a decent job difficult, so Tyler hired him to overhaul plane engines instead. There's logic for you.

"He told Tyler that this pilot in the plane that crash-landed didn't go up alone. I think I'll talk to Murphy myself first thing tomorrow. What are you going to do, hang out with Nan?"

"I thought I'd go into the office. I'm not here for a vacation, you know."

"Well, it is Labor Day, the last day of the rodeo. Half the town, not to mention the staff, will be there. Sure you don't want to wait 'til I can go into the office with you?"

The Labor Day weekend rodeo in Dillon was the largest in the state, and it attracted whoever wasn't already out of town. But Mesa had reason not to drag her feet. "Why?" she asked. "Nobody there bites, do they?"

Chapter 3

Between swigs from the orange juice carton the next morning, Chance made two phone calls. The first was to Consolidated Controls, Inc. of Lincoln, Nebraska, an agricultural equipment outfit, which held the crashed Cessna's registration.

Chance had checked the tail number on the FAA website, but what he had learned was irritatingly uninformative. When he called Consolidated, a recorded message informed him that the corporate offices were closed for the Labor Day holiday and would reopen on Tuesday, September 8. So much for direct sources.

Next he called Nick Philippoussis, hoping to meet him for breakfast. His wife answered and said Nick was asleep and she wasn't about to wake him. He had been out most of the night with a traffic accident. Somebody driving to Helena on I-15 had hit an elk, then careened across the highway and hit a pickup. Two dead, not counting the elk.

So much for phone leads. Pavement pounding was next, but he would need some hefty fare to soak up the rotgut coffee he would have to drink while listening to Kev Murphy. Chance decided to stop by the Butte Hill Bakery for one of its giant cinnamon buns before heading out to Silver Bow Aviation.

He hopped into the Land Rover and turned left onto Silver Street, taking a quick, two-block detour south to drive by the crash site. The plane remained intact, the morning sunlight reflecting off its windows. Yellow police investigation tape still surrounded the southwest corner of the block, but the wooden barriers had been removed from the middle of Washington Street. Instead, a black, Butte Silver Bow police cruiser was parked strategically at the corner of Washington and Porphyry, keeping a silent vigil.

He pulled up next to the police car where Brock Van Zant, who had gone to high school with Chance, sat hunched in his seat. Only in Butte would somebody try to strip down a plane at a crime scene in the middle of the night.

"I'm headed for a cinnamon roll," Chance said after greeting the yawning cop. "Want one?"

Brock sat up and declined the offer. He was getting ready to go off duty, explaining that the sheriff had asked him to baby sit the scene to keep the federal crash investigator happy.

The sheriff was back. Now that was news, Chance thought moments later, while he waited in line at the bakery. Sheriff Solheim was building a retirement cabin on the Wise River. Coming back into town before the end of the long weekend had definitely been a concession.

By the time Chance reached the airport, nothing was left of his cinnamon bun but the brown-sugar glaze on his fingertips, which he meticulously licked off. He parked in the small lot outside Silver Bow Aviation and went inside. The office, the reception area and the pilot's lounge, all of which he could see from the doorway, were deserted.

He meandered through the pilot lounge, which reminded him of the lobby of a dingy hotel. A gray, metal, government-surplus desk and chair took up the wall space under the window from which the runway was visible. A couple of worn upholstered chairs that had come from Tyler's mom's basement, accented by a perennially stained coffeepot and a sink that had long ago lost its shiny stainless steel luster, completed the ensemble. A rumpled copy of the *Montana Standard* and an empty paper coffee cup on the desk were the only signs of human presence. The place had a 'last outpost' feel to it, save for the smell of recently brewed coffee which hinted that somebody might be around.

He stopped at the door of the hangar, where he saw Kev working on a Beechcraft's engine. As usual, he had plenty to say about the plane that had gone down.

"You could fill your pilot's log with obits when you're in the aviation business," he said when Chance described the pilot being extracted from the plane.

"What happened to the other two?" Kev asked.

Stunned by Kev's matter-of-fact question, Chance wasn't sure how to answer. It wouldn't be the first time Kevin had been known to hallucinate. He might not even have gone to bed the night before. "What are you talking about?" Chance asked gingerly.

Kev pulled his head out of the engine compartment and stood up. He was looking eye to eye at Chance. "There was two other guys went up in that plane. I was on my way to the can when I saw the three of them walking across the tarmac toward the tie-down area."

The can was in the lobby, which meant Kev must have seen them through the picture window in the pilot's lounge, which was also where the door to the tarmac was. He must have missed them by seconds. "Did you recognize these guys? Were they from around here?"

Kev shook his head and went back to working on the engine. "Didn't see 'em up close. Besides, I wasn't that interested."

"Well, what did they look like?" Chance asked, trying to hide his impatience.

Kev looked up from the engine for a moment, thinking. "One guy looked like your typical knock-around, about your age and size," Kev said and returned to the engine, then spoke between turns of a socket wrench. "Another one was taller, ramrod straight. Could have been ex-military. The third guy looked older. I think he wore glasses. I only saw them for a split second."

"You talked to the sheriff about this yet?" Chance asked, not surprised by the tirade that followed about what had the cops ever done for Kev but give him a hard time.

Finally, Chance left Kev to his overhaul and walked back to his car, a mixture of concern and indignation engulfing him. He drove back uptown, wondering what kind of guys would walk away from a crash-landing into a house, leaving a dead man. He also wondered if they knew they had been seen.

Granted, Silver Bow Aviation was not the world's busiest place. Few people in Butte could afford their own planes, let alone hire a pilot. Out-of-towners and their passengers came and went without much notice unless they needed to refuel, or the weather was bad and they had to lay over.

Without a traffic tower, a pilot could fly in and out of Bert and Ernie's without checking with anybody. All you had to do was avoid the commercial traffic, which was easy enough, considering it consisted of two flights a day from Salt Lake. And a fair number of private planes flew visual flight rules, so even the radio traffic was light.

That was partly why some celebrities, like David Letterman and Hank Williams, Jr., flew into Butte. If you wanted to get noticed, you flew into Bozeman. Whoever these guys were, they apparently had something to hide.

❧

The last time Mesa had spent any serious time at the *Mining City Messenger* office, she had just finished her freshman year in college back east. That had been more than ten years ago, the month after her grandmother had decided to buy a newspaper.

The paper's offices occupied the old Cleveland Building, which had once housed Butte's grandest car dealership, with a fancy showroom for the Cadillacs and Oldsmobiles. The building, repainted in brick red, still maintained its dignity in the middle of Mercury Street, redefining the once famous center of Butte's red-light district. From the outside, Mesa saw no hint that the *Messenger* might be in any trouble.

Nana had bought the weekly paper for a song from Solomon Ramey—Sol to his myriad drinking buddies. After Grandpa Ducharme died, volunteer work aside, Nana needed more to occupy her. She might not be a newswoman like Clare Booth Luce, but like Sol had said, you didn't need to be able to write to own a newspaper. You just needed cash flow. Together Mesa and her grandmother had spent the summer getting the *Messenger* offices into shape.

The *Messenger* quickly picked up where Sol Ramey had begun to slow down. The paper was free, supported by a loyal base of local advertisers. Each issue usually ran at twenty-four pages with lots of homespun interest. Its peak circulation was ten thousand strong, with two hundred distribution points all over the county. But lately, according to Chance, advertising had taken a dive. Local speculation about the paper's future, given their grandmother's illness, no doubt contributed to the decline.

Mesa took a deep breath and entered the small reception area. The smell of stale coffee hung in the air. A faded, tan vinyl sofa with cracks at the seams took up most of the room. The only welcoming feature was a Big Sky water cooler in the corner.

She reached for a copy of the *Messenger* on the coffee table. The headline read, "Two More Mine Frames to Be Lit by Christmas." The story was tightly written with vivid details about the preservation of the iron gallows that dotted the mountainside—revered symbols of Butte's mining heritage. She was relieved the paper had at least one decent reporter.

Mesa had begun to inspect the rest of the front page when scurrying footsteps from the connecting hallway distracted her. A buxom, no-nonsense woman appeared, herding a thin young man with bowlegs and dusty boots out the front door.

"You listen up, cowboy. Here's two words for you—paycheck," the woman called after him. Mesa remembered the woman from the airport the day before, taking photographs. But they hadn't recognized each other then.

Her miniature, feathered, dream-catcher earrings jostled when she spoke. "You tell your boss that if those inserts aren't ready by Wednesday noon, you won't see one thin dime. Now get the hell out of here and get busy."

The door closed and the woman tossed her jet-black hair over her shoulder with a palpable sigh of frustration and turned to withdraw the way she came. It was then, from the corner of her eye, she spotted Mesa. She paused for an instant, straightened her burgundy blouse collar, and then said, "Sorry about that." She cleared her throat and smiled. "Can I help you? I'm Irita Yellow Robe," she said, obviously impatient to get the conversation going. Her voice was a rich alto, tempered by more than a few years of smoking.

Mesa smiled back and returned the newspaper to the cluttered coffee table. The last time Mesa had seen Irita was the summer after college graduation. Mesa had no intentions of coming back to Butte then either, but that hadn't stopped her grandmother from trying to lure her. Irita had been a scrawny, anxious-to-please new employee. An extra thirty pounds now rounded out her upper body and face. The transformation, both in physique but especially in attitude, was startling.

"Beautiful name," Mesa said and offered a hand in greeting. She decided to string Irita along for just a minute.

"It's Crow," Irita said. When Mesa didn't respond immediately, Irita continued, "You know, like Indian. Feathers? Teepee?"

"Of course," Mesa said. She thought back to the ceremonial welcome at the airport, surprised in a way. When Irita had taken the job at the *Messenger*, she described herself as a city Indian who had left the reservation years before. Maybe her attitude about that had changed too.

"Do I know you?" said Irita, her expression a mixture of curiosity and worry, as if a creeping awareness was bringing an unwanted realization to light.

"Irita, it's me, Mesa."

"Holy crap," Irita said with an air of self-derision. "Of course. God, it's been forever," she said and reached out to hug Mesa. "I've seen your grown-up photograph in Mrs. Ducharme's office but, well, it doesn't do you justice. Come on in. God, I'm sorry about that little sideshow just now. We've been having some distribution problems, and I've got a ton of ads in this week's issue, and if they're delayed getting on the street even an hour, our advertisers will be ringing the phone off the hook."

Irita reached for Mesa's elbow and pulled her down the hall into the depths of the *Mining City Messenger* offices. Mesa let herself be carried along in the whirlwind. They stopped in front of a large office with half-glass walls.

"I thought we could put you in here for the time being," Irita said sheepishly.

Mesa looked at the rich, mahogany desk and chair, family photos on a credenza next to the wall. "This is grandmother's office," she said with an air of finality that suggested she did not intend to use it.

Irita sighed and then said, "It's not like we don't expect her back but . . ." She gestured toward the pool of several desks in what Mesa remembered was the newsroom and said, "But that's it, unless you want a desk in our personal version of the Pit."

Mesa took a step inside the office and looked around. Irita followed. "Look, you're gonna need an office and one with a door you can shut. Trust me." This last caveat Irita delivered with a tone that came right out of The Godfather: Part II.

Mesa smiled. "Okay, for now." She felt uneasy about moving into Nan's office on the first day, as though this were a signal that big change was afoot. But maybe Irita was right. Privacy might not be such a bad thing.

"Chance won't be in right away," Mesa said. "Nan said you could give me the lay of the land."

"Chance is never around when you need him," Irita said with a smile, "like most of the male species. He's probably off rescuing some old building from the brink of destruction."

On the one hand, Mesa wasn't surprised to hear this. But on the other, she wondered who was running the paper if he wasn't around.

Chance parked behind the KXLF-TV Bronco. He could see Ashley Carroll, the latest TV news blonde, lugging a video camera and struggling across the vacant lot in her high heels toward Sheriff Solheim.

Messenger staff did not routinely attend the sheriff's daily press conferences, leaving coverage of the local crime beat to the *Montana Standard* and the local TV stations. But if Chance wanted to know more about this plane crash, he knew the sheriff would provide whatever the police wanted the public to know.

It might not be cutting-edge journalism for the police department and local reporters to cooperate, but Chance was prepared to let Mesa worry about that. He just didn't want to miss what the sheriff had to say.

For some reason, which the department's receptionist didn't know, the sheriff had abandoned his office and the usual behind-the-desk conference to move to the crash site. Chance couldn't blame any elected official for taking advantage of a little free TV time.

He joined the other media reps around Sheriff Solheim. At his full Nordic height, an imposing six foot three, Roland Solheim reached easily across Ashley to shake hands when Chance appeared.

"Thought I might see you today," the sheriff said with a wry grin. His steely gaze and lanky build made it easy to imagine him facing down a trigger-happy gunslinger. In truth, Sheriff Solheim rarely stared down anybody but the Council of Commissioners and an occasional TV camera. A western sheriff in the twenty-first century, even in Butte, was more politician than lawman. He was open and affable and told everyone, except those who worked for him, to call him "Rollie."

"You know Noah Gilderson?" Solheim said and nodded to the square-shouldered, fair-haired reporter with wire-rimmed glasses and a gentle smile. Chance liked Noah, a transplant from South Dakota who covered the courthouse and crime beat for the *Standard*. Like most of its reporters, he was young and energetic and woefully underpaid. But the two papers, at least as far as the hard news went, rarely competed, so theirs was a symbiotic relationship— back scratching all around.

Chance thought Rollie was a first-class lawman. Silver Bow County's ninety square miles made it one of the smallest counties in the state, but the sheriff had his hands full trying to stretch a limited police force to cover all the terrain. By all accounts, he did a better job than most of his predecessors.

Sheriff Solheim rubbed his stubbly silver-gray crew cut with a bear-sized hand and waited politely for Ashley to balance the camera on her shoulder. When the red light came on, he began reading from several sheets of paper he had rolled up in his hand.

"The occupant of the Cessna 180 that crash-landed at 303 Washington Street on Sunday, September 6, was dead at the scene. An autopsy is pending. The victim is identified as Lowell Austin, age 54, most recently of the Idaho Correctional Institution in Orofino.

"Investigators from the National Transportation Safety Board will arrive today to assess the wreckage to determine the cause of the accident. Special agents of the FBI are investigating the whereabouts of the last known pilot of the plane, which is believed to have been stolen from Moab, Utah. We are looking for any witnesses to the crash who might have information. They can contact the police department directly, etc., etc."

"Thanks, Sheriff," Ashley said, swinging her camera within an inch of Noah's head, and then moving away to get a shot of the crashed plane.

"THE Lowell Austin?" Noah said after he ducked.

Chance looked at Noah, whose expression was a mixture of surprise and delight. "Wait, did I miss something?" Chance said. "Who's Lowell Austin?"

"Don't you read the newspaper?" Noah said with a smile. "We ran a wire story about Austin's release last week. He did twenty-plus years for killing two Idaho game wardens in 1984. He left an Idaho prison a free man last Wednesday." Noah turned to the sheriff. "What kind of injuries did he have?"

Solheim hesitated, leaning on the wooden fence at the back edge of the lot and said, "None really. No gunshot, not a lot of blood at the scene at all. I've worked a few auto accidents like that. It's usually a heart attack. Again, don't quote me. This is my first plane wreck."

"What do you think he was doing in Butte?" Chance said, surprised by the victim's identity, but glad that the dead man was no one local.

The sheriff looked up from his prepared statement with the smug expression of a police officer who couldn't help appreciate the irony of the situation. Half Irish and half Swedish, he had a subdued, gallows sense of humor about work and life. "Beats the hell out of me, but he should have stayed in Idaho, that's for damn sure. But don't quote me on that either," he said with a chuckle and shook his finger at Noah.

Solheim entwined his fingers and stretched his arms in front of him as if the conversation had begun to wake him up. "Put your pens away."

Chance and Noah silently obeyed, knowing that Solheim just might give them something off the record to tickle their imaginations.

"As far as I can see it, Mr. Austin went on a plane ride that ended tragically. Doesn't look like he was flying the plane, so obviously we still have a few dots to connect. His next-of-kin is an elderly mother in Virginia who didn't know anything about what he was doing here. But he wouldn't be the first ex-con who decided to light in Butte, and he sure as hell won't be the last."

Chance knew this was one of Solheim's pet peeves. Butte already had its share of ex-cons thanks to the Pre-release Center, a locally contracted correctional service that housed compliant convicts on parole. The center helped the cons find jobs in Butte and kept track of their AA meetings, counseling sessions and literacy tutors, until pre-releasers were ready to rejoin society. All too often, according to Solheim, they ended up staying in Butte once emancipated.

"What about the owner of the plane, Consolidated Controls?" Chance asked. He suspected Rollie, or more likely an FBI agent, had been able to get through to someone who would say something other than "No comment," which was all Chance had heard that morning.

"Hell, they know less than the mother. At least she knew who Austin was. The comptroller of . . ."—here Rollie hesitated and looked at his statement again—"Consolidated Controls says they own the plane and that the president of the company flew it to Moab, Utah for some Outward Bound type deal. We found his gear in the plane. The guy's not due to come out of the Canyonlands until Friday noon unless the FBI wants to spend a small fortune searching for him in the back of beyond."

Canyonlands was 300,000 acres of wilderness of countless canyons where people went to get away from civilization. The plane's owner might as well be on the moon.

Chance had to give Lowell Austin credit though. He had made the rounds all right. Released on Tuesday, he had gotten himself from the penitentiary in Orofino, Idaho to Moab, Utah and then to Butte, Montana in five days, and in a stolen plane. He had covered a lot of miles. Too bad he hadn't lived to talk about the trip.

Chapter 4

"I'd be glad to bring you up to speed if you're ready," Irita said to Mesa. "Want to start with what's lined up for this week's issue?"

"How about the staff? Who's in today?" Mesa said. She knew what it felt like to have a new boss. She thought she might ease the anxiety, at least temporarily, of any edgy employees curious about her. "Can I meet whoever is here?"

"Dealer's choice," Irita said. "Follow me."

The two women snaked through a half-dozen desks, mostly unoccupied, while Irita talked. "You probably remember the newsroom. These empty desks are just temporary. We've had some desertions since your grandma's heart problems. You probably heard about Rolf quitting, the old weasel," Irita scoffed.

A retired Forest Service hydrologist and supposedly confirmed bachelor, Rolf Andervald had written a popular column called "Outta Doors." Rumor had it that he had been soft on Nana all along, but when she took sick, he decided to face facts, and quit to move back to North Dakota.

"Then our so-called ace reporter, Fiona Curnow, defected. To her credit, she came and talked to me about it beforehand. The *Standard* lured her away. You know how it goes."

Mesa understood. Reporters still interested in print journalism cut their teeth at weeklies and when their writing skills become sufficient to attract attention, they headed for any daily that was still hiring, for even a small raise in pay. The same thing happened at her old paper, the *River City Current*, whose staff of experienced reporters migrated to the Cincinnati *Enquirer* when an opening occurred.

A waiflike young woman, who looked no more than fourteen years old, sidled up to Irita and handed her several phone messages and then whispered, "And Anna said to say she decided to take the day off after all."

"Here's your first victim," Irita said and looked at her watch. "Mesa Dawson, meet Erin O'Rourke. She covers the local news and does most of our features at the moment."

Deep green eyes peered through what seemed like enormous horn-rimmed glasses for such a small face. Erin wore a thin yellow sweater, a slightly darker shade than her hair. The cartoon character Tweety Bird came to mind.

"I'm looking forward to working with you," Erin muttered and then practically curtsied.

Mesa had the distinct impression she had gone back in time a hundred years to the hired help meeting the ranch owner.

"I'm surprised about Anna," Irita said in low tones as if she were thinking out loud. Then realizing she had witnesses, she spoke up. "She's the business manager. She handles payroll and accounts. She's one of our most reliable employees. I mean, not that we have anyone who's unreliable. It's just weird that she'd duck out like that when she knows you're expected."

Nana hadn't mentioned any staffing problems, but then she had not wanted to discuss the newspaper so much as she had wanted to make sure Mesa felt at home. As usual, Nana put the comforts of her family first.

"Anyway, there's you, and Chance and me. I got promoted to publisher's/editorial assistant after a couple of years. I handle personnel, circulation, write an occasional story, and empty the trash." She stopped at the end of the newsroom at a doorway to a closet-sized office, poked her head in, and said, "Meet Arnold Cinch. Just plain Cinch to all that knows and still loves him. He handles the classifieds and whatever advertising Chance or I don't snag."

A wiry looking man glanced up from the phone and feigned a smile. Tufts of white hair covered various parts of his head like patchy spring snow. His office had the air of a bank vault—no windows with shelves from floor to ceiling.

"I don't have anything to do with what goes into the paper," he said matter-of-factly. "I just try to see that it makes a few bucks. I certainly hope you're not planning to sell the paper like Irita is afraid you will."

Irita whacked Cinch on the shoulder, at which point he covered his head and turned back to his phone conversation.

"Don't pay any attention to that old goat," Irita said with a wave of her hand, as if to dispel the notion that she was worried about the fate of the paper.

Mesa wasn't surprised. If the paper's advertising revenues were on the skids, Irita's supposition was logical.

"That leaves Delilah," Irita said and threw her head back dramatically. "She covers arts and entertainment. She usually rolls in around noon. You can't miss her. Just look for the black outfit wrapped in some flashy scarf. She can't help herself. She's from Seattle."

They strolled back toward Mesa's office when an eager, well-scrubbed face, a crust of toothpaste still in the corner of his mouth, bounded in with four cups of coffee in a cardboard holder. "Your latte with a double shot," he said and bent forward in mock supplication as he handed Irita a cup.

"Oh yeah, we usually get a couple of interns from the college," Irita said. "This is . . . what's your name, kid?"

"Micah. Micah Bradley," he answered and moved toward the back of the newsroom, not the least bit intimidated by Irita's feigned snub.

"From Montana Tech?" Mesa asked, though she was unsure what the once-famous Montana School of Mines had to offer in the way of journalism, even with its name changed.

"Missoula even," Irita said. "The university's journalism program is still pumping 'em out. And, of course, we have a stable full of freelancers, of which two or three are usually dependable about deadlines. Mrs. Ducharme always handled them, so I figure you could pick up on that."

"What about layout and graphics?" Mesa asked.

Irita let out a deep breath. "I was hoping you wouldn't ask." She motioned around a carpeted divider and into a cubicle. A red and black bumper sticker thumbtacked above an oversized computer monitor read, "You know you're Serbian if at least one of your friends is named Dragan."

A young man, maybe twenty-five, sat dressed all in black. A tattoo of questionable design crept down his arm from under the sleeve of his tee shirt to his elbow. "This is Phadron Draganovich, the resident geek."

Phadron looked up over thin, stylish, black-framed spectacles. A sterling silver loop pierced the left side of his lower lip but his smile seemed genuine. He offered his hand to shake. "Nice to meet you," he said. "People call me Phade."

Mesa smiled back. Finally, someone she could relate to. Phade would have fit in easily at the *Current*. "That a blog you're working on?" Mesa asked and pointed to the monitor.

"Nothing official *yet*." He rolled his eyes toward Irita as if he were awaiting approval. "I think the *Mess* could definitely support one. We got some younger readers out there with plenty to say."

Irita nudged his shoulder. "That's *Messenger* to you sir and that's enough for now,"

They walked back to the office, where Irita said, "Phade may not look like much, but he knows his stuff. He's bailed us out of more than one computer headache. Mrs. Ducharme didn't let him wear that lip thingy when she was here. I kind of let it slide."

"Fine by me," Mesa said. "It's what's in the paper that counts." She gestured to Irita to sit. "Okay, what are we working on for our next edition? What's the lead story?" Mesa felt an urgency to get to work, as if she might be able to whip the paper into shape in three days and be on her way to Portland and life on a grander scale without feeling the least bit guilty.

"Good question," Irita said with a tone that suggested she had her own notion of how the paper should run—a notion Mesa was not inclined to dispel for the moment. "That's your first decision. Apparently, your brother is feeling his oats and wants to run something on yesterday's plane crash into a house in Uptown. We don't normally cover breaking news, but I guess Chance has some angle on the victim. I can tell you right now your grandmother's not gonna be happy to see any photos of plane crashes on the front page."

"We can run the story without a photo or bury it on page two. What else?"

"We were sort of planning to have a background piece on you on the editorial page. Erin's waiting in the wings to interview you today."

Mesa shrugged. The idea of having an article that focused on her was not particularly appealing, especially since she didn't plan to stick around.

"I know Erin seems young," Irita said, "but she's a good kid, and she can turn it around like you won't believe."

"That's not it," Mesa said. Best not upset the apple cart yet. "I'm sure she'll write a fine piece. It's just that I'm the shy, retiring type. But I'll adjust. What else?"

"We're running part two of a feature on the resurgence of live poker in the Mining City." Irita rolled her eyes. "There was a Texas Hold 'em tournament over the weekend at the Depot, and some Butte rat won a bundle."

Mesa couldn't help but smile at the phrase "Butte rat" despite the unpleasant image it conjured up. The moniker was carefully bestowed only on those born and bred in the Mining City.

"The Depot?" Mesa asked. The number of bars in Butte had been steadily declining for years, but this sounded like some place new.

"Over on Arizona Street. It used to be the Great Northern Railway Depot. Somebody remodeled it last year, hauled that 24-foot walnut long bar from whatchamacallit's in Walkerville. Now they've set up a few card tables, broken open the poker chips, and supply the booze and the bouncers. The rest is up to Lady Luck.

"We'll round out the edition with the usual football scores, AA meetings, shindigs and assorted other hysteria, birth announcements, anniversaries and, of course, our bread and butter—the classifieds and advertisements."

Mesa said nothing and Irita paused. "You didn't want to write anything, did you?" This question came quickly, as if she suddenly realized she had forgotten to set a place at the table for the guest of honor.

Mesa let out a whoosh of relief. "No way. I'm a fish out of water for the time being. If I had to write anything about Butte, I might break out in hives. When's deadline again?"

"Tomorrow night, preferably by 11 p.m.," Irita said. "Ads had to be in on Friday."

"So, let's go ahead with the rest of the week's schedule," Mesa said. "When's the editorial staff meeting?"

Irita stared at Mesa and then looked quickly from side to side, moving her eyes and nothing else. "Surely, you jest," Irita said finally. "You *are* the editorial staff. This is Montana, honey. When you're the boss, whatever you say goes."

"Don't you discuss feature ideas? How do you decide what the paper's lead is going to be?" Mesa knew her grandmother had not a dictatorial bone in her body. She hardly ever told anyone what to do directly. She had this way of getting you to tell yourself. Maybe she ran the *Messenger* that way.

"Of course we discuss things, but it's usually over a shot and a beer at the Silver Dollar. This is not the Butte of old with ninety thousand people, political corruption, corporate intrigue, and five papers competing for the biggest scoop. Everybody in town pretty much knows what's going on as fast as we do. You can pretty much guess what the *Standard*'s going to cover, which leaves pretty much everything that's local and not mayhem to us."

"Guess that pretty much covers it," Mesa said with a grin, then added, "Humor me anyway. Wednesday morning, let's have an editorial staff meeting. Say, 9 am. You, Erin, Delilah, Phade, and I want Chance there, too. Where's his office, by the way?"

"Pork Chop John's," Irita said and excused herself to answer a ringing phone on her desk just outside what was now the editor's office door.

Chapter 5

An hour later, Irita had dragged Mesa to Stodden Park to observe the passing of summer, Butte style. "Come on, it's the Labor Day picnic. You gotta eat," Irita said while they waited in the chow line where the mayor and several city commissioners were dosing the crowd with baked beans, potato salad, and hotdogs.

"One hotdog won't kill you," Irita said, "even if they *were* donated by Terminal Meats." Mesa smiled and hoped the owners of Butte's oldest butcher and wild-game processing store weren't within hearing distance.

The last time she had attended a Labor Day picnic, her mother had been alive. They had spent the afternoon sunbathing at the swimming pool on one of the rare, truly hot summer days. Her mother had been so happy to be back in Butte.

"You'll meet some new people, maybe see some old friends, and get heartburn," Irita said. "It's what neighborhood news is all about."

In the span of twenty minutes, Irita had introduced her to every other person in Stodden Park. Locals of all ages basked in the warm sunshine, playing Frisbee, drinking Bud Lite, and otherwise trying to ignore the speakers at the mike.

The stock-in-trade for the labor unions that had once held sway in Butte, political promises nowadays seemed to fall on deaf ears. Shabby and thin on the ground, much of what she saw spoke of little money and hard times. Butte was ten percent romantic notion and ninety per cent grim reality. Now that the mines were closed, the sponsors of the picnic had dwindled, but the number of hungry mouths had grown, and filling them was everyone's priority.

Irita and Mesa waded through a sea of picnickers, babies on blankets and elderly people in lawn chairs. They perched themselves on one side of the brick foundation of the Korean War Memorial.

Mesa gazed up at the idealized, larger-than-life bronze sculpture of an infantryman. Montanans had a proud history of serving their country, including her own father, whose career choice he readily admitted was partly the result of the state's notorious lack of decent, steady employment. Unlike her father, she suspected her views on international relations were decidedly left of many Montanans, even in Butte, which was the state's Democratic stronghold.

Mesa felt the gentle nudge of an elbow into her side. "Stop thinking and eat," Irita said, her mouth full of hotdog oozing with mustard, ketchup, and sauerkraut. She was ready for bite number two when a woman about thirty appeared with two kids in tow. Both children broke free, calling "Grammy, Grammy."

Irita eagerly traded her plate of food for children and smothered them with hugs. Their mother quickly intervened. "Let Grammy eat," she said gently. Lean and graceful with long dark hair, the woman apologized for interrupting.

Mesa blushed as Irita introduced her as the new boss and was surprised to find that the other woman, Kathy DiNunzio, was Irita's daughter-in-law. Kathy smiled warmly and stepped aside. A taller male version, with more muscle but without the smile, nodded. "You remember Garrett, my brother," Kathy said, her voice slightly too enthusiastic. "He's on leave."

Irita stood up and said, "Sure do. Sorry I didn't get to wish you bon voyage before your trip to Kandahar. Welcome home."

That explained the short haircut, Mesa thought as Irita introduced him by saying he lived in Billings but was now in the Army National Guard. He mumbled a greeting and then stood by stoically, not unlike the statue in front of the memorial. His gaze indirect, he waited without a word while his sister chatted easily with Irita.

Mesa, feeling vaguely uncomfortable, searched for something innocuous to say. She had met plenty of airmen in her day but no one who had served in the more recent deployments to the Middle East. For sure, she hadn't met any recently returned, frontline soldiers, which somehow she knew he was. "I haven't met anybody who's been in Afghanistan," she said.

He looked up at her, his brow thick. His hazel eyes filled with a weariness that made her want to hug him. "It's all right," he said almost apologetically, as if he understood what she felt.

She didn't think conversation about American foreign policy was appropriate. Especially to this soldier who seemed uneasy, not like the ones that made the cover of *Time* and *Newsweek*. Finally, she said, "I'm sorry for the trouble we've put you to." She felt strangely inarticulate, but she knew she would have regretted saying nothing, letting the moment pass.

When he spoke again, his voice was raspy, as if he had spent the previous day shouting orders nonstop. "I'm sorry too." Then he retreated to the number one question in every Montanan's mind. "How about this weather?" he said with the tiniest hint of a grin at the corner of his mouth.

Before she could answer, the kids tugged at him, each pulling on a different finger of his large hand. He clapped his free hand to his shoulder and held it, feigning injury. The children laughed, and then pleaded with him to take them to the swings. The trace of a smile crept across his face, and he said goodbye to her. Then he turned and quietly followed the children, who were already skipping toward the colorful jungle gym. She watched him walk away and wondered what horrors he had seen or perhaps committed so far from home.

She thought about her dad who, contrary to his military career—he would say because of it—had taught her long ago that no soldier wants to go to war. They always argued about the so-called all-volunteer army. She thought everybody should serve and then politicians would be less likely to send their own kids off to war.

Her dad believed some men, and maybe some women, although he still wasn't entirely sure about that, were more suited to combat than others were. He had no illusions about the fact that, despite all the expensive technological advances, soldiers on the ground were still a necessity. Mesa's reply was that it was too bad more people didn't discover their lack of a temperament for battle before getting sent into one.

Mesa turned toward the makeshift stage by the outfield fence of the softball field. She tried in earnest to pay attention to the congressional candidate, a mint farmer from Kalispell, who was assailing the crowd with the faults of his Republican opponent. Standing several feet behind the mike, and apparently waiting to speak, Mesa saw Shane Northey.

Irita was deep in conversation with Kathy and Mesa thought about going up to say hello. He had a pleasant, clean-cut look to him, dress shirt and jeans again. She wasn't immune to attraction, short-term as it might be. A quick smile accompanied his ready handshakes with others on the stage. He turned his attention to the speaker, and so did she. Predictably, the Democrat needled the Republicans, demanding better-paying jobs and attention to health care reform—not that she didn't agree.

Mesa turned when she heard her name being called in an unmistakable, high-pitched voice. Tara McTeague came hurtling precariously toward her in toeless, cork-wedged sandals. On her hip rode Kelly, her blue-eyed, blonde-haired daughter, an exact image of her mother. Connor, an almost identical little boy, tottered along, pulling on his mother's hand. Mesa embraced as many of the trio as she could, having only seen photos of the twins previously.

"When did you get in and what is going on?" Tara asked over her shoulder with mock indignation as Connor immediately began herding them toward the giant jungle gym with remarkable determination for a two-year-old. "Chance wants me to look for a place for you, and the last email you sent said you were thinking about moving to Portland."

Tara was her usual whirlwind self, juggling several pieces of life at once. Married and the mother of twins right out of the shoot, and now she was pregnant with a third. Their lives were completely different, but Mesa had learned long ago that she could always count on Tara to keep her mouth shut. "God, my butt's really in a sling this time."

"What a shocker," Tara said with gentle sarcasm. "Tell me everything." If life was too full for Tara, she didn't show it. She still had a wide grin and time to offer a ready opinion about the guys who found their way into Mesa's life.

"Remember Derek Immelmann?"

"Your boss that you had the hots for all this time?" Tara's voice brimmed with anticipation.

Mesa nodded. "He quit and moved to Oregon at the end of June to work for *Pacifica* Magazine."

"Never heard of it," Tara said.

Pacifica was the most progressive magazine on the west coast, but social commentary wasn't Tara's strong suit. "It's a cool magazine, and it pays well," Mesa said.

"So what are you doing here?" Tara asked while depositing Kelly and Connor on the bump slide on the jungle gym. "You and Derek got together before he left, right?" Tara said with a smile.

Mesa nodded. It had been two weeks of nonstop sex, usually fueled by too many beers after endless late nights at the *Current*. "I said I'd follow him anywhere, which may have been a slight exaggeration."

"The sex really wasn't that good?" Tara asked.

Mesa shrugged. "About as good as my timing."

"I know I'm not Einstein," Tara said, "but I still don't see the problem."

"The day after Derek left, Chance began his campaign to get me to run the *Messenger* until Nan's back on her feet. Now that I'm finally here, Derek wants me to come to Portland. He submitted my resume for a job that's come open, and I fly in for an interview on Friday."

"Can't live with them, can't live without them," Tara said.

"You're telling me. He's the hard-drinking, married-to-the-job type," Mesa said. "But the job screams real potential. I'm just not sure how I'm going to explain the change in plans to Chance."

"Well, I'm glad you've kept your options open because you'll never guess which old heartbreaker is back in town, and headed right this way."

Mesa tried to ignore the slight increase of her heartbeat. Then she turned to look straight into the eyes of Hardy Jacobs.

"How's she going?" he said to them both. Then to Mesa he murmured, "I heard you were back in town."

Brown hair tipped blond, no doubt by a summer of biking all over southern Utah, framed Hardy's youthful good looks and blue-green eyes. He looked like he belonged in one of those Ralph Lauren ads in *Rolling Stone* magazine.

"Not too bad," Tara said. "How 'bout yourself?" she said and nodded toward his foot.

"Ended up on the wrong side of some reckless slick-rocker who should have been walking instead of riding." Hardy held up a bandaged left ankle. "Twisted it a bit."

"Can I get either of you ladies a drink?" He held up an empty Mountain Dew can. "Time for another. Don't you move," he said to Mesa. "Be right back."

Tara and Mesa watched him hobble toward the drinks tent, each waiting until he was out of hearing distance. Tara was the first to react.

"Oh my God. He is too smooth. He acts like he just saw you yesterday. How long has it been?"

"Your birthday party at the McQueen." Christmas four years ago, the last time Mesa had been in Butte. Hardy had shown up halfway through the evening, fresh from a weekend's work as a snowboard instructor at Big Sky. Tan and buff as ever, he looked half his age dressed in baggy ski pants and a long-sleeved tee shirt advertising some brand of snowboard. A stocking cap completed his ensemble, with errant wisps of hair peeking out at the ears and neck.

"Oh yeah, now I remember. Didn't you hook up with him and take off to Big Sky? I was so bummed. I hardly saw you at all that Christmas."

After a few quick beers, she and Hardy had drifted together, reminiscing about old times. One thing led to another. How could she blame herself when the next day she had gone to Big Sky and stayed the weekend at the cabin Hardy shared with two other ski bums? They had pledged seriously to see each other again soon. At least Mesa thought they were serious.

She had returned to her job at the *Current* with perma-grin. Then, in the next four years, she had received exactly two postcards from Hardy, who spent May through October working for an outfitter in southern Utah, and continued to winter in Big Sky.

"Good thing he never misses any free food, or it might be another four before you see him again."

The two women stood next to the ladder of the slide, helping Kelly and Connor. "Tara, don't get evil on me. We had a lot of good times together."

"If you can call watching baseball all summer a good time."

A decade ago, Hardy breathed baseball, playing shortstop for the Miners—Butte's double A American Legion team. With a handful of other female fans, Mesa and Tara had spent the summer pretending to be devoted to the great American pastime.

"Excuse me, did you or did you not meet your husband while he was playing third base for the Helena Saints?" Mesa countered.

Those were the days when ball players and fans alike drank beer at the Vu Villa. The closest bar to the baseball field, the team, and their followers naturally gravitated to the Vu, drinking til midnight if they lost, til closing if they won.

Hardy's older brother lived in an apartment on Park Street where they invariably crashed afterward. Mesa often snuck home in the pre-dawn, barely able to get a few hours' sleep before work at the paper the next day. No easy feat in her grandmother's creaky, old Victorian house.

She knew Hardy took a lot of grief from his teammates when he would walk her the six blocks home from the bar. But she had fond memories of those long summer evenings when they would walk hand in hand down Platinum Street, when neither had a care in the world.

ৎৣৣ৵

"Jesus H. Christ, if it's not one thing, it's another," Irita said. She sat back down next to Mesa, who had retreated to the war memorial when Tara had decided to take the twins home for their nap, and Hardy had gone off to talk baseball with an old teammate.

"Anything newsworthy?" Mesa asked, resisting the instinct to look for bad news.

"Not for the moment," Irita said and picked up her cold hotdog.

"I had no idea you had grown children," Mesa said with a smile, "and grandchildren, too?"

"Why, thank you," Irita said. "Aren't they adorable?"

Mesa looked over at the playground where she could still see the little girl being pushed in a swing by her Uncle Garrett, who was now accompanied by a blonde woman in blue jeans and a western shirt. She looked familiar, and though Mesa couldn't remember her name, she felt reassured by the woman's presence. That soldier needed some TLC.

"So, what's the problem?" Mesa probed while Irita attacked the rest of her hotdog.

Irita sighed and looked around as if she wanted to be sure no one overheard. "Turns out Garrett was supposed to report back to his unit already. His sergeant called Kathy, as next of kin, this morning looking for him and to say if Garrett's not back in 48 hours, he'll be AWOL. So, naturally, she told his sergeant she didn't know where Garrett was. She wasn't going to rat out her own brother, at least not 'til she talked to him first."

"What's the brother say?" Mesa asked, marginally surprised to hear that Garrett was not looking forward to a return to duty.

"Well, that's part of the problem. Apparently, he's wound tighter than the inside of a golf ball. Hasn't slept a wink lately and isn't eating or talking much either."

Mesa looked at Garrett, who did seem to take a more-than-passing interest in those around him— maybe a touch of paranoia. Of course, from the way the Army operated recently, people really were after him or would be shortly.

"What happens to somebody who goes AWOL these days?" Irita asked half out loud.

"I think they stopped shooting deserters after World War II," Mesa said, trying not to sound sarcastic. She had a long enough association with the Air Force to understand the gravity of regulations, though her father had never broken any, at least not to her knowledge. "Maybe they send you back to the frontlines, although I'm not sure if they know where that is in the Middle East anymore. I think you have to be gone for a while before they consider it desertion."

"I'm surprised to hear he'd pull a stunt like that," Irita said. They were both watching him swinging his niece. "He's not a bad guy. The kids idolize him. Before Afghanistan, he was talking about going into business for himself.

"I told Kathy I'd ask around. See what she can do to help him get back into the good graces of the Army."

"What did he do in Afghanistan?" Mesa asked.

"Drove a truck is all, as far as I know. But I did hear he had some buddies blown up by one of those roadside bombs a week after they were deployed. Kathy says he never talks about it. She heard about it from a friend who read it in the Billings *Gazette*."

"Well, I think you better tell him the Army called."

"That's what I said, but Kathy's afraid he might do something drastic."

"Sounds like he already has."

Chapter 6

That afternoon Mesa reviewed the proofs for Wednesday's paper. She shook her head and wondered how she could be dumb enough, once again, to allow Chance to talk her into having him take her photograph. At least it was inside on the first page.

Irita had argued to put the whole story on the front page. "Hell's bells," she had said, "A new editor is a big damn deal. People in town need to know who she is, that she's Butte connected, and that she's not some Easterner trying to reinvent herself."

Mesa wasn't so sure what the photo conveyed. To get her to relax, Chance had posed her leaning on the office credenza. Too relaxed, Mesa thought. She had slouched instinctively so as not to accentuate her height, and now her bony shoulders stood out.

Her head was cocked just to the left and she sported one of those "I can't believe you're making me do this" smiles. Thank goodness, for a thick head of dark hair and the money she spent to get a decent haircut. At least she didn't look like a pinhead.

Never mind the photo. The bottom line was that her appointment as editor was not a story she wanted to publicize . . . period—not with the Portland interview looming—but she didn't have the heart to tell anybody on the first day. But Irita was right. The newspaper business these days, especially a local, neighborhood newspaper, relied on stability. You couldn't have your readers wondering if the paper was going to be out on time. Or God forbid they should worry that the story about their nephew might get left out. The paper needed to reflect her arrival somehow.

Mesa scanned the piece, which sounded less like the usual bio and more like a sweet homecoming story—up-and-coming journalist leaves a thriving career in cutting-edge journalism. She definitely couldn't leave that story line in. She would have to come up with something else.

Mesa sighed and flipped through the remaining pages of the paper. Micah had written a short piece about the challenge faced by fourth graders starting at a new school after the closure of their beloved Longfellow Elementary. The story hit at the heart of one of every mining town's dilemmas. The ebb and flow of the population, along with the inevitable aging of those who stayed behind, meant the children had to toughen up. School closings were unavoidable.

Erin had contributed part two of the saga of the Butte Jazz Society, a group of well-meaning, musically inclined citizens. The society had hoped to preserve and renovate the now defunct Presbyterian Church across from the public library. A board member had hoodwinked them all and diverted their grant funds to cover gambling debts.

The building showcased a beautiful stained-glass rose window. Everybody had been heartened to see that it might be rescued. Once again, some outsider had made off with the loan money and robbed Butte of an opportunity to improve its community. So much for the good news.

Irita stuck her head in the door and interrupted Mesa's musings. "On the first day, you don't have to burn the midnight oil." She smiled. "I'm assuming Mrs. Ducharme gave you a key?"

Mesa nodded and smiled back.

"Good, looks like you're the last one out, so lock up, okay?"

Irita disappeared down the hall, leaving Mesa grinning and offering a mock salute. Her father would call Irita a piece of work, someone who did things her way and expected other people to oblige. But as far as Mesa was concerned, Irita did it in a charming way. Local Irish blarney had rubbed off on her.

In fact, Irita could probably run the *Mining City Messenger*, despite Chance's attempts to make the job sound tough. That could be Mesa's salvation. Irita would step up, at least until Nana came back.

Mesa's mind began to spin in the stillness of the empty office. Maybe there was a way after all to extract herself from Butte and the *Messenger* without disappointing too many people.

She felt exhausted after her first day on the ground. She had moved enough in childhood and in college to know it would take a while to feel comfortable. But if she took the Portland job, then her transition was just beginning.

She looked at the family photograph on her grandmother's credenza, a portrait of the Dawsons. Chance looking like Dad, handsome well-proportioned features sitting above high cheekbones and a strong chin. She stood next to him looking like their mother, except bantam size and freckled. They were all so lean and healthy then.

Mesa glanced at the desk calendar. It was September 7th, her mother's birthday. She would have been how old? Mesa did the math, feeling slightly guilty that she didn't know by heart.

In the weeks after her mother died, Mesa had struggled to imagine life without her. It still made her uncomfortable to think about that time, when her father had returned to his assignment in Germany, throwing himself back into his work to avoid showing his own grief.

Without giving much thought to it, she picked up her cell phone and called his office at the Pentagon. All she heard was an answering machine. Silly, she belittled herself; it was nearly eight o'clock in the evening on the East Coast. Even Colonel Nathaniel Dawson wouldn't be in the office at that hour. She got the same response at his apartment in Crystal City. She left a simple message: "I'm at Nana's. Miss you. Call me."

◆◆◆

Chance meandered through the token "after work" crowd in Muldoon's. A perennial St. Patrick's

Day favorite, off-duty cops and other law enforcement types held the bar in high regard, mainly because the bartender always seemed to have a connection to the department. In this case, the current barkeep, Casey Van Zant, had a brother on the force.

Chance scanned a group of guys standing under the moose antlers and looked for Nick Philippoussis. He had promised to hook up after a quick trip to the mortuary to prepare one of the Elk Park traffic victims for cremation.

Chance wouldn't describe himself as a barfly, but that didn't mean he was uncomfortable in any of the local drinking establishments. Bars in Butte performed a peculiarly social function, more local and familiar than the bars Chance had frequented in eastern cities. Each place had its regulars who, on any given evening, appeared like clockwork.

He often wondered if this was a legacy of the days when miners frequently went from work to the bar and, sometimes, vice versa. In its heyday, Butte had one bar for every twenty miners. And after every mine accident, no doubt a silent tally of customers took place to see who, if any, were missing.

At this point in the day, Chance felt the need to quench his thirst. After an hour of knocking on doors in the neighborhood around Porphyry and Washington Streets, he had come away frustrated. Less than half the residents were even at home. The ones he had talked to had seen nothing of the plane crash, let alone anyone walking away from it. He told himself to be patient and to try again the next day when people would be back from their three-day weekend.

Nick was still nowhere to be seen. Surveying the crowd again, Chance didn't see any off-duty cops either. He wasn't likely to pick up any new information on or off the record. It looked like he would have to take potluck and check the word on the street. Otherwise, he would have to wait until tomorrow's press briefing when with any luck the crash investigators might be forthcoming.

He sat at the bar and turned his attention to Casey. She was certainly the best looking among Butte's many barmaids, and well informed particularly about police matters. But she had a prickly side, and even Chance had to work to get a smile out of her.

"What happened to your Red Sox this year?" he asked when she delivered a bottle of Moose Drool to him.

"They're not my Red Sox anymore, and consequently I could care less what happened to them."

"After all these years, a devoted fan such as you?" Chance teased gently.

"I've turned over a new leaf on numerous fronts."

Casey had broken up with her live-in, a guy named Mattie Gronauer. He was a washed-up forward with the Roughriders, Butte's hockey team, who now worked construction. He had been working out of town in Bozeman, so one night she had driven over to surprise him. Instead, she found him doing the horizontal mambo with a casino girl from a joint over there. That was Mattie, always lazy. He never looked far for women, not that he had to.

"Mattie never seemed like your type," Chance said quietly, not wanting to open their conversation to others. He knew he was taking a big risk. Casey might just tell him to shove it, or she might just appreciate the support. He was counting on the latter.

She stopped in front of him, wiped the bar, and said, "Thanks, Chance." She looked at him with a sigh.

He could see the loneliness in her, the small lines around the corners of her eyes, evidence that she had not been sleeping well.

"Funny how you can get used to having a son-of-a-bitch around all the time," she said.

"Never mind, what you gotta do is get back in the saddle," Chance said and held an imaginary set of reins in front of him while he made a slight bucking motion on his barstool.

She broke into a smile, which he returned.

"What you up to yourself?" Casey asked. "I hear your sister's back in town."

News was traveling at its usual pace. "Yeah, she's helping out at the paper til Nan gets back on her feet. She has me working this story about the plane crash." Chance knew this wasn't entirely true, but he liked promoting the idea that Mesa was in charge.

"Brock told me about it," Casey said. "A stolen plane, no pilot, and a notorious but dead ex-con. One too few you, if you want my opinion."

Chance drained his Moose Drool and said, "Leave it to Butte to attract the most infamous ex-fugitive in three decades."

Casey shrugged and brought him another. "I hear the station is crawling with investigators from the plane manufacturer to the FAA. I'm sure they think they'll have it all figured out in no time." She glided toward the other end of the bar to customers clamoring for refills.

"Hey, hotshot, how ya doin'?" Nick Philippoussis sat down on the stool next to Chance. Nick called out to Casey for a Shawn O'—Buttese for a shot and a beer—and a couple of pickled turkey gizzards. Then he turned to Chance and said, "Sorry I had to blow you off yesterday. I didn't want to keep the medical examiner waiting even an extra second when he was coming back from vacation for us. He's one hell of a good guy. Plus, I knew he'd want me to stay 'til it was over with."

Chance grimaced. He had no stomach for the blood-and-guts part of Nick's job. "How did it go?" he asked and hoped Nick would skip the gruesome details.

Nick downed the shot of whiskey, took a pull from his longneck, and then pulled apart the turkey gizzard while he talked. "Pretty clear that Lowell Austin wasn't flying the plane. The medical examiner says that pilots who die in crashes sustain particular injuries on their hands and feet, which Austin didn't have. Still not sure what killed him though. I'm betting drugs.

"They were pulling fluids for the tox screens when I left to cover the Elk Park massacre. They probably won't know the exact cause of death until the results come back. They're plenty backed up at the lab, but they'll put a priority on this one since it involves the Feds."

"I thought it was weird that whoever left him in the plane tried to make it look like he was the pilot," Chance said.

"I told you something was sketchy about it," Nick said. "Why would they do that? As soon as you know who the guy is, you know he wasn't the pilot unless they're giving flying lessons in the joint."

Chance nodded. "Buying time to get away is all I can figure. Even if it was only twenty-four hours."

"Which, if that's true," Nick said, his voice rising with curiosity, "then what was the real pilot needing to get away from?"

Chance sipped on his beer and wondered the same thing.

Mesa spooned several scoops of the aromatic, black P&G Tips into the porcelain teapot, and then grabbed milk from the fridge for the creamer while waiting for the water to boil. Impatient and chastising herself for it, she searched in several kitchen cabinets before finding the sugar cubes her grandmother always used.

Normally, she loved fixing the tea, one of those quaint English traditions that made her cherish her grandmother. Today she was grinding her teeth. It wasn't that she didn't want to be a comfort, but she couldn't help feeling that's all she'd become.

Now that she had begun to consider the real possibility that Irita could run the *Messenger* without anybody's help, she wondered if Chance hadn't realized the same thing a month ago. Why then had he applied the pressure to get Mesa to come back to Butte?

The water boiled, Mesa filled the pot, found some shortbread biscuits, assembled the rest of the tea tray, and carried it into the parlor. Nana put down the proofs from the *Messenger* and smiled at Mesa as she placed the tray on the coffee table in front of the settee.

"I can't tell you how wonderful it is to have you here at home again. Come sit by me," Nana said.

As usual, Mesa's resentment temporarily vanished when she sat next to her grandmother and felt her warm hand on her own. Nana reached for the teapot to pour, and Mesa quickly interceded. "Here, let me do that. Give me your thoughts on this week's edition."

Nana folded the galleys on her lap, and then said, "Perhaps I should be asking your opinion. I'm hoping you can elevate the level of our journalism a bit. I'm tired of reading about courthouse squabbles and who's mad at whom about the blasted animal shelter."

Nana took the proffered cup of tea with milk and two lumps and said, "I know if a person can write honestly, have a curiosity about the world around them and can keep their facts straight, that should be enough to produce thought-provoking stories, but I think the *Messenger* needs a bit of a shake-up. Just because we're small doesn't mean we can't be good.

The market is out there for us. Not everybody in this town has gone electronic. Plenty of people want to pick up a paper and read about their neighbors. God knows the *Standard* runs enough canned stories; there's plenty of good local color that goes unnoticed."

Mesa knew what she meant. She had worked as a stringer for a daily straight out of college. It didn't take long to notice the mediocrity, less and less in-depth features, less and less national coverage, twice the space devoted to comics and more coverage of the weather than serious news. And now with the Internet, everybody was scrambling.

The *Montana Standard* publisher's main concern had to be the bottom line. Keeping the payroll to a minimum, hiring young reporters fresh out of college and boosting coverage with wire stories and editorials were tried-and-true strategies for every daily from Massachusetts to Montana. Unless you were the *Washington Post* or the *New York Times*, the only thing that was cutting-edge at newspapers was their accountant. "To tell you the truth, Nan, I think the *Messenger* is doing just fine."

"Now, Mesa, you don't have to worry about hurting my feelings. You wouldn't have left that paper back east just to come to Butte to be with me. I know you're a professional now, and I want you to take over completely. My name can remain as publisher on the masthead, but I don't want to come back to the office."

Mesa almost spilled her tea but recovered before Nana noticed. She took several sips to buy time while she thought about just how much to say. This was a well-intended offer, and the last thing Mesa wanted to do was offend her grandmother, the person who had been the one true anchor in her life. But she couldn't find it in herself to reveal her Portland plans.

Instead, for the moment, she decided to counterpunch. "But Nana, I thought you enjoyed working on the paper. Why do you want to give it up all of a sudden? Your recovery is progressing well. The staff wants you back."

"I'd been thinking about it even before the heart attack. Chance and I talked about it a while back. Butte's economy is making a comeback. The *Messenger* has the potential to be more than just a neighborhood paper, but it needs an experienced journalist like you who understands both print and electronic media."

There was Chance's hand in this again, Mesa thought.

"I'm not sure I'm ready for all this responsibility, Nan. Let's not make any rash decisions."

"Actually, I was quite surprised when Chance suggested calling you," Nana said. "I rather thought you might be too involved with that young banker of yours."

Mesa poured her grandmother more tea and leapt at the opportunity to take the conversation in another direction, even toward her muddled love life. Nana's heart attack had put her out of the loop as far as Mesa's love interests were concerned. The banker had been pre-Derek. "The banker lost interest some time ago," Mesa said with a smile.

She saw a slight grin budding on Nan's face. "Now that doesn't mean you should start any matchmaking," Mesa said. "I can make my own company."

"Wouldn't think of it, dear, but I had hoped to meet Philip for dinner tomorrow night. He wants to go to The Derby, something special for my first night out, you see. Of course, I really shouldn't drive. I suppose Shane could pick us both up and then come back for us. Reminds me of when your mother was a teenager." Her voice trailed off as she realized she was thinking out loud.

"All right," Mesa said with a smile. "I'll go along. But no more matchmaking, promise?"

"I'll call Philip straight away," Nana said and picked up the phone next to her on the lamp table. Mesa shook her head and wondered if Shane Northey knew Hardy Jacobs.

Chapter 7

By the time Mesa had walked the eight blocks to the *Messenger* office on Tuesday morning, she had decided she would come clean. Chance would have to face the fact that she did not intend to spend the next thirty years running the *Messenger*. At the very least, she would have to figure out how to pull that "new editor" story.

Irita appeared at Mesa's desk and placed a double latte in the middle of it even before Mesa sat down. With an air of deference to the new boss, Irita said, "Anna Takkinen has deemed to grace us with her presence this morning. I told her to bring you a copy of the annual budget like you asked."

Mesa nodded and sipped the coffee. Irita was still standing by her desk. "And?" Mesa said.

Irita looked as if she were seriously contemplating what to say next. "Anna's a hard worker," she said finally. "Her old man was the last owner of the Helsinki Bar. She grew up in Finntown, so she knows what it's like to keep your nose to the grindstone."

Mesa leaned back in her chair and tried to dredge up whatever she could recall about the Finnish part of

Butte—photographs of lanky, taciturn Nordic miners in front of the gigantic boarding houses that had dominated the east end of Park and Broadway Streets. All that remained now was a single building that had housed the Helsinki Bar, a faded monument to the once bustling neighborhood, which the Anaconda Company pit mining operation had gobbled up forty years before.

Wallace Stegner had once written that more than half a place is memory. In the case of Butte, Mesa thought it was more like ninety-nine percent. Everything and everybody in Butte had a history that had significance to somebody. But she still couldn't figure out what Irita was trying to tell her. "So?"

"Well, just keep in mind she would never do anything she wasn't told to do, okay?" With that caveat, Irita backed out of the room, quickly replaced by a tall, gray-blonde woman clutching a set of hanging file folders to her bosom like they were a flotation device and she was on the Titanic.

Anna seemed paralyzed, feet and eyes fixed to the floor. Mesa finally had to ask her to sit down. "I've been meeting all the staff. No big deal, just wanted to put a name to a face."

Anna said nothing, still clutching the files. Surely, this was more than Scandinavian reserve, but Mesa wasn't sure what the problem was. "What's that you brought with you?" Mesa asked and resisted the urge to reach out for the files, lest her movement result in Anna's fainting.

"Irita said you might want to take a look at the budget. I made you a copy," Anna said with a slight stutter. She opened the top folder on her lap. "There are the spreadsheets for the projected budget and then a monthly breakdown."

Mesa smiled and nodded. One thing Stu Friedman, her managing editor at the *Current*, and she did agree about was a newspaper's finances. No matter what size the budget, he would say at their quarterly meetings, make sure more money comes in than goes out. "Why don't I take a look at what you've brought me, and then if I have any questions, I'll get back to you. Okay?"

Mesa shuffled the few papers on her desk and made several other "meeting's over" gestures. She thought sure Anna would fly out of there like a shot.

Instead, Anna moved to the edge of her seat, handed the copy of the budget across Mesa's desk and said, "I think I should explain a few of the entries under advertising. I have pleaded with Chance, but it just doesn't do any good."

Chance took a seat at the counter of the Copper Pot, where the counter girl brought him a cup of coffee. He didn't recognize her. The owner, Lars Schogren or Shug, short for Sugar, earned his nickname in toddlerhood when he had routinely stuck his fingers in the sugar bowl. Shug now had six kids of his own—four of them daughters. Maybe this was one of the younger ones who had grown up without Chance noticing.

"Is Shug around? I want him to look at this week's proof," Chance said, opening a manila envelope and removing the galley for the restaurant's upcoming ad in the *Messenger*.

The counter girl had retreated to take a customer's money. Chance went back to a quick study of the menu and wondered what was keeping Shug.

"Pops says you should leave the ad," the girl said when she returned moments later. "Our cook didn't show this morning. Pops says to say he's busier than a one-legged man in an ass-kicking contest." The girl blushed and chuckled at the same time.

The *Messenger* had run numerous ads for the Copper Pot since its grand opening two months before. Shug had asked if Chance could sit on the bill through Labor Day when the restaurant was sure to be on its feet.

Rose Ducharme had a soft heart, and an iron pocketbook. But she knew that nobody who did business in Butte could avoid carrying somebody sometime. She condoned the practice on a rare occasion when a local business really needed a helping hand. In this case, Nan had been in the hospital when Shug Schogren had asked for some slack, so Chance decided the Copper Pot qualified.

"Oh, and he says to give you one of these Danishes." She lifted the glass cover on a mound of icing-covered confections that made Chance's mouth water.

Chance sighed inwardly then grabbed the top Danish, cherry, gulped the rest of his coffee and said, "I'll be back at lunchtime to pick up the galley.

And tell Shug my sister's running the paper now, so I need him to pony up."

Chance trotted outside. He had to make three more stops, all at businesses like Shug's that were behind on their accounts. In Mesa's world, the word "behind" didn't exist unless it was followed by "the eight ball," which was where he would be if he didn't collect what was owed.

ᱛᱷ

Mesa flipped through the monthly balance sheets for the past four months and wondered what went through her brother's head sometimes. The actual number of new advertisers was up over the last three months. That was the good news. The bad news was that ad revenues were half what they had been this time last year, with three particular accounts overdue to the tune of nearly seven thousand dollars. That might be peanuts in Pittsburgh, but in Butte, that was more than half of Erin O'Rourke's salary.

The Dumas Brothel and Sex Museum caught Mesa's eye first. Nana, not wanting to seem old-fashioned, had confided to Mesa about the audible sigh of relief from the country-club end of town when the oldest continuingly run brothel in the country had closed its doors in the spring. Thieves had broken into the museum and stolen most of the antique sex toys. Mesa was sorry the Dumas had finally closed, especially since that meant twelve hundred bucks the *Messenger* probably wasn't going to see anytime soon.

But what really steamed her was the Mountain Gallery and Frames whose *Messenger* account had an outstanding balance of eighteen hundred dollars. She reached for the *Standard*'s Labor Day insert. She stared at a half-page ad for Mountain Gallery and Frames, offering fine art, supplies, and custom framing. Sure as shooting, the *Standard* wasn't handing out free ads.

She went to the door of her office and called for Irita, who was in animated discussion with Anna at her desk. Irita responded with a wave, and Anna quickly turned her attention to her computer screen.

Irita appeared a moment later, shut the door, and sat on the sofa across from Mesa. "Anna feels bad because she knows Mrs. Ducharme carried her dad for several months when the Helsinki Bar was in its last days. Mr. Takkinen went to your grandmother and said his word was as good as the Finnish government, which, as you may know, was the one country to pay their war debt back to the United States after World War II. Mrs. Ducharme figured she could count on Paavo Takkinen."

"And don't tell me, he paid off his tab eventually?" Mesa said and rose from her desk to close the slim Venetian blinds, so that the piercing September sunlight didn't roast them. She was saving that torture for Chance.

"Businesses have been up and down in Butte since the first mine closure," Irita said. "Everybody does what they can."

"I know that," Mesa said. "But I don't like the *Messenger* being taken to the cleaners. Just who is it that owns Mountain Gallery, and why have we been carrying them for three months when apparently they can afford to take out ads in the daily paper?" She held up the *Standard*'s insert and shook it in the air.

Irita pressed her lips together and said nothing. Mesa may not have seen her in six years, but they had quickly bonded. Maybe it was the realization that neither of them minded hard work, or suffered fools. Whatever it was, Mesa knew she could be candid with Irita and expect the same in return. "I understand that Anna is only the bearer of bad news," Mesa said. "I don't intend to shoot the messenger. I'm saving my bullets for Chance."

Irita smiled nervously.

"So how about evening the odds a bit. Who thinks they can take advantage of us like this?"

"It's one of those California investors," Irita said in a burst of stored-up annoyance. "Name's Adrienne DeBrook, one of those artsy types. For reasons I am not sure of, nor really give a shit about, six months ago she came to town and bought the Imperial Building over on Park for a song."

Mesa knew the source of Irita's irritation. She had heard it all from Chance before. In the early 1900s, when Butte's mining economy supported nearly a hundred thousand people, Butte companies commissioned eminent architects to design their buildings. Their gargoyled cornices, clock towers, and delicately inlaid arches rivaled buildings in San Francisco and Chicago.

Unfortunately, many of those structures had fallen into disrepair. Few local residents could now afford to restore these building themselves, but that didn't stop the rest of the world. Outside investors from both coasts had begun buying precious but decaying old buildings in the Uptown historic district.

"At least she started renovating it right away instead of mothballing it," Irita said with some envy. "I have to admit it looks like she's done a damn good job. She's opened this framing business on the first floor, and now I hear she's turned the upper floors into studio loft apartments."

That still didn't explain how DeBrook had run up an advertising bill with the *Messenger*. "So who suggested we cut her a deal?"

Irita shook her head. "Nobody cuts deals around here except your grandmother. Of course, after the heart attack ..." Her voice trailed off. "Maybe Delilah was anxious to support another gallery and talked Chance into it."

Mesa and Delilah Tate, the *Messenger*'s arts and entertainment reporter, had yet to meet, so Mesa could make no judgment about her. Chance, on the other hand, although not immune to a sob story, was neither dumb nor careless. He would never let anyone take advantage of the family business.

Irita had the answer in her expression. Her piercing eyes were always sizing up a situation. When she talked, she never took her eyes off you. And when she wasn't talking, if she had something on her mind, it was impossible to hide.

"Mountain Gallery and Frames is into us for three months of quarter-page ads and has paid for one week. Come on, what do you know?"

Irita sighed and then said, "You didn't hear it from me."

Mesa nodded.

"I think Chance and she might have something going," Irita said and turned her head away as if she expected Mesa to yell or throw something.

True, women adored Chance. That wasn't news. Even Stephanie, who had divorced him, still loved him. Women sensed they could trust Chance— not that he didn't have all the usual male blind spots, but he was not a steamroller, and that was rare. He had manners and he knew how to treat women. "What do you mean, 'thing'?" Mesa asked. "You mean 'thing' thing?"

Irita rolled her eyes. "I hate talking about stuff like this. I think you should ask Chance."

"You bet I will. I'm not asking you to gossip," Mesa said matter-of-factly, as if she knew Irita wouldn't dream of such a thing. "Just tell me what you do know."

Irita sighed and Mesa had the sense that her newly found confidante was genuinely reluctant to reveal the story. "We've been having these Art Walks the last few summers, once a month, on Fridays. Local artists set up exhibitions of their work in different stores around town. Well, these last two months Adrienne DeBrook has been showing her own work, and at least one of her paintings is of Chance. Apparently, she has a cabin north of town, up on Moulton, where she goes to paint. So I guess he's spent enough time up there to get his portrait done."

Mesa was taken aback. She had suspected that Chance might be giving a break to yet another local who was down on her luck. She might have gone along with trading ad space for a new set of golf clubs. But romance? And with an artist, no less? What surprised her even more was that he hadn't told her about the woman himself.

His only real interest in art had been limited to architecture. Their parents had dragged them, as kids, to every museum within a half-day's drive from the various Air Force bases where they had lived. They had visited most of the great museums of Europe, but Mesa was the one who liked art.

The phone rang and interrupted her quandary.

"Mesa?"

She recognized Chance's voice. "Where have you been?" she asked, trying not to sound too snarky.

"Don't leave for lunch yet. I need to talk to you."

"Likewise," she said, but he had already hung up.

When Chance walked into the editor's office barely five minutes later carrying a white paper bag filled with Pork Chop John sandwiches and fries, Arnold Cinch was haranguing Irita and Mesa about "local hooligans" who had vandalized a *Messenger* distribution stand.

"The airplane that crash-landed didn't belong to the guy in it," Chance announced with animated gestures. "And, there was no ID on him either. So the National Transportation Safety investigator had a fingerprint check run on the guy," he said and began offering the bag of fries around to the trio. "Guess who the victim was? Go on, take a guess."

Mesa shrugged her shoulders. "Jimmy Hoffa?"

Chance rolled his eyes. "None other than the criminal who caused one of the biggest manhunts in the West in the past thirty years."

"Now wait a minute, did I miss something?" Irita asked. "Last I heard, Ted Kaczynski's in federal prison in Kansas or some damn place."

"Ha, ha," Chance said. "This is someone who served his time and was released. Come on now, don't you people read the newspapers? Cinch, you're the resident historian. Help 'em out. Who caused the biggest stink in poaching history in the Northwest in the last twenty-five years?"

"If this is Final Jeopardy," Arnold said, his face deadpan, "I'd like a new category."

Chance grabbed the front section of the *Standard* from Mesa's desk and tossed it onto the sofa. Lowell Austin in his last prison photo stared out from the bottom corner of the front page. "You mean you haven't read the morning paper today?"

Irita sat quietly, pensive, for once.

"You know, don't you, Irita?" Chance said, turning toward her. "Apparently women loved this guy. That's probably why he got off so light. They even wrote a country and western love song about him, for God's sake."

"You don't mean Lowell Austin?" Irita said in disbelief.

"One and the same."

"They're teaching flying in prison now?" Cinch said.

Chance plopped down between the two employees and put his arms on the sofa behind them. "I didn't say he flew the plane, but he's who they found in it, very dead."

"Well, I'm sure every Fish, Wildlife, and Parks warden in the Northwest will be ecstatic," Cinch said. "May I go now?"

"Somebody want to fill me in?" Mesa said with her arms folded.

Chapter 8

Mesa had never been particularly drawn to tales of rugged, western individualism, with the exception of Brad Pitt and "A River Runs through It," but this story had her attention. Cinch summed up the life of Lowell Austin like it was a made-for-TV movie, which apparently it had been.

"Killed two law officers and led the FBI around by the nose before charming a nearly all female jury into convicting him of the least severe charge possible," Cinch said in a disinterested monotone. "Unrepentant, Austin thumbed his nose at the parole board and served his full twenty-five years, minus three years for so-called good behavior, so he could be released a completely free man."

Mesa quickly did the math. This had all happened long before she began reading newspapers. "He must have had a good lawyer," she said.

"I don't remember hearing anything about this guy either," Chance said to Mesa. "Maybe we weren't stateside. Must have happened, what, in the mid-'80s?" He looked to Cinch for confirmation.

Cinch nodded. "I was a stringer in DC at the time. I was sipping my bourbon in some dive bar in DuPont Circle one afternoon when somebody showed me an article in the *New York Times* about the trial. They glorified Austin, the loner with good manners, a vivid imagination, and a mean streak. You've seen that kind of journalism back East," Cinch said with a nod toward Mesa. "Look at the animals in the zoo kind of thing," Cinch said with disdain. "That kind of romanticized reportage would make even open-minded Montanans want to repeal freedom of the press."

Unfortunately, Mesa did know. Happenings in the western states rarely made the front page of an eastern newspaper, unless you counted news from California, which might as well be a foreign country as far as most Montanans were concerned. The other news that was covered tended to be as Cinch described. "I can imagine what the Fish, Wildlife and Parks types thought," Mesa said quietly.

"They still haven't forgotten," Cinch said. "I was at the Nite Owl last week when the news broadcast that Austin was getting out. You know Hoyt Rawlins, who works in Fish, Wildlife and Parks?" Cinch said to Chance in a way that suggested to know him was not necessarily to love him.

Chance nodded. Rawlins was a monster of a guy who had spent several years as a boxer before he had taken up a career as a game warden, a job he loved more than money.

"The general consensus in our local Fish, Wildlife, and Parks office is that Austin was a rattlesnake and a murderer who should have been hung," Cinch said. "Of course, in Butte, just as many people would say he's done his time, leave him alone."

Mining towns were notorious for their tolerance of those down on their luck, even those who had been rightfully convicted. If you did a hard day's work, no one cared about your past. "Judging from what happened to him," Mesa said offhandedly, "he was safer in prison."

"Exactly my point," Chance said. "And obviously, he wasn't flying that plane. Unless, like Cinch said, they're teaching something in prison besides furniture making."

"So what are you saying?" Mesa asked. A hint of curiosity began to arouse in her.

"A pilot, who apparently didn't want to be associated with the crash or Lowell Austin, walked away. That's the story I'm interested in."

"That's not a crime, is it?" Mesa asked. "Like leaving the scene of an accident if you're driving a car and somebody gets hurt?"

"Ask the FAA," Chance said. "Maybe if you're dazed and confused, you could wander off. But if it was my plane, I'd stick around."

"Speaking of being responsible," Irita chimed in, "Cinch and I have work to do."

The two departed, and Chance stood up to follow.

"Hold up," Mesa said. She wasn't about to let Chance walk away without hearing about Adrienne DeBrook. "I need to talk to you about the advertising revenue. Seems we have some accounts that are in arrears."

"Okay, but let me get Erin going on this story first," Chance said between French fries.

"Anna showed me the budget this morning," Mesa said, not relenting. "You've turned her into a nervous wreck."

"Not to worry," he said over his shoulder. "The Copper Pot will settle up at the end of the month. The Dumas, well, I'm putting them on a long-term payment plan. Plus, they may reopen. The antique sex toys have turned up."

"And what about Mountain Gallery and Frames?" Mesa asked, trying not to seem any more concerned about it than the other accounts. She handed the insert to Chance, who stopped in the doorway and looked at the ad "We haven't lost that account," he said. "The owner just decided to diversify her marketing strategy."

"Well, you don't suppose the *Standard* ran that ad for free, do you?"

"What do you mean?" Chance said. He sounded genuinely puzzled.

"Mountain Gallery and Frames owes us twelve hundred dollars."

"They do?" Chance said and took the spreadsheet that Mesa held out to him.

"She's good for it, I'm sure. I'll get on it right away," he said with a big smile and headed down the hallway with Mesa after him.

Anna Takkinen called to Mesa from her cubicle. "A check arrived in the mail from Mountain Gallery this morning. Paid in full."

"See, I told you," Chance said with a grin.

"Who is the owner anyway?" Mesa asked. There was nothing for it but to be direct. "I've never heard of the place."

"Name's Adrienne DeBrook," Chance said in his usual casual way. "She's an artist. Moved to Butte last spring."

And then he was gone before Mesa could ask any more questions. So be it. She would find out more on her own.

Around 1:30, Mesa walked up Wyoming Street, deciding she needed to reacquaint herself with the ambience of Uptown Butte from the point of view of the pedestrian. The fact that her route took her to Park Street and directly past the Mountain Gallery was purely coincidental. She peered through the tall front windows into the long gallery. At the back, she could see a counter with sample frames mounted neatly on the walls behind, but no one was about.

She entered the shop, telling herself she would never pass up a new art gallery, not even in Butte. On one wall, half a dozen large portraits by a local artist she had heard about, Bonnie Rummenthal, caught her attention. The features of the figures were brash and bold—miners wearing headlamps, a ranch hand wiping his brow—the subjects teeming with enthusiasm for hard work.

Mesa turned to look at the opposite wall, on which hung dozens of smaller pieces—watercolors of street scenes and mine head frames in Uptown

Butte, suitable for souvenir-seeking tourists. Clearly, Adrienne DeBrook had some marketing sense. Mesa had to concede that the establishment felt comfortable—unpretentious but appealing, not to mention prosperous, which was how she liked to think of their advertising customers, especially if they paid on time.

Toward the back wall mounted on an easel, Mesa saw the painting Irita had called Chance's portrait, or at least the painting he had posed for. It was less a portrait than a painting with a figure in it, though anyone who knew Chance would know he had posed for the artist. Mesa wondered why that bothered her.

Bare-chested, grappling with a fence post with a head frame in the distance, his deerhide-gloved hands drew the viewer's focus into the center of the watercolor. High-contrast greens, golds, and dark browns made Mesa think of an Andrew Wyeth exhibit she had seen once at the Smithsonian. This one, titled "Whiskey Ridge Gulch," was priced at $1600.

She wasn't sure how long she had been looking at the painting when she heard a measured voice say, "I'm not sure I like the title."

Mesa looked up to see a woman standing behind her and gazing at the same painting. Dressed in a denim skirt and lavender, short-sleeved silk blouse, she wore amethyst earrings, accented with diamond chips, and looked like she could afford to plop down sixteen hundred bucks for a painting without any trouble.

"I think using numbered titles or geographical names is a good idea," Mesa said, trying not to sound proprietary, as though the fact that her brother was the model for the painting gave her some special insight. "Otherwise the artist overstates the work, like she's trying to tell the viewer what to think. Wouldn't you say?" This last statement sounded more perfunctory than she meant it to.

The woman smoothed her well-coifed, silver-gray hair away from her tanned face and nodded, not so much in agreement as in consideration. The scent of expensive perfume wafted through the air.

"How can you tell a woman painted it?" she asked.

Mesa shrugged. "I can't really. I mean I'm not sure I would say a woman did. I just happen to know the artist."

"You do?" the woman said, her face lit up in a curious smile that made her look younger than the graying hair would suggest.

"I know of her, I guess I should say," Mesa said, not wanting to seem as if she was trying to impress this stylish woman.

"Are you from Butte?" the woman asked.

Mesa shrugged. "Might as well be. I have family who live here, and I spent lots of time with them as a kid. I moved back for a while just recently."

Mesa suspected this woman was from the West Coast—L.A. or Seattle. She moved easily, inviting the space around her—poise you didn't see often in Easterners out of their element. She wasn't afraid to strike up a conversation with a stranger in some out-of-the-way place either. That was confidence that came from living in urban quarters. "Where are you from?" Mesa asked.

The woman moved toward the counter, adjusting a watercolor of a gallows frame along the way. A queasy feeling engulfed Mesa, like the time she had discovered Chance's stash of girlie magazines under his bed and wanted to believe they didn't belong to him.

"I live here in Butte, though I'm a transplant. I was born in Kalispell, but I have to confess I spent thirty years in dreaded California. And I'm working hard to recover and fit in again," she said with a smile. "I just opened this gallery."

Mesa took a deep breath and tried to think what she should say next. A heart-pounding moment of fight or flight finally passed. Mostly she thought about telling the truth, but even that was hard—the order of things, what to say first. Thankfully, Adrienne DeBrook seemed to have some task at hand, or at least she had the good grace to pretend she did.

Finally, Mesa just blurted it out. "I'm Chance's sister, Mesa." She stepped forward to the counter with her hand outstretched and hoped she didn't look as much like someone's kid sister as she felt, and probably sounded. Why hadn't she said, "I'm Mesa Dawson" and just left it at that?

Adrienne immediately broke into a smile and came back around the counter. She took Mesa's hand in both of hers.

"Of course, I should have known. The resemblance is obvious. I've been looking forward to meeting you. Chance speaks of you so often, I feel like I practically know you. So what do you think of 'Whiskey Run Gulch'?" She reached with her hand toward the painting as if she were remembering how it felt to touch him. "Chance says you're the one in the family with the artistic sensibility."

She was so relaxed that Mesa was filled with envy. "I like it," Mesa said. "I'm impressed with your technique. Dry brush, isn't it?"

"Yes," Adrienne said and talked for a few minutes about why she chose the method, which involves squeezing most of the moisture from the brush and painting with a few bristles to intensify the hues, especially in the detail of the gloves and the belt buckle.

Mesa's mind was abuzz. The issue of the gallery's accounts had faded to the background. All she could think about was what kind of relationship Chance might have with this woman, who had to be easily fifteen years older than her brother. She barely heard Adrienne's question.

"Do you paint?"

Mesa shook her head. She probably never would either as long as someone as accomplished as Adrienne DeBrook was in Chance's life. "No, I lean toward the written word for artistic expression." She sounded so lame. God, how was she going to get out of this?

"Chance tells me how good a writer you are. I'm looking forward to what you can do with the *Messenger*."

This was the segue Mesa needed to retreat gracefully, expressing gratitude for the Gallery's advertising business, mentioning specifically the most recent payment. Speaking of the *Messenger*, Mesa was about to say, when the bell at the door rang and an equally well-coifed woman in matching linen blouse and shorts entered, carrying several rolled canvases and demanding attention.

Adrienne excused herself to attend to her customer, and Mesa backed out of the shop, promising to return soon. Once on the sidewalk, she hurried back around the corner and leaned against the building to gather herself, all too aware of her hyper-physical reaction to the idea of Chance with an older woman.

Her mind spun with self-criticism. If Chance were seeing a woman fifteen years younger, would she react this way? How could she call herself a feminist if her ideas about sex and age were so narrow? And would she feel this way if the younger guy involved with Adrienne was somebody besides Chance?

She stared out across the valley to the East Ridge and took several deep breaths. The bottom line, she decided, was whoever Chance chose to see was none of her business, pure and simple. Letting out a long sigh of relief, she barreled down the hill and back to the office.

The hot afternoon sun had just passed its zenith when Chance knocked at the door of yet another duplex on Porphyry Street, seeking witnesses to Sunday's crash. At the two miner's cottages he had already approached, the inhabitants had been away for the long weekend, so the appearance of a crashed plane in the neighborhood had come as quite a shock when they returned on Monday. In the third cottage, a God-fearing Christian, on whom the feint smell of alcohol hidden by mouthwash was evident, had left for church just before the crash.

Chance had already canvassed the two houses on the east side of the street. He had heard about one lady's family reunion in Helena, and had spoken to a retired welder who had been surprised as hell to find a plane across the street when he returned from a weekend fishing at Georgetown Lake.

At the last house, a bungalow that could use a new porch, Chance had knocked twice before a disheveled twenty-something guy answered the door. He shared the house with three other guys, all of whom had gone to the Oredigger football game, where the Montana Tech team had beat the crap out of Carroll College, resulting in two days of nonstop celebration. The guy had seen nothing, though he thought a plane in the middle of a house was "trippy."

Chance turned from the porch and began walking up Washington when a man on a black Harley roared to a stop in front of the house with its newest appendage wrapped in yellow crime-scene tape. The rider dismounted slowly. Tall and broad of shoulder, he wore a black leather vest with an emblem on the back that read Riding for Christ. He moved almost in slow motion up the sidewalk toward the house.

"Mr. Mandic?" Chance called out, remembering the Tutty kid's comment about the man living in the house liking motorcycles. "Are you Mr. Mandic?" Chance called as he crossed the street. "Could I talk to you?" he called again.

Finally the man turned. He looked confused, an expression made more menacing by several days of beard and a red, white, and blue bandana pulled low on his forehead. "This better not be your plane," he said. His voice was as rugged as his appearance.

"No way," Chance said in as amiable a voice as he could muster. "I'm trying to find out who flew it into your house. This is your house, isn't it?"

"Maybe. You a cop?"

Chance quickly shook his head. "I'm with the *Mining City Messenger*. We've been following the story since Sunday when the crash happened. Looks like this is the first you heard of it."

Mr. Mandic turned back toward the plane, ducking under the crime-scene tape, shaking his head as he came back around to the front of the house. He muttered, "What the hell?"

"I was wondering if I could come inside and see the damage," Chance said. "Maybe get a statement from you for the article we're doing." His gut told him the crash didn't have anything to do with Mandic or his house. That would be too bizarre. Even if Austin had harbored some grudge against Mandic, why choose dive-bombing his house to get even? "I don't suppose you know a man named Lowell Austin by any chance?" Chance asked.

Mandic scowled in response, and then walked up to the front door of the single-story house. He pulled off a pink piece of paper taped on the door. On it, "Police Notice" was printed in black letters large enough that even Chance could read the words. "Get away from me. I got enough problems," he said, waving the notice at Chance. "I been in Dillon helping my brother in the blacksmithing contest all weekend. He lost and then I come home to the police on my back. I go away one damn weekend and this is what happens." He spread his hands wide and shook his head, then entered the house, slamming the door in Chance's face.

Chance turned away and sighed. He couldn't blame Mandic for being irritable. Who wouldn't need a little time to adjust to a plane sticking out the side of his house?

He looked up and down Washington Street for about the fifth time. Somebody must have seen something. He just hadn't found them. Then something up the hill caught his eye.

On the third floor of the Virginia Apartments, a block north, someone had just peeked through the curtain. Chance had been concentrating on the houses that were at street level where the crash had occurred. Maybe this witness had a completely different view.

Chapter 9

By mid-afternoon Mesa had recovered from the astonishment of meeting Adrienne DeBrook enough to compose two hundred words for the editorial page. She picked up the office phone and dialed Irita. "I want you to pull the new editor story, the photo too," Mesa said. "We can run it next week, if need be."

Irita was in Mesa's office in a flash. "You want to pull a story now?" Irita said. "What are we going to run instead?"

Mesa handed her a hard copy of a short editorial titled "News that's Always Fit to Print," which extolled the virtues of the *Messenger* and how any upcoming changes in the editor's chair would not affect the quality of the paper.

"But I thought you were going to be all about change," Irita said when she finished scanning the article. "That's what Chance has been saying your grandmother wants."

Mesa sighed. It had taken a mere day and a half for her to remember why her grandmother had always liked working with Irita. She was as straightforward as they come. Mesa was awash with the uneasiness that came with trying to dodge such frankness. Finally she said, "Look, Irita, I need to tell you something, and I need you to keep quiet about it."

Irita shook her head and collapsed on the sofa. "Jeez, you know I'm no good at keeping things quiet. Look how easy it was for you to whittle that stuff about Chance and that DeBrook woman out of me."

Suddenly, the tone of her voice changed. "What do you mean, 'if need be.' What are you trying to tell me?" Her voice had become a whisper. She spoke quickly, as if racing through the words might save her from their impact. "The paper's not folding, is it?"

"That's the last thing I want," Mesa said in her most encouraging voice. "It's just that my level of involvement with the paper might decrease, which I'll know more about after I fly to Portland on Friday. And I need you to cover for me while I'm gone."

Irita's eyes were now the size of cow pies. "What's in Portland?"

Mesa gave a quick rundown of the Portland situation, although she skimmed over the two weeks of sex with Derek. Instead, she said that her former boss thought highly of her work, which was true, and expected her to come out as the top candidate.

"If I do get the job, I may have to leave in a relatively short time." She watched the color drain from Irita's face. "Hopefully, I can convince Derek to give me a couple of weeks to make the transition."

"Just when I thought this job was picking up again," Irita said, making no effort to hide her disappointment. "I thought it was too good to be true when Chance said you were coming back."

"That was my original intention, Irita. And I wish like hell that the timing on this Portland job could be different. If I could be here for a couple of months, I think that you could be more than ready to take over as editor yourself."

Chance hustled up Washington Street into the marble-walled foyer of the Virginia Apartments and pressed each of the doorbells for the third-floor apartments. On the fourth doorbell, an elderly woman answered. "Yes?" she said in a lilting voice.

He read the name on the mailbox and said, "Mrs. Penmarron?" Then, in case she didn't like the sound of his voice, he quickly introduced himself and said, "I'm with the *Mining City Messenger*."

"Are you the young man who has been knocking on doors about that airplane?" she asked. The women spoke with a soft English accent.

Chance smiled, sure that he had found himself a witness, albeit an elderly one, judging from the sound of her voice. She must have been watching him canvassing the street, even noticing him point to the plane. "That's me," he said triumphantly. "Mind if I ask you a few questions?"

"Do you have any identification?" she asked.

"Yes, ma'am," he said in his most proper voice, and he heard the buzz to signal that the foyer door had unlocked.

Chance had read about the Virginia Apartments, along with every building on the Historic Register in Butte. He stopped to admire the art deco lamps in the hallway and delighted in his ride to the third floor in the fully functional 1921 Otis elevator with its accordion door.

Mrs. Edith Penmarron, slightly stooped but still tall and thin, answered the door on the first ring. "You're with what paper?" she asked through the narrow opening of the chained door.

"The *Mining City Messenger*," he said, and then quickly adding to reassure the woman, "I'll bet you know my grandmother, Rose Ducharme. She owns the paper."

Penmarron was a Cornish name, and while Mrs. Penmarron's accent wasn't the distinctive Cornish, he knew she was English, in which case she surely knew Nana. After World War II, more than twenty war brides had immigrated to Butte and they had started a club. His grandmother had been invited to join when she came to Butte in the fifties.

"Oh yes, how is she doing these days?" Mrs. Penmarron said and closed the door for a second to unchain it. "I knew she had the heart attack."

"She's well on her way back to her former self," Chance said and hoped this wouldn't get immediately back to Mesa. Not that Nana was completely out of the woods, but he wanted Mesa to have every reason to stay in Butte.

He followed Mrs. Penmarron past an antique hutch filled with china teacups and an array of bric-a-brac covered in Union Jacks and likenesses from Winston Churchill to Princess Diana. "Penmarron is a Cornish name, isn't it?" Chance asked.

"My husband was descended from Cornish tin miners who immigrated here in the 1890s. But I myself am from Buckinghamshire, not terribly far from where your grandmother was born. Would you like some tea? I've just put on the kettle."

Chance knew better than to refuse. He was sure Edith would be on the telephone to his grandmother after this visit, and he didn't want to be found wanting. He sat on the sofa and drank hot, milky tea from a fine bone-china cup with a pink rose on it and listened to Edith's story.

She had lived in her present surroundings for the last twenty years since her husband had died of a stroke.

"He never recovered from what the Anaconda Company did to Butte," she told Chance. "It broke his spirit and nearly the town's too."

Her lovely family of children, grandchildren, and great grandchildren lived all over Montana, with a few still in Butte. But she enjoyed living on her own. She didn't want to be a burden. And since she'd had her cataract operation, she had plenty of reading to keep her busy. She motioned to two walnut bookcases jammed with books. Mysteries were her favorite she told him with a smile.

"My distance vision is still quite good," she assured him. She invited him to the window where he had seen her ten minutes before.

"I didn't see the plane crash, but I certainly heard it. I was putting marmalade on my toast. I came over to the window to see what the noise was. Haven't heard anything like it since the Blitz. It sounded like a building collapsing."

The Blitz? If Mrs. Penmarron could remember the bombing of London, she had to be more than eighty. He hoped her short-term memory was as good. He looked down on the street from the window. Mrs. Penmarron had a clear view of the street, but he was doubtful how much she might have seen of the cockpit of the plane. Still, he listened.

"I can't tell you much except there were two men, and I think they were both hurt but not so badly they couldn't walk. The dark one held his right elbow like this." She let her right arm go limp and then grabbed her elbow at the joint with her left hand.

"Dark one?" Chance asked wondering if maybe, she meant Native American.

"His hair," Edith waived a thin, veined hand toward her head then continued. "He walked right away, quite deliberately. He crossed Washington Street and walked toward the hospital. Didn't stop to see if anybody was hurt in the house or anything. Maybe he was delirious, do you suppose?"

Chance shrugged but had wondered too. No one from the crash had come into the emergency room of the hospital. He and Noah had both checked there.

"The other fellow was lighter, sandy-haired, and taller," Mrs. Penmarron said softly. "He seemed to have a bit of trouble walking and he held his wrist."

Again, she demonstrated by clasping her left wrist with her right hand. "At least he took the time to look inside the window on the porch of the house, to see what damage had been done, I think. But he didn't stay long."

If they knew Butte, Chance thought, the direction they headed might help him narrow down who the jerks were. "Which direction did the second man go?"

"Toward Montana Street, away from the other man." She turned and walked back to her rocking chair. Over her shoulder she said, "I don't think they were friends. They'd been through a frightening experience, and they didn't seem to want to have anything to do with one another."

Mrs. Penmarron sat down slowly, and Chance sat on the sofa across from her. "Maybe they had already discussed what to do before they exited the plane?" Chance offered.

Mrs. Penmarron held her hand under one elbow, the other hand touching her chin. She was seeing the moment all over again. "Well, I do think they knew where they were going."

"What makes you say that?" Chance asked. This old girl was well schooled in mystery all right.

"They didn't even look around. That's what most people do, isn't it, when you need to find your bearings? But they simply took off on their own as though they'd walked the streets every day."

Chance thanked Mrs. Penmarron, promising to remember her to his grandmother, then left her with the sheriff's phone number and told her she should call his office right away. He didn't want the feds accusing him of withholding information. Then he trotted up along Silver, to Montana Street and over Park, all the while thinking about what Butte's own Miss Marple had told him.

He put little credence in the likelihood that Lowell Austin, at 54 years old and four days out of prison, had died of a heart attack, or that his two companions had done anything to give aid to him if he had. He wondered what they had planned to do with the stolen plane and what complications had occurred, now that the crash had obviously thrown a wrench into their plan. Or had it?

He had barely worked up a sweat by the time he reached the Imperial Building. Cast-iron columns, graceful upper story arches and decorative brickwork reflected the elegant details of another time. As architecture went, it was classy, just like its owner.

He saw her standing behind the work counter at the back, holding a sample frame against a matted drawing. Classical music played in the background. He looked to the right of the L-shaped shop to the section where she displayed greeting cards and small-framed pieces. No customers. Afternoons were often slow.

The Imperial's previous owner, an antiques dealer from Minnesota who had to sell fast when he'd been diagnosed with cancer, had gutted the building's upper floors. After years of living in San Francisco, Adrienne knew a good deal when she saw one. She had grabbed the Imperial up the week she came to town.

She had been persuasive convincing Chance to oversee the restoration of the upper floors, not that he needed convincing. His involvement with the *Messenger* when Nana ran the show was light enough that he had spent five months happily overseeing a crew of pre-releasers who finished the renovation of its first floor into an art gallery and the construction of her loft apartment upstairs—a rush job so she would have somewhere in town to live.

She had developed the habit of coming upstairs each evening after closing the gallery to check on the construction progress. Then one night she picked up a hammer and started helping out. He found himself staying longer and longer each evening, and so did she. They talked about everything—construction, architecture, history, Butte, art, life.

One evening when the rest of the crew had gone home, he was tearing out a rotted joist and she was telling him about her medical practice. A joist buckled and snapped, hitting him across the brow.

He had staggered back. Immediately she became the doctor again, giving him the once-over, making him watch her finger as she moved it in front of his eyes. "Why did you stop being a doctor?" he had asked.

"You never stop being a doctor," she said with a smile. "You just stop practicing. I still have a license. I could go back to it tomorrow if I wanted." She put a Band-Aid on the abrasion on his forehead and pronounced him fit to return to work.

"But you don't want to?" he asked.

She shook her head. "In the second half of my life, I'm going at my own pace."

And now, four months later, she was in the gallery business.

"Excuse me, ma'am," Chance said and walked up to the counter. Adrienne looked up and gave him a smile like the sun breaking through clouds.

"Why Mr. Dawson, what brings you here on this fine Butte afternoon?"

"A medical question." He leaned on the counter and thought about the previous Saturday night they had spent together. She was not like any woman he had ever known. She felt no need to have a hold on him, didn't call him, or expect to be called. Didn't want to make plans or dates. She was completely spontaneous.

"If it's not too complicated, I might be able to help you." She leaned toward him to listen.

He couldn't help himself when her low-cut blouse allowed his gaze to take in her cleavage. "I'm listening," she said and lifted his chin so his eyes were level with hers.

Her eyes were bright with curiosity and she moved with ease. No games. He felt so comfortable around her that he was disarmed by it. Sometimes he didn't feel the need to talk at all.

"A medical question?" she said with a grin.

"Right," he said, recovering his train of thought. "It's about this plane that crash-landed on Sunday. Since there was so little blood, the sheriff thinks the victim might have died before the crash. What could cause that?"

She shrugged her shoulders in conjecture. "Any number of things in flight—heart attack, cerebral hemorrhage, diabetic coma, maybe a drug interaction. God knows they kill more people than doctors would like to admit."

"Hmm. What about if it was a homicide, like if somebody killed the guy and then left him in the plane to make it look like he died in the crash? How would you do it so that it didn't look like he had been murdered?"

"Chance, you're such a gentle soul," Adrienne said. "Why such sinister questions?"

Chance did not like to admit to his morbid curiosity, though it did seem plausible that an ex-con who died in a likely stolen plane hadn't died of natural causes. "It's background for a story for the paper. That's all."

"I thought you didn't like that tiresome stereotype that Montana is full of anti-government types who like to take the law into their own hands?" Her voice was earnest but laced with a dash of sarcasm. "I can think of a lot more likely possibilities than murder. Maybe this man went into cardiac arrest or had a stroke. Maybe the pilot was his son, and he lost control of the plane when he tried to help his father."

Chance considered this for a moment. Of course, Lowell Austin had not even been married according to the stories Chance had read online in the Idaho *Statesman* at the *Messenger* office. He shook his head. "Good, but if that's the case, why did the son do a disappearing act?"

She wagged a finger at him and smiled, "Not a medical question."

"Plus, in this case, I think we can rule out the family angle. The victim was an ex-con who is sure to have had serious enemies."

She tapped her lips with her first two fingers and considered these implications. The gesture took him back to the first time he had kissed her a month ago.

It was early August, the last night of the Irish festival. He had just finished the final touches on her loft apartment. Sanding the joint paste on the drywall, he had spent much of the evening wondering how he might manage to see her again. He had almost convinced himself that she probably wouldn't care if she ever laid eyes on him again, when she reappeared.

She carried a four-pack of Guinness she had won from a street vendor. Blushing, she told him how people in the crowd had teased that she should find a man to share her winnings. "At this point in my life, you're the only man I seem to share anything with. So I came back to see if you'd like a Guinness."

He had never seen her drink anything stronger than herbal tea. They drank to his job well done. Then, as if she were reading his thoughts, she said she would miss him.

The Guinness must have gone to his head, because finally, he told her, "You know, I've wanted to kiss you every day for the last month. Since I don't officially work for you anymore, would it seem too forward of me to kiss you now?" Pondering his question, she had tapped her fingertips to her lips then too.

"Strangulation," Adrienne said, thinking out loud. "But you'd see bruises around the neck probably. Spinal shock of some kind, maybe?" she mumbled, and then looked up at him. "Aren't they doing an autopsy?"

It was Chance's turn to shrug. "They're working on the preliminary report. But they still need the tox screens. They'll have to wait for the logjam at the state lab to break," he said, his voice trailing off. "Who knows if they'll ever figure it out."

"Speaking of mysteries, guess who I met today?"

Before Chance could answer, Adrienne announced proudly, "Mesa."

"She showed up here, did she?" Chance wondered offhand what had prompted her visit. "How did it go?"

"Fine," Adrienne said. "She seemed a little shy. Why? How would you expect it to go? She likes your painting."

Chance said a silent prayer of thanks. The last thing he wanted was for Adrienne and Mesa to get off on a bad footing. "There seemed to be some confusion about the Mountain Gallery's account with the *Messenger*." He gestured toward a stack of bills on a large oak desk behind her. On it, he could see a stack of unopened mail. "Planning to get to those anytime soon?"

She turned quickly to follow his gaze and then sighed. "Check's in the mail, honest."

"I'm teasing. It came today," he said, his mind no longer on Mesa. "Too bad, too. I was thinking about taking what you owed in trade. Just as well. I

wouldn't want to have to explain it to Anna
Takkinen."

"Maybe I should hire her to be *my* business
manager," Adrienne said. "You really think that's
why Mesa came to the gallery?" She feigned a
grimace when he didn't answer. "Guess I blew my
chance for a good first impression."

Chapter 10

It was mid-afternoon by the time Chance drove out to the Fish, Wildlife, and Parks office on Meadowlark Lane. The office manager had said, "Wait right there," and disappeared to find one of the wardens before Chance could protest. The Fish, Wildlife, and Parks officers shared a building with the bigger and better outfitted U.S. Forest Service, and it might be awhile before she or one of the wardens returned from the bowels of the building.

Chance eyed the pelt of a mountain lion that lay draped over a chair in the corner. He had seen a lion in the backcountry several times, but never up close. He wondered if he dare sneak behind the counter for a closer look. You could never tell what kind of mood these game wardens might be in.

Proudly displayed around the office walls were mounts of animals that had been poached and subsequently recovered by the game wardens—an antelope, a mule deer, a mountain lion, a peregrine falcon, and an elk with a gigantic rack. Chance thought about the grizzly that had been shot near Mill Creek last month—turned out to be the *Standard*'s front-page story the next day.

In the minds of some, killing a human being could be justified far more easily than slaughtering wild game out of season, let alone shooting an endangered animal. Sure, game regulations could stir a heated debate, but no one could doubt the wardens' dedication to the animals they protected.

Chance looked at his watch. He had been waiting for a good ten minutes and no one had appeared. Apparently, the Fish, Wildlife, and Parks officers could be as hard to track down as a lot of the animals whose welfare they were charged with guarding.

Still, he thought that asking for a comment on Lowell Austin's death might make for some colorful quotes. Chance had spent a good part of the previous evening at the Idaho *Statesman* website, reading the news articles covering Austin's trial and its aftermath. The game wardens' murders had changed forever the way they would do their jobs. Idaho wardens wore side arms from then on. No more forays into the wilderness without fear of confrontation from humans. Chance wondered if that was when the Montana Department of Fish, Wildlife, and Parks had decided to adopt similar practices.

His thoughts were interrupted by Sam Waldau who wandered into the office, looking like a bear that had been awakened unexpectedly from hibernation. Sam had spent years working part-time for Fish, Wildlife, and Parks during hunting season until he had finally gotten on full-time. He rubbed his beefy forearm and said, "What?"

Chance ignored the typical Butte guy bluster. "Hey, yourself. Thought you might have a comment about the guy who died in that plane on Sunday."

Sam motioned behind the counter to a chair in the office that the three wardens shared. "Why?" Sam looked genuinely befuddled. "Is it somebody I know?"

"I thought you might have heard," Chance said. For once, the jungle drums were beating slowly.

"I been out on the Big Hole all weekend keeping track of flatlanders."

"It was in the *Standard* this morning. But let me be the one to fill you in. A Cessna 180 crash-landed into a house on Washington Street. The one fatality was a guy by the name of Lowell Austin."

"No shit," Sam said. His voice a whisper, he sounded genuinely astounded. "I heard they thought he'd go back to California where they caught him when he escaped that time."

Cole Sheehy, Sam's office mate, appeared. He tended toward the tall, silent type, but in this case, he joined the conversation. "Why the hell didn't he stay in Idaho?" he mumbled. Chance and Sam nodded.

"Probably met somebody from Butte doing time," Cole said with an ounce of sarcasm. "He was out of prison a week, wasn't it? Think he was headed to Butte?"

Chance had wondered about this himself. Initially he had assumed Austin was on his way to Butte when the pilot had problems with the plane, or landed to refuel. But if Kev had seen the trio rendezvous at the airport, Austin must have already been in Butte, if only for a short while, and had gone up in the plane after he arrived. "I'm still trying to figure that out. The guys at Silver Bow Aviation say the plane flew into Butte on Saturday, but whether Austin was a passenger then, I haven't asked yet. That's my next stop."

"Well, if he was coming to Butte because he has friends here, they better never cross my path." The gruff voice of Hoyt Rawlins interrupted the conversation. Hoyt was the warden sergeant, a man who clearly seemed to prefer the company of animals to people. Nobody bucked him. "That bastard should have gotten the death penalty the first time around. He flat out murdered two wardens, hid their bodies, and then got off with manslaughter. That's the jury system for you." Hoyt ducked under the counter gate, grabbed his cowboy hat off a hook on the wall, and went out the door without saying goodbye.

"Hoo, hoo," Cole said with a big grin. "Trust Hoyt not to sugarcoat it."

"Should have asked him if he saw Austin at the airport," Sam said. "Hoyt flew down to Dillon on Sunday to check out this tip somebody called in about a poachers' camp."

Chance hadn't expected much sympathy from the wardens or anybody associated with the agency. Even if Austin's crimes had been committed long before any of these guys were in uniform, their outrage was still intense, even if not personal. Could it be possible that one of them might be involved with Lowell Austin's death?

❧

Chance walked into Silver Bow Aviation ten minutes later, still pondering the possibility that Hoyt Rawlins might have seen something or someone at the airport on Sunday. He poked his head into the office, then the pilot's lounge. As usual, the place was empty. A raspy voice crackled over the office radio console, making Chance jump. "Butte area traffic, this is Sky West 147 approaching from the south 7 miles out," the pilot announced. The customary afternoon commercial flight from Salt Lake was inbound.

Butte didn't have enough air traffic to warrant a radio tower. Pilots quietly and calmly relied on their own communication—an arrangement that might terrify the average plane passenger like Mesa. But no pilot, especially a commercial one, would approach even a small airstrip without announcing the plane's arrival on the appropriate local frequency.

Chance could see how someone like Hoyt Rawlins, who had been flying planes for Fish, Wildlife, and Parks ever since he had been transferred to Butte, could waltz through here and fly in and out unnoticed. More than a few local pilots even fueled up their own planes and simply left a note for Tyler to charge the gasoline to their account.

Chance opened the door that led into the hangar where Kev was working on the Beechcraft 99 cargo plane that made regular contract flights to Billings for FedEx. "You talk to the police yet?" he asked after saying hello.

Chance had tried to call Rollie Solheim for information about the coroner's report but couldn't get through. At the previous day's press conference, Rollie had volunteered nothing about the possibility that the plane had other occupants.

"They were in here this morning," Kev said, in a voice tinged with irritation. "Making a lot of noise and acting like I ought to know who the bastards were." Kev leaned into the engine cavity, busy with a socket wrench.

"I hear Hoyt Rawlins flew out early Sunday morning," Chance said quietly. "You know Hoyt, right?"

"Big guy. Doesn't say much. I like him," Kev said, "and I didn't see him on Sunday either, okay?"

So much for speculation about Fish, Wildlife, and Parks on a vengeance mission.

Tyler appeared from behind the Beechcraft. "Hey, man. How's she going?" They left Kev mumbling over the engine and went back into the pilot's lounge.

"I'm still picking over this plane crash." Chance knew his excuse to Mesa was just that. He had no burning ambitions as a journalist—he was just out-and-out curious.

"Cops were here this morning asking about it. Turns out some company in Kansas or some damn place owns the plane. They wanted to know if anyone here had seen it touch down."

"What did the pilot's log say?" Chance asked. He had tried to get a look at the log himself, but Rollie was having none of it. He was saving everything for the FBI evidence team that was expected at any moment.

"Rollie said the last entries was four days ago," Tyler said.

Which was not exactly unheard of. A pilot's log was supposed to be a record of a pilot's hours in the air, which included stopovers and fueling locations. But no one official ever checked it. More than once, Chance had written down his log entries on the back of an envelope or a map and transferred them to his log later. But he figured whoever was flying this plane had no intentions of keeping the logbook up-to-date.

Tyler walked over to the window that looked out over the runways. "Wonder what they do to you if you walk away from a wreck like that?" Tyler said almost to himself. "Nobody around here would pull that kind of stunt."

FAA regulations required the reporting of any kind of mishap in an airplane, even one where nobody was injured, let alone dead. "Maybe the pilot didn't really go biking in Canyonlands after all," Chance said, theorizing out loud. "The Outward Bound story could be a cover while he was making a run for it, and now he's busted. He could have been headed to Canada. You know, absconding with the company's payroll."

"Maybe he doesn't want to own up to what happened is more likely," Tyler said.

"I can see why," Chance agreed. "Did you hear who the dead guy is?"

Tyler walked over to the pop machine, shaking his head as he went. He took a key from his pocket, opened the machine, and took out a can of Bud Lite, one of several he had stashed behind the cokes to keep cold. "Want one?" he asked Chance.

Chance shook his head. "Lowell Austin."

"Don't know him," Tyler said. "Should I?"

"Fitz will know." Tyler's dad, Sumner Fitzgerald, was an orthopedic surgeon with a deep and abiding love for flying who had started Silver Bow Aviation when Chance and Tyler were teenagers. "Austin led the FBI on a wild goose chase for nearly two years back in the eighties," Chance said. "All over the Sawtooths. People had to have helped him out for him to avoid capture for that long. Then when they finally did catch him, he got off with voluntary manslaughter when he flat out shot these two game wardens. Sounds like he pissed off a lot of people."

"You think he crashed that Cessna?" Tyler said with a sly grin.

"Well, he was sitting in the front seat. They're doing an autopsy to figure out what killed him for sure. But what I'm wondering is who else was in the plane."

"Whoever it was, I'm surprised somebody didn't see them hightailing it," Tyler said and took a long pull from the Bud.

"Somebody did. This little old lady up in the Virginia Apartments saw two men near the plane just after it crashed. She didn't actually see them get out of the plane, but I doubt it was anybody snooping around, or if they were, they weren't talking about it when I showed up ten minutes later. That time in the morning on a Labor Day weekend, the neighborhood was pretty well emptied out or asleep. I woke up about seven to go biking, and I bet you I didn't see three cars in 45 minutes."

"I sure as hell wasn't around," Tyler said and leaned on the edge of the desk.

"Whoever they were, they apparently escaped without a scratch. At least they weren't hurt bad enough to need help."

"Pretty goddamned amazing, if you ask me," Tyler said. "Walk away from something like that. Must be Irish."

"Must have been scary." Chance still had dreams about crash landings, though he had never made one. Fitz, ever vigilant of impending or imagined disaster, had schooled them all on what to do in such an emergency, but Chance had managed to avoid catastrophe.

"Remember all those emergency landings your dad used to make us practice over by Rocker." Fitz had taught his son and a couple of his friends to fly, Chance included. Their lessons usually took place west of town over empty, sagebrush flats far from any buildings.

Fitz had seemed like a fanatic about pilot preparedness in Chance's sixteen-year-old reasoning. But looking back now, he appreciated his instructor's wisdom, if not his humor.

Fitz had made them work off the cost of flying lessons by requiring them to be at his beck and call for the bulk of their teenage lives. Chance had done every odd job at Silver Bow Aviation from clean out the toilets to paint the tie-down lines on the tarmac every spring.

Tyler smiled. "Used to scare the shit out of me, flying under those utility wires."

Chance laughed. "You never said anything—you or Hardy."

"I think Hardy enjoyed it. He'd probably do it for fun now."

"Maybe. I don't think he does much flying down in Moab. Even he's not dumb enough to go barnstorming when he hasn't been in the saddle for six months. He's back in town by the way. Saw him yesterday."

"So I hear. He was at the Hoist House knocking 'em back 'til the wee hours Saturday night, according to Colleen."

The Hoist House had always been one of Hardy's favorite hangouts. The bartenders were always women, and he was always the recipient of more than his fair share of free drinks. Tyler's sister, Colleen, known to have a ten-year crush on Hardy, tended bar there on weekends.

"He usually stops by here at some point," Tyler said in a sullen voice, as if he were jealous of Hardy's attention elsewhere.

"Speaking of which, how many other planes stopped over on Sunday and Monday?"

"I don't know, a couple, I guess."

"Kev said all along there were three guys boarded that plane on Sunday morning." Chance felt badly that he wondered if Kev was seeing double. "So, how did they get to the airport?"

"Maybe they all flew in together," Tyler said. "Kev wouldn't necessarily have seen them if they came in early. He comes in late half the time when

I'm not around to ride his ass. Maybe they walked over to the Copper Baron and stayed there for the night. Then walked back over in the morning. You check over there?"

The Copper Baron Hotel sat directly across the highway from the airport, a five-minute walk at most. The commercial crews always stayed there, some fly-throughs too. "Reporter from the *Standard* printed the dead guy's prison mug shot from the prison press release off the Wire Service. Nobody at the front desk recognized him from the photo."

Noah Gilderson had been quick to think of that idea, even if it hadn't gotten him anywhere. At least it had eliminated one possibility.

"Could be that one of them is local," Chance said. "If they drove to the airport, then they left a car here unless they somehow managed to retrieve it after the crash. Did you notice a vehicle parked overnight?"

"I was out at the lake all weekend." Tyler's family owned a cabin on Georgetown Lake where he and his latest girlfriend, Rachel, spent every spare moment. Tyler had long ago mastered the art of relaxation.

Chance and Tyler walked over to the window that overlooked the parking lot and silently surveyed its two pickups and Chance's Rover. "Yours, mine, and Kev's," Tyler said. Then he added, "Somebody could have dropped them off."

"Maybe." If that was the case, somebody in Butte was harboring material witnesses in a murder case, no petty crime. "If they did drive here, then how would they get back here to get their vehicle after the crash."

"What difference does it make anyway?" Tyler said, in a mildly irritated voice. "All you're doing is putting together a story for the paper. You don't have to know every detail, do you?" He turned away from the window and walked into the office.

The dismissive note in Tyler's voice hit home. What difference *did* it make? The truth was, the crash had unnerved Chance, especially the fact that the pilot had disappeared. The pilots he knew were serious, safety-conscious people. They certainly wouldn't abandon a plane they'd wrecked, let alone someone who was critically injured, even an ex-con.

"Maybe somebody picked up their car for them," Tyler added as an afterthought.

"Or maybe they had someone drive them out here, and maybe somebody saw them pick up the car," Chance said in a probing tone.

"Well, it wasn't me." Tyler plopped down at the desk back behind the counter shuffling through an in-basket of file folders. Then he stopped and looked at Chance. "Which is why you asked about who else came in," Tyler said and sighed. He reached for a black binder that showed a record of fuel sales. "A guy from California came in on Monday in one of those new Beechcrafts. He wanted to go down to Melrose to look at some property. We set him up with a rental car."

"Is that it? Nobody else was with him?"

"I think I heard Kev say some young guy hopped a ride with him. I'm not sure."

"A rabbinical student," a voice from behind them said.

Chance turned around to see Morris Untermann standing in the lobby by the door to the tarmac. He and three other dentists in town owned a Cessna they kept tied down at Fitz's.

"Hey, Mo. Long time no see," Chance said.

"That's because you missed your appointment to have your teeth cleaned," Mo said and shook his hands in the air in mock distress. "I can't be held responsible."

Chance smiled. Dr. Untermann had a light touch with the drill, but he was still a dentist. Chance always dragged his feet when it came to visits, even routine ones. "You talked to this rabbinical student?"

"Sure I talk to him. I see him at synagogue."

"Where's he live? I'd like to ask him a few questions."

"He lives in L.A," Mo said with a smile. The dentist and his wife had moved to Butte from Brooklyn twenty-five years before. His accent had softened, but his appreciation for an occasional sarcasm had not.

Chance's heart sank.

"But he comes to Butte once a month for services. That's why he was on the airplane. This time the lucky schmuck hopped a ride with some rich guy from Santa Monica."

"Did he go back with him?" Chance asked, ready to be disappointed.

"Nah, he doesn't fly back 'til Sunday."

༺ঌ৵༻

When Jake Brinig was in town, the rabbinical student who provided religious guidance to the B'nai Israel Congregation stayed in a home in Butte's "Mediterranean Block." On the west side of Broadway and Granite between Washington and Idaho Streets, the area's houses, many nearly a hundred years old, had almost all been renovated. One of Chance's favorite neighborhoods, it demonstrated so well what a facelift could do to the rest of the city.

Jake's host owned the gray stucco Victorian home with a red and white decorative façade, which reminded Chance of a wedding cake. Its renovation had just begun when he had returned to Butte after his divorce. He had watched with admiration the progress of the restoration of the down-on-its-luck home to its former glory.

"I wouldn't have even noticed the car," Jake said while he and Chance sat on a metal glider on the porch under the house's arched entrance, "except that we followed it right out of the airport and onto Harrison Avenue for a few miles."

Brinig's stylish horn-rimmed glasses clashed with his short-sleeved, white dress shirt and brown suit pants. He hardly seemed old enough to be leading a congregation. Chance knew no Jews in Butte besides Mo Untermann, who he could not imagine seeking Jake Brinig's advice on much of anything. But Brinig had an eye for detail, and that was what Chance needed. "When exactly was this?"

"Monday, around noon. I came in early this month. I'm officiating at a funeral tomorrow. One of my Yeshiva teachers has a brother who's a plastic surgeon in Los Angeles, and owns his own jet. He gave me a lift," Jake said with a smile. "They all think I'm crazy for coming out here."

Chance knew little about B'Nai Israel, Butte's congregation, except that its synagogue had been renovated recently for its one-hundredth anniversary. The congregation had sunk a lot of money into the project and done it right. The gold domed building was in tiptop shape. "So why do you?"

"My great grandfather owned a clothing store here in the twenties. Can you believe that? On Main Street. They moved back east after World War II."

Chance smiled. He always thought the Jewish community had to have been a lot bigger to support a building like the synagogue. Like the Finn, Croatian and Serbian communities that had shrunk once the mines started to close in the early 1950s, others moved away too. Not that many Jews worked in the mines. Like Jake's great-grandpa, they were the retailers and professional people whose services were needed in any bustling metropolis. "Butte family ties go far and wide."

No doubt people in L.A. couldn't imagine what the Mo Untermanns of the world saw in a place like Butte now. But then they didn't know that Mo worked four days a week and went fly-fishing without fail on the fifth. "What do you think of Butte?"

"I enjoy the history of the place, but I couldn't live here," said Jake. "Don't get me wrong. I like the congregation, but the town's too small and too slow," he said with a sheepish grin.

"I understand," Chance said. "It takes a certain kind of person to survive here. Whether you're born here or transplanted, you get this feeling about the town, and you just can't leave. It defies explanation."

"That what happened to you?"

"Well, my mother was born here, and I visited a lot when I was a kid. In the end, I couldn't find another place I'd rather be. I guess it gets in your blood."

Jake smiled in a way that made Chance think he was envious. Feeling unexpectedly self-conscious, Chance broached the real reason he had come to talk to Jake. "When you left the airport on Monday morning, did you happen to notice the cars parked in the lot? Usually there are two pickups in the lot, one white, one red. Did you see any others?"

"Just the one we followed out of the lot when we left," Jake said nonchalantly.

Chance perked up. It was a long shot but it was possible the car that had transported the men in the plane had also ridden in that car. "Did you recognize the model of the car? Anything distinguishing about it?"

"Maroon Ford Bronco. A guy in our building has one, not that you'd need an SUV in L.A., of course. It had one of those special Montana license plates."

Chance smiled and pulled out his notebook.

"I probably wouldn't have noticed, but Mr. Samuels, who gave me a ride, didn't know his way around that well so he drove pretty slowly at first. Plus, it being a holiday, traffic was nonexistent. The place felt like a ghost town." He paused for a moment as if trying to visualize the car. "Oh, it had one of those ribbon magnets. You know, support the troops."

Chance couldn't write fast enough. "Wait," he said. "Let's go back to the license plate." There were easily twenty or thirty different specialty license plates in Montana—those that said Support the Griz, or the Bobcats or one of the other colleges. Rocky Mountain Elk foundation plates, all different ones. "Do you remember which particular plate it was?"

"It's that one with the sunset and the trees. Support the parks, something like that."

Chance made a note to check the state's web site. But he was pretty sure Jake was describing the Fish, Wildlife, and Parks Foundation's license plate. Hoyt Rawlins? Chance thought for a moment. No, that couldn't be. Rawlins and other Montana game wardens drove those lime-green, heavy-duty, club cab trucks with government vehicle license plates. They even drove them to and from home so they could take off in the middle of the night if somebody called with a tip about a poacher.

"You say you followed this car for some time. I don't suppose you remember which way it was headed? Did it turn somewhere?"

Jake's quick smile made Chance's day as if he was proud that he could find his way around town. "We came up Harrison Avenue from what you call the Flat and turned onto Dewey, followed it all the way up to Montana Street. The Bronco turned left just before the Town Pump at the light. I forget the name of that street."

"Platinum Street," Chance said. The car was headed in the direction of the west side and the college. "How about a description of the driver."

Jake stopped with a quizzical look on his face. Apparently, he had been more interested in the car than the person driving it. He stopped and put his hand to his forehead as if he were trying to halt the lighting quick details of his mind and go back to the picture he needed.

"Man or a woman, young or old?" Chance asked, trying to narrow the possibilities.

Jake shook his head. "I didn't notice."

Chance was surprised. The kid had paid more attention to the car than the person in it. Though in truth, that's probably what Chance would have done.

"Why the interest in this car?" Jake asked. "What kind of story are you working on?"

Chance explained about the Cessna's crash landing, which seemed to amuse Jake.

"That sounds like a stunt for Evel Days," he said with a smile. "Did you ask the guys at the airfield?"

The kid was right about Evel Days. Every dare devil outfit in the West showed up at the end of July to honor the memory of Evel Knievel, arguably Butte's most famous, or infamous, favorite son. As yet, they had not attracted any aerial acts, unless you could count the stunt guy who had jumped off the Finlen Hotel roof. Chance wasn't about to make any suggestions.

"They were the ones who told me about you. Or at least Mo Untermann did."

Chance's cell phone rang, and he stood up to answer it. The call was from Nick Philippoussis.

"Right," Jake said and ran his hands through his thick, dark hair. "Mr. Untermann." His words trailed off, as if he were wondering what Mr. Untermann might think of the conversation that had just taken place. Then he added quickly, "What's your phone number? If I see the car again, I could call you."

But Chance did not hear Jake. What he heard was Nick saying, "The call just came in from Missoula. Your barnstormer definitely did not die of natural causes."

Chapter 11

Tuesday evening marked the first night out in Butte in a while for both Mesa and Nana. Fine dining had not been one of Butte's strong points since about 1950, unless of course you were looking for a thick, juicy steak. The Derby, serving one of the best ribeyes in town, was one of her grandmother's favorites while Mesa had not eaten at the steakhouse since she was in college, not that she ate much steak anywhere.

Like most Butte restaurants, the Derby was attached to a bar and casino, and the bells and whistles of one-armed bandits had greeted them at the front door. Mesa surveyed the patrons, wondering who she might run into, as she followed her grandmother and their escorts into the dining room to a booth in the dining room.

Shane Northey glanced at Mesa over his menu, and then nodded toward their respective grandparents who were conferring about the early-bird specials over a single menu. Shane stifled a grin as did Mesa.

The last time she had eaten dinner with anyone's grandparents, they had been the banker's. It was

Valentine's Day, seven months ago, and they had gone to Pigall's, a five-star French restaurant in Cincinnati, famous for its snooty waiters.

All that evening she had felt she was auditioning for membership in the family. The banker's grandfather still actively ran the family's banking business. His patrician attitude would not have made him popular in Montana.

When Mesa spoke French to the waiter, the grandfather had been suitably impressed. Later she had silently cursed herself for showing off. All things considered, she decided she was much happier dining in Butte.

Nana did her best to showcase Shane's suitability. She kept asking him to talk about the legislature and how the governor had encouraged him to run for office.

"I met him at the Weed Whackers' Ball in Wise River last summer," Shane said after his blush subsided. "He probably said the same thing to half a dozen other people there."

Mesa doubted that. The way Shane talked about his work for the Big Hole River Foundation, she could tell he had mastered the delicate balancing act needed to talk to Montana ranchers about environmental concerns and its world-class trout stream. He had skills a legislator needed in this state. "Don't be so modest," Mesa teased.

"Seriously, all I did was pet his Border collie," Shane said. "Next thing you know, he's telling me Helena needs some younger blood."

Soon Mesa found herself having a meaningful, two-way conversation with a man about a serious subject. They talked about environmental regulations and the equally important and sometimes conflicting need to bring new companies and more jobs to Montana. They talked about art and music. He played bass guitar in a jazz trio. She had just begun to think Nana had the right idea about Shane when she saw Hardy Jacobs pass through the restaurant and into the casino.

ও-ও

On his way into the Copper Baron Hotel, Chance had called Adrienne. He had never been one to call women. His ex-wife had said it was one of his passive-aggressive traits. He seemed to call when she didn't want him to.

Maybe that was why he found himself calling Adrienne more often. She never expected him to do anything.

"You're lucky. I was just about to turn my phone off," she said when she answered on the third ring. She frequently turned the phone off when she painted.

"Had dinner yet?" he asked. She never seemed to eat unless he did. She appeared to exist on herbal tea and an occasional bowl of soup.

She chuckled. "Is this an invitation?"

"Always, and open-ended, although not at this particular moment." Then he explained where he was.

"I need you to clear something up for me," he said, sounding more serious than he meant to.

"Not another medical question?" she said.

He could imagine her leaning against a windowsill chewing on the end of a paintbrush, her usual curious self, inquisitive without being intrusive. He gave her the details of the state medical examiner's report that had been faxed to the coroner's office just before quitting time. Nick had read him the pertinent sections over the phone.

Lowell Austin had died of spinal shock, caused by a puncture wound between the second and third cervical vertebrae. "He had some cuts and scrapes from the impact," Nick had said. "The entry wound must have been hidden by his hairline. I watched the doc going over that body, and they didn't see anything that unusual while I was there."

"That's gruesome," Adrienne said. "And certainly not something the average person would be able to do, except maybe by sheer accident. The neck is the boniest part of your body. If you're trying to sever somebody's spinal cord, which is what must have happened, you need to know where to poke."

Chance thought about this and felt that queasy sensation of the day before returning. "Somebody who knows what they're doing, you mean like a hired killer?"

"Or some trained medical person, God forbid," she said in a quiet voice. She had become serious too. "The victim would become like a puppet with its strings cut. They would be paralyzed almost immediately, unable to move, or talk or breathe. The mercy would be that death would come quickly, which answers your question about why so little blood."

"Right," Chance said and wondered for the first time just how interested he was in this story. Whoever had killed Lowell Austin had done so in a stealthful way, designed to discourage any attention. He was no longer sure if he wanted to be on that someone's trail.

"I could give you a hands-on demonstration about the cervical vertebrae in question, "Adrienne said, "if you'd like to stop by later."

Happy for the moment of distraction, Chance said he would, and then he went into Shoestring Annie's.

For the second night in a row, he found himself searching through a bar for someone. Nick had suggested this would be the likely place to find the NTSB investigator after hours. "Now that this is a homicide investigation, the FBI takes over. The crash investigators are pulling up stakes and getting the hell out of Dodge," Nick had said.

But they wouldn't be leaving soon. The last commercial flight out of Butte had left more than an hour ago.

Unlike Butte's many neighborhood bars, Shoestring Annie's catered to the city's contingent of overnight out-of-towners. The Copper Baron's clientele consisted mostly of business people who disdained all that Butte had to offer, and looked to fly in and fly out as soon as possible. Such folks were hardly the type most Buttians wanted to drink with, even in a bar named after one of Butte's legendary street characters.

Known for her tirades at the tightfisted, Shoestring Annie had sold shoelaces on the streets of Butte in its heyday. Grown men, including police officers, were known to avoid the corner where Annie sold her wares for fear of her outbursts.

The bar's walls were covered with news photographs of Annie and other street characters from Butte's past, their legends a testament to the color of the city's glory days. The atmosphere was sufficiently quaint to attract at least an initial visit by most of the hotel's patrons. Even on this Tuesday night, many of the oak tables and chairs were filled. Unlike most of the uptown bars, this one on the flat, as locals called the area on the valley floor, encouraged its patrons to sit down to have a conversation.

Chance scanned the crowd, looking for the truly out of place, and settled on a table with three men, two in their mid-fifties, with closely trimmed haircuts and not a pair of blue jeans or cowboy boots among them.

This was no time to be reticent, Chance knew. He walked over to the table to introduce himself to the trio as a representative of the local press. Immediately he realized he had hit pay dirt.

The senior of the three, at least in age, was the National Transportation Safety Board investigator, Martin Zlokovic. With a broad grin, he introduced the two men seated with him, FBI agents. Roy Perryman, an expressionless man dressed in a suit and tie and sporting a crew cut, shook hands more out of politeness than interest. The other agent, who was closer to Chance's age, had a steely gaze and a handshake to match. Perryman lost no time explaining that they were from the Helena FBI Field Office, and that was all they could say to the press.

"I was just looking for comments about Lowell Austin's murder. We haven't had any infamous criminals in these parts since the Unabomber. Thought you might like to assure the public about their safety."

Perryman shook his head, encouraged Chance to check with the sheriff's office, and then excused himself and his partner, leaving their Diet Cokes behind.

Zlokovic continued to sip his drink. "Forgive my colleagues. They're shy. Besides, they're making an early start in the morning," he said with a grin. He was clearly amused by the FBI's sudden departure.

"Can I get you another one of those?" Chance said and gestured to what looked like a vodka tonic. Zlokovic nodded. "Why not. I'm flying out later tomorrow."

Chance liked Zlokovic, who was obviously more relaxed than the FBI agents. "So does that mean your job's over?"

"Just delayed. The FBI Evidence Team likes to handle their own investigation. When they're done, the whole shebang will get trucked to Seattle, and we'll examine the wreckage there. We still need to find out exactly why the plane crashed."

"I'm mostly interested in who else was in the plane, particularly if it turns out to be someone local. Don't suppose you saw anything that might lead to the identification of the other passengers?"

Zlokovic smiled again and deflected the question. "You from around here?"

"Mostly," Chance said and drank from the Moose Drool he had ordered. "I can't technically call myself a Butte rat since I wasn't born here, but I been around off and on since I was a kid. Why do you ask?"

Zlokovic shrugged. "No particular reason. I've never been here before. The old buildings uptown remind me of old San Francisco, not exactly what you expect in Montana. And I hear you have a Serbian Orthodox Church."

Chance thought about the agent's last name, smiled, and nodded. "You Bohunk?"

"A 120-gallon barrel of wine and cabbage is aging in my garage even as we speak." The agent's laugh sounded like a hyena with a head cold. "Born in Chicago."

"Stick around," Chance said. "I can line up a tour of the church for you tomorrow. You gotta see the murals they just had done." Phade Dragonovich's mom, who was a member of the Circle of Serbian Mothers, had told him all about the muralists who had come from Czechoslovakia. She liked to stop by the office usually with sarma or povitica. Naturally, Mrs. Draganovich had been enamored with Chance and his appetite for her baking. "Butte's not like anywhere else in the state," Chance said. "Miners made her what she is and she's proud of it—Irish, Norwegian, Finn, Serbian, Cornish, grit and all."

"Wish I'd known sooner. Maybe I'll come back on my own time."

Chance couldn't tell what, if any, information he might get from Zlokovic, but at least he had him warmed up to the town. "You surprised somebody tried to land a plane uptown?"

Zlokovic smiled again. "That what you think happened?" he said in a voice that suggested he drew pleasure from listening to people's theories about what was his job to figure out.

"I saw it in the air just before it went down. I was at the top of Park Street, so I had the long view, but that's what it looked like to me."

"Aha, a witness," Zlokovic said and raised his glass in a toast. "Now I can talk to you."

"I also saw the body in the plane," Chance continued. "It looked like somebody had tried to make it seem like the dead guy was the pilot. Which, once you know who the guy is, is downright stupid. No way, a guy who's been in prison for twenty years can walk out and then fly a plane. Not this guy anyway."

"Probably some drug deal gone wrong," Zlokovic said. "That's usually the reason these size planes get stolen, if in fact that's what happened. That I don't know so much about, but lots of things can go wrong with a plane, and I know about all of them," Zlokovic said with a grin, ready to school Chance on the dangers of flying.

Chance nodded and then added. "I think I understand. I fly a Cessna 152. But I saw those skid marks on the street. I think something went wrong with the people in the plane, and that caused a problem for the pilot. He lost altitude for some reason and had to ditch it."

"You think maybe?" Zlokovic said, his voice softer as the vodka began to relax him.

Chance shrugged. "You're the expert. Plus, you've seen the controls and the instruments. Air speed and angle of descent would tell you something, wouldn't it?"

Zlokovic hunched over his drink. "You're a pilot. You know about CFITs, right?"

Chance nodded. "Controlled flight into terrain" was official language for a flying accident where a perfectly operational plane flies into an object or the ground. In this case, the object was a house.

"About half the small-plane accidents we investigate, the plane worked fine but the pilot's situational awareness was compromised, like he lost visual contact with the ground for some reason, and bam, into a side of a mountain or the treetops. But we can't know for sure about this one until we find out if the plane or its engine malfunctioned."

Chance couldn't help thinking, for easily the tenth time, about what the pilot's last seconds must have been like—trying not to panic, to figure out what was happening and what to do. That kind of concentration was to be envied.

"I don't know what brought the plane down, but the pilot did his damnedest to land the sucker," Zlokovic said. "Might have managed it too, but he must have hit something in the street. That took him into the lot and the house. Either by luck or design, the back wheel hooked into a roll of chain-link fence. Like a fighter landing on an aircraft carrier, the drag minimized the impact. If I was you, I'd be looking for somebody with a serious case of whiplash."

"Which brings me back to my original question," Chance said with a smile. "You see anything inside the plane that might give an idea about who else was in it?"

"Oh, no," Zlokovic said with a sly grin. "You better talk to the boys from Helena about that. They don't like it when information from their investigation gets leaked. They'll kick my Serbian butt all the way back to Seattle. Besides, your cops took plenty of photos. They can tell you what was there." He whispered this last little gem as he stood up.

"So something was there?" Chance asked.

Zlokovic patted Chance's shoulder. "You didn't hear it from me."

Mesa slipped out of her grandmother's house around 10 p.m. Careful to close the back door gently, she felt like a teenager again. Crossing Excelsior Street, she looked back at the dark sitting room at the front of the house and relaxed.

She could have driven her grandmother's intrepid Trail Blazer, a vehicle that could and did go everywhere. But Mesa couldn't bring herself to ask to borrow it. She didn't want to have to come up with answers for Nan's inevitable questions about their night out.

Dinner had gone well, even if doubling with a couple of grandparents didn't seem like the most auspicious beginning. Shane had good-naturedly agreed on that front. They had adjourned to the porch when it was time to say goodnight, leaving Nana and Phillip Northey in the parlor. Shane joked about how he didn't want to cramp anybody's style.

For a moment, she had actually thought about kissing him. He had been so accommodating. But it was barely nine-thirty, though why that made a difference, she couldn't say. Instead, he saved them from the awkward moment by extending a generic invitation to have coffee, and she had agreed to an undetermined get-together in the next week. Then his grandfather appeared for the ride home.

Maybe it was because she had ignored all her hormones in an attempt to resist Hardy's clandestine invitation to meet later at the Hoist House. He had stopped by their table at the Derby and greeted Nana. He knew the Northeys too, apparently. At least Shane's "In town for long?" implied they knew of each other's existence.

On the way out of the restaurant, Mesa realized she had forgotten her sunglasses. Had that been subconscious? When she went back inside, Hardy appeared at the door as she left and invited her to come to the Hoist House later. He wanted to catch up.

Catch up with what, she wondered, as she walked along Silver Street. Where he left off four years ago in Big Sky? Think again.

Hardy was the king of the conquest. No woman would ever catch up to him. Mesa now had the perspective to see that. She had smiled at him, said nothing, and then spent the next two hours losing her resolve.

Resolve that had been hard-won. Her predilection for "bad boys" had blossomed not long after she left high school and Butte. Her alma mater, Damascus College, had attracted more than its fair share of anti-establishment, rebellious students. Their desire to test the system at every turn beguiled her. Her military-base upbringing had produced a meticulous child who knew the rules, but now she began to bend them. When she returned home for the summer, Hardy Jacobs' rough and tumble ways seemed irresistible.

Ten years later, she now understood Hardy's antics and where they led. She no longer had expectations of him, and she wanted to test herself. Like the recovering addict, she wanted to prove to herself that she could go to the well but not drink.

Hugging her arms to her chest to stay warm, she reached Galena Street and walked toward the Hoist House on Montana. She had forgotten about the eighty-degree days and forty-degree nights in September in the Rockies. At least she could count on Hardy to give her a ride home, if necessary. Then, she chastised herself as she fantasized about not needing a ride home at all.

The blue neon sign outlining a gallows frame beamed over the Hoist House's entrance. The door opened, and two women too scantily dressed for the cool night air walked out into Montana Street. Music and laughter trailed after them.

Mesa walked into the bar moments later, surprised by the amount of people out on a Tuesday night. The off-key crooning of some forty-year-old singing "Brown-Eyed Girl" explained everything.

Karaoke night, a phenomenon she felt was overrated, and which she knew Hardy had no patience for either, had reached the uptown bars. Butte miners must be rolling over in their graves, she thought.

At the far end of the bar, she saw Hardy in all his glory. He wore a long-sleeved tee shirt with a Head Case cycling helmet logo and a pair of convertible hiking pants that could be made into shorts by unzipping them at the knees. The blue shirt highlighted his eyes.

Without even trying, he was a walking advertisement for mountain sports, or at least the lifestyle associated with them. The irony was that Hardy never seemed to care about clothes. Whatever he wore hid his taut, muscular physique, about which he was otherwise totally unconscious even when naked.

His lack of fashion sense didn't bother the many women he attracted, as was the case this evening. He leaned on the bar talking to the bartender and another woman, younger and blonde. Mesa felt a twinge of jealousy, which she hated. It signaled that some part of her, however small, still clung to the adolescent notion that Hardy should long for her company and hers alone.

She considered heading to the bathroom, then making an unobtrusive exit. He could go to hell.

But Hardy had spotted her and motioned her to join him and his growing harem. When she didn't react, he even got up from his stool and met her halfway. He embraced her, his arms pulling her

close and, surprisingly, held on for that extra
moment as if he had been waiting weeks to see her.

He introduced her to the other two women, both
of whom were from Butte. The foursome then
played Butte's version of six degrees of separation to
figure out how they were all connected.

The bartender was Tyler Fitzgerald's sister,
Colleen. The blonde worked as a nurse and knew
Rose Ducharme from her recent stay at the cardiac
unit of the hospital. They all read the *Mining City
Messenger*. Mesa would have hummed "It's a Small
World After All," except she feared that someone
might hand her the karaoke mike.

Instead, someone else began singing a throaty
rendition of Otis Redding's arrangement of "Down
in the Valley." Mesa found a table and watched
Hardy, still walking gingerly on his left foot, bring
her an Amstel Light while he clung to his usual Bud.

Hardy had a notoriously tough constitution. In
high school, he had played the entire last quarter of
the state football championship with a crack in his
collarbone. Call it hard-headedness or strong will,
his reluctance to quit cemented his reputation. It had
also cost him a baseball scholarship when he re-
injured himself. "How's the leg?" she asked.

"Inconvenient as hell," he said and sat down.

She wondered how long he would be in Butte
with ski season just three months away. "Nothing
serious, I hope."

"Nope, bumps and bruises with a twist," he said
with a sarcastic chuckle.

She'd seen enough of Western resort towns like
Moab, Jackson Hole, and Durango, not to mention

the ski towns. Recreational Mecca's with a transient population, they got old eventually for someone like Hardy, who knew what it meant to have roots. "Life in Moab getting you down?"

He cocked his head to the side before he answered. "Business was slow. Decided I might as well come home." Then he added, "Maybe see you."

She laughed out loud and tried not to feel embarrassed—as if he actually meant it.

Hardy was even cool when he sipped his beer, putting the bottle to the left side of his mouth when he drank. "Speaking of limping home, what brought you back to town? I was afraid we had lost you to the big city forever."

Normally, Mesa would not let a crack like that one go, but Hardy said it in such a subdued, offhanded way, as if he had something else on his mind. "Don't get excited," she said. "It's not permanent. I'm helping with the paper until my grandmother gets back in the saddle, as they say."

"I thought maybe you came back for Shane since he got dumped."

"Jesus, Hardy. Invite a girl out and give her a hard time, why don't you?" She flicked a beer cap on the table toward him.

"I'm just teasing," he said and snatched up the beer cap and handed it back to her gently as a peace offering. "Although I was surprised to see you with him. That's all."

Mesa was taken aback to hear Hardy express what sounded like a genuine feeling. She was used to his Butte-boy toughness. She leaned her arms on the table and looked at him. "Hardy, I've gotten all of two postcards from you in four years. Why would you suddenly care who I have dinner with?"

"Well, it's not like you didn't know where I was or how to get in touch with me." He sounded like a ten-year-old in trouble on the playground. "When was the last time I heard from you?"

"Okay," she said and pushed back her chair. "I can see this was a bad idea. Thanks for the drink. I'm out of here." She didn't relish the idea of walking home in the cold, but she was not in the mood to trade any more barbs with Hardy.

"Wait, wait. I'm sorry. Truce. Honest, I won't say another word. I mean, I just thought we could talk about old times. Please, don't go."

Now she *was* curious. Hardy never pleaded for anything, especially from a woman—not his style. She pulled her chair back toward the table. "Hardy, what's up? You don't seem like your usual self."

He sighed, and then slumped back in his chair, his resignation as halting as the karaoke singer in the background. Finally, he spoke. "I been going through a rough patch. Looks like my so-called career in Moab is going bust."

Mesa was stunned. Hardy's life as a slick-rock biker guide, leading convoys of bicycling tourists through Arches National Park and other local cycling attractions, had meant he could cling to some part of his image as an athlete, not to mention that it was a ticket out of Butte.

"My dad and my brother are at me to come to work with them. Maybe it's time."

Hardy's family owned a plate-glass repair business. Over the years, when he wasn't playing one sport or the other, he had worked for his father part time. He had also once told her he would never want to make a living replacing windshields. The boredom would kill him.

What had changed his mind, she wondered? "I thought you were going to open your own bike shop in Moab." At Christmas, Chance had told her that Hardy had met a millionaire dot.com couple from Seattle who were going to finance the business.

"Didn't work out. Customers love me, but I need capital, and I haven't been able to get the kind of backers I want."

Hardy was smart but had no real credentials. He couldn't flash around a college degree, let alone an MBA to instill confidence in potential investors he might meet slumming in Moab. Plus, Hardy, like most Butte rats, was no good at hiding his disdain for guys with money who had done little to earn it. Or, more likely, it could mean that the husband had figured out that his wife had more than a business interest in Hardy.

"Besides, my dad's thinking of retiring. He's got some heart problems, and my brother could really use the help."

Mesa wondered if this change of heart signaled a change in attitude in other ways. "Don't tell me you're thinking of settling down in Butte."

Hardy shifted in his seat, stretching his shoulders. "Let's just say I been thinking about making a few changes. What about you? I heard you were running some paper back east and gonna marry a banker."

That was bar talk. Tyler had probably repeated something Chance said, which Colleen turned into her own version and then repeated. "No on both fronts," she said with a chuckle.

This banter felt deceptively comfortable, and Mesa allowed herself to fall into it as she separated truth from fiction, her job at the *Current* and her semi-defunct love life, explaining bits and pieces of the conflicts.

"Funny how things work out," Hardy finally said, "or don't."

Two hours and three beers later, Hardy agreed to give Mesa a ride home. Standing outside the Hoist House, she had put her hands into her pockets, and felt the spare key to Chance's duplex, which he had given her on Sunday. At that moment, Hardy had turned to her and said, "Be nice to curl up in front of a fireplace about now."

Hardy never mentioned sex directly, though it all but oozed from his pores, which of course was what made him so hard to turn down. At least that was how Mesa saw it when she slid next to him in one of his father's Yukon Glass pickups.

అప

Hours later, Mesa opened one eyelid to stare at moose-covered, navy-blue flannel sheets, a parade of antlers marching by. She had given the sheets to Chance right after his divorce. Stephanie had always made him sleep on sheets with flowers on them.

She could hear Hardy's steady breathing next to her. She rose from the bed, careful not to wake him, and tiptoed down the stairwell to peek into the downstairs. The sofa was empty. The clock on the nearby desk read 4 a.m. Chance had not come home.

She couldn't decide if she was more relieved or curious. She would not have relished the crap he would have given her if he had found Hardy and her in his bed. But that didn't stop her from wondering where he was.

She retraced her route upstairs and crawled under the covers, where she lay awake for another hour. She had once told Tara that sex with Hardy was like bungee jumping. You weren't sure why you did it until it was over, and then the thrill would stay with you for days.

She had to admit she still felt the same, but his days of extreme sports were catching up with him. He still looked good, but it took him longer to heal from his bangs and scrapes. Eventually, her thoughts drifted to Chance and Adrienne, whose bed was where she ventured her brother was currently laying his head.

Chapter 12

When Micah, the intern, arrived with Mesa's double latte on Wednesday morning, she was so grateful that she had included him in the editorial staff meeting. After all, she wasn't planning any bloodletting, that was for sure, and she liked the idea of the big happy family, despite the fact that she herself felt like a fallen woman.

Erin was first to arrive with a fresh reporter's pad and pen, followed by Phade, who looked like he had slept in his clothes. Chance appeared on time, looking decidedly chipper. Mesa exchanged muted pleasantries with Delilah, the arts and entertainment editor, who arrived predictably dressed in black with a teal and mauve silk scarf fashionably draped over the left shoulder.

The office felt so crowded that Irita had them all adjourn to the reception area, where she locked the front door so they could avoid any interruptions from their adoring public. Mesa did her best, despite the fact that her beauty sleep had suffered from having to get up at 5 a.m. so Hardy could drive her home. She gave a passable pep talk about how local weeklies were holding their own compared to the rest of the newspaper world. She talked about smartening up the paper, beefing up their advertising revenue, and encouraged everyone to think creatively. After all, their fate would soon be in their own hands, although she hadn't said that out loud.

Delilah was quick to establish her turf, and suggested she could expand the arts and entertainment section of the paper with more profiles of local artists. Mesa agreed, provided Delilah worked with Chance to bring in more paying advertisers to support the extra space.

Chance appeared to take no notice of this dig in his direction. Instead, he reported on the continuing saga of the plane crash and the information he had gathered the day before including the two men seen leaving the plane like they knew where they were going, and the maroon Bronco. He asked if Erin could pal with him and work up a feature.

"Isn't the *Standard* all over this story?" Mesa asked. She had not gotten to the office soon enough to scan the daily, but the story about Austin below the fold on the front page the day before had clearly been written with hopes that it would get picked up on the wires.

"It's still breaking news," Delilah chirped in. "What can we say that the *Standard* hasn't already? What direction are you going with the story? Do you have any leads?"

Mesa thought about cutting Delilah off. Her tone reminded her vaguely of her former publisher, a man with no heart. And she suddenly felt protective of Chance.

Chance nodded. "I'm sensing there's a local angle to this story," he said, which brought even more reactions from Irita and Delilah, both of whom were playfully derogatory, if not negative.

"Mr. Engineer has intuition," Irita said.

"At least he admits he can't write," Delilah said and crossed her arms.

Mesa looked at Erin, who had made no protest. "How many stories are you working on already? Do you have time to work on another?"

She nodded timidly. "I'm working on a feature about the new animal shelter, but we can run that anytime. Micah's ready to cover the city council meeting this week, so I have time. And I already drafted a couple of paragraphs from notes Chance gave me yesterday."

Mesa knew what it was like to be hungry for a story about something completely new, and she could see that look in Erin's eyes. "Okay. Let me see what you have. Chance, give it another day. Micah, Erin will have oversight over all your Court House assignments."

The meeting was over in forty minutes, with Irita giving Mesa a congratulatory nod. The staff dispersed, walking a little taller and with a sense of purpose. Everyone seemed so eager, trying so hard, that Mesa felt rife with guilt.

❧

Chance headed toward the front door, but Mesa caught up with him before he could get away. "Where are you going?"

"Pork Chop John's, of course." Aside from its prime location, one block south of the *Messenger*'s office, Chance loved the restaurant, not just for its homey atmosphere, but its historical significance. For eighty-plus years, the uptown spot had been Butte's answer to fast food before the term even existed.

On any given day, you never knew who might show up—the sheriff, the mayor. Even the governor had stopped by before last year's St. Paddy's Day parade and had a chop sandwich. And, the part Chance liked best, they treated everybody the same.

"I've got just enough time to grab a bite before the sheriff's press conference," he said, licking his lips. "Come on. I'll treat."

"I haven't seen you alone for more than five minutes since I came to town," Mesa said. They walked quickly along Main Street.

"Yeah. I've been humping on this story the whole time." He tried to sound contrite.

"Is that what you were doing when I stopped by your apartment last night?" Mesa asked just as they crossed Mercury Street and entered Pork Chop John's.

The patrons greeted Chance as they entered the restaurant, which sported a Formica counter circa 1950, ten red vinyl and chrome stools, and a walk-up window.

He tried to act nonchalant, but he could tell from Mesa's manner that she had something on her mind. Before he even reached his regular seat—the stool next to the wall at the back—the latest counter guy, a Butte rat with a pierced eyebrow and tongue, said,

"The usual?" To which Chance, thankful for the diversion, replied, "You betcha."

"As a matter of fact," he said to Mesa, "I was out at the Copper Baron Hotel talking to the National Safety Board crash investigator."

"All night?"

Chance smiled. "Is there a problem?"

The counter boy appeared to take Mesa's order before she could answer. "You guys remember my sister, Mesa," Chance said. "She's back in town to help out at the paper," he said, addressing his introduction to either side of the counter.

Mesa felt her neck redden, but everybody tucked back into their sandwiches almost immediately.

"What'll it be?" said the counter boy in a soft voice that suggested he understood her embarrassment.

She looked for a second at the monumental plateful being placed in front of Chance and then said, "Just coffee."

"There's no problem," she said turning back to Chance, her voice high-pitched and petulant. A long pause ensued, during which Chance took a large bite of his pork chop sandwich, mustard oozing from its edge.

Mesa finally said, "I met Adrienne DeBrook yesterday."

"I know," Chance said with another grin, which seemed to irritate Mesa more.

"Why didn't you tell me about her? I had to hear it from Irita."

Chance could hear the hurt in her voice.

"Usually when you start dating somebody, I get a day-by-day commentary," Mesa said.

Chance paused for a moment to think about what Mesa had said. Dating hardly seemed to cover his relationship with Adrienne. It was too direct. She had entered his life through a side door, not head-on at all.

The first time he had met her, she was in a fix, and he was all business. She had bought one of those self-contained cabins, designed like the Sherpa huts in the Himalayas. In all-too-common Butte fashion, the local contractor who was supposed to pour the foundation had crapped out on her.

The cabin's builder, from Thompson Falls, had gone to engineering school with Chance. He called and asked for help. It blew Chance's mind to meet this sophisticated, big-city lady who was prepared to live in a fourteen by twenty-six foot cabin next to the national forest for the rest of her days.

"This is different," Chance said as Mesa fixed her attention on her cup of coffee. "It wasn't like I was asking her out on dates. We started out doing business together, then we became friends and then it grew into something else."

He had spent two weeks putting a daylight basement under her cabin. Twice she had come into Butte to consult with him about the work. Then a week later, she had told him she was interested in buying the Imperial Building and would he look at it with her.

Whenever he spent time with her, he found something else about her that was so different from any woman he had ever met. "Why does it matter, Mesa? Is there something about her you don't like?"

"I don't dislike her," Mesa said while she stirred her coffee. "I haven't known her long enough to form an opinion. I don't really know any women her age that well. Sure you're not just another boy toy?"

Chance's brow furrowed. "Adrienne struck you as someone who's shallow and frivolous and primarily interested in sex?"

"No," she said, "I guess not."

Her voice had taken on a serious tone. Chance wiped his mouth with a napkin, surprised to feel fire rising in his gut.

So that was what was bothering Mesa. He had to admit he was taken aback. What did age have to do with the fact that Adrienne could carry on an entire conversation without ever mentioning money, clothes, or the local gossip, all the things that women talked about that could make a guy crazy. "What do you mean 'her age'?"

"I don't hang out with anybody"—here Mesa hesitated and then focused on straightening the napkin under her coffee cup— "anybody as old as her. Maybe I would if Mom were still alive."

"It may come as a surprise to you, Mesa, but I don't think about Adrienne's age. What I think about is how much I enjoy her company. How she doesn't play games, how she says exactly what she means." Chance put his sandwich on the plate. "Maybe that's why I didn't tell you about her, because subconsciously I knew you would have an attitude about it. Turns out I was right, I guess."

Mesa stopped stirring her coffee mid-swirl. "How . . ."

Here, to Chance's surprise, Mesa, usually the champion of underdogs everywhere, stumbled.

"How much older is she? It's just that, well, she has gray hair. Why didn't you tell me? I could have been prepared."

Chance tried not to show his disappointment. He didn't want to give Mesa the satisfaction. "There's nothing to tell except I like her a lot, and you need to relax about the age thing. She's fifty-one. You do the math. Here," he said and tossed a ten-dollar bill on the table. "Coffee's on me. Sheriff's press conference starts in fifteen minutes." He turned to go.

"Aren't you going to finish your pork chop?" she asked.

Chance could hear the astonishment in her voice. "No, for once, I think I've actually lost my appetite."

Moments later, Mesa walked slowly up Main Street to the office. The midmorning sun fell on her shoulders, but she felt oddly chilled. For the first time since she could remember, she had found herself trying to filter out what she wanted to say to her brother, mindful that she might say something that could hurt his feelings. Over the years, they had often disagreed about the people they dated, but they had always confided in each other. He made the usual big-brother inquiries about the guys she dated. Mesa had been the first to hear about Chance's divorce.

She had told herself to choose her words wisely, but she had not suppressed the underlying tone of disapproval. She felt embarrassed, surprised by the resentment that welled up in her. For the life of her, she couldn't understand where all these feelings were coming from. Adrienne DeBrook seemed like an attractive, intelligent, creative person, someone Mesa might otherwise find appealing. Except for the minor detail that Adrienne and Chance were sleeping together.

"Somebody local was flying that plane. You don't just land in the middle of a neighborhood and then disappear," Chance said in a low voice, "not unless you know the vicinity. Even a little old lady in the Virginia Apartments knows that."

"And you think you know who this pilot was?" Rollie Solheim asked. They were standing in the hallway outside the sheriff's office. The press conference had been predictably short. Agent Perryman had sat in at the beginning but then gave a "No comment" to any questions from Noah or Chance, including the one about what was found in the plane.

Chance's question about whether the FBI were aware of a witness who lived in the Virginia Apartments merited a different response from Perryman—a brusque "We're on it."

Apparently, Edith Penmarron had called the sheriff's office right after Chance had left her the day before. Perryman even responded with "No comment" to Chance's inquiry about what Mrs. Penmarron had said—information Chance already knew and which he was sure Mrs. Penmarron had told the FBI that she had told him.

Hoping Rollie would be more forth coming, Chance cornered him in the hallway afterward. "I think I know just about every pilot in town, not that I think any of them is so coldhearted, not to mention dimwitted, as to leave a dying man in a plane crash."

"So you don't know who it was?" Rollie said with a sly grin.

"I think I might be able to find out. Whoever was flying that plane may have walked away, but not without any scratches. And if there's any evidence that was left in the plane, maybe I could help you come up with a lead or two."

Rollie nodded imperceptibly. "Hang on a minute. Let me talk to Perryman. Maybe you can give him the benefit of your wisdom," Rollie said with a laugh and a slap on Chance's shoulder.

Moments later, Roy Perryman reappeared. He, Solheim and Chance went back into Solheim's office, with Agent Perryman closing the door behind them.

Chance explained his connection to Silver Bow Aviation, and gave a quick rundown of his efforts to identify the pilot so far. He covered everything from seeing the plane moments before it went down, what Kevin had said about three men taking the plane up, and Jake Brinig's seeing a car that they might have driven to the airport. Chance punched home his usefulness with the fact that he was the one who had found Mrs. Penmarron and told her to call the sheriff.

Perryman sat silently for a moment, sizing Chance up as if the agent couldn't decide if he were trustworthy or not. Finally, he said, "All right. But whatever information I give you now, I share with you as part of an ongoing investigation. None of it goes into your paper. You can write your story, but the details I'm giving you now are directly pertinent to the investigation, and if they find their way into print before we've made an arrest, I'll have you charged with obstruction. Do we understand each other?"

Chance nodded. He, for one, wasn't expecting the *Messenger* to get any kind of scoop anyway. He knew it was his own curiosity, and pilot's integrity, that was driving this story. If the *Messenger* ran anything later, it would be a feature after the fact.

"We were able to lift a good set of prints from the plane's steering controls. If they are in fact the pilot's, he's not in our system, which means he doesn't have a criminal or military record. We're working on identifying the other prints that have been lifted," Perryman said in a tone that suggested he had said these words a thousand times before. "We think the murder weapon was some sort of small but sharp object, and the attack came from the rear seat of the plane, but we haven't found anything but smudged prints there." Perryman leaned on the doorjamb of the sheriff's office and crossed his arms. "That give you any ideas?"

Chance thought for a moment. "So, whoever took the plane wasn't a known criminal?" he said.

"Not known to us. He could be Canadian or Mexican, if you buy the drug-running scenario, which I don't, since we found nothing in the plane to corroborate it. Still, we're checking. All we found in the plane were the usual items you'd expect—maps, the pilot's log, the registration, and an owner's manual. Other than some junk-food wrappers and soda bottles, that's it." He paused again. "Having any insight yet?" Perryman's tone was not so much sarcastic as bored, as if this whole case meant less to him than somebody's dog getting run over.

Chance inhaled deeply, and then shook his head.

"You don't seem to know as much as you thought you did," Perryman said with a sigh.

"What about the two guys Mrs. Penmarron saw and the Bronco?" Chance asked.

Perryman nodded. "We're following up, but don't get in our way. If you should actually think of anything that might help, you call me. Got it?" Perryman peeled himself off the doorjamb and rolled out the doorway.

Chance muttered under his breath, "Prick."

Rollie smiled and then opened a folder on his desk and took out a couple of glossy eight-by-ten photos, which he tossed on the table. Chance looked at the photos of the plane's interior. A couple of candy wrappers and empty plastic soda bottles lay in various corners of the plane. He shook his head as if to say there was nothing he could add. He looked at Solheim and said, "Still no word from the guy who owns the plane?"

Solheim shook his head and then said, "But we heard from his insurance company. Their investigator is in Moab today and here tomorrow."

The sheriff leaned back in his desk chair, his arms behind his head, and said, "Look, Chance, do me a favor. Don't rub these Fibbies the wrong way. They don't like it in Butte now any more than they did when Hoover used to banish them here fifty years ago. I don't want them around any longer than necessary. Let them do their jobs and you stick to yours, okay?" This last request was a gentle, Dutch uncle, plea.

Chance walked down the cool, stone stairway of the police station. He was vaguely aware that it was lunchtime. However, he was not hungry. What with Mesa and now the surly FBI agent, his appetite had not returned.

The FBI agent had worked one case too many. But Mesa, the defender of every oppressed group in America, if not the world, had no excuse. Had she really given him crap about Adrienne's age?

"Boy toy" was the term she had used. If only Mesa knew, not that he ever planned to tell her.

Adrienne had been reluctant about their sleeping together, at least at first. And even if he chose to be somebody's sex object, it was none of Mesa's business. He was deep in thought about Adrienne when he almost ran into a man pacing back and forth in the lobby.

Chance excused himself and then realized he knew the man. "Mr. Swoboda," Chance said and smiled. The "preacher," as the kids at Butte High always called him behind his back, had taught biology until his recent retirement. He'd gotten into some flap about not teaching evolution. A kind, soft-spoken man in a school filled with too many drill sergeants and dragon ladies, Chance had thought of him as a good teacher whose comments about how the world was created had largely been ignored by his students. At this moment though, Mr. Swoboda looked agitated. "How's it going?" Chance said. "You're the last person I would expect to see at the police station."

Swoboda held a copy of Tuesday's *Standard* and tapped the photo of Lowell Austin with his knuckle. "This man, I know him. He was staying at my house."

Chapter 13

Daniel Swoboda recalled with vivid detail his journey to Butte with Lowell Austin on the previous Thursday evening. They had met at the bus station in Drummond, fifty miles west, and driven back along the interstate, probably the only vehicle doing the speed limit.

When they reached the outskirts of Butte, Lowell had asked about Our Lady of the Rockies. The ridgeline was indistinguishable from the night sky, and the statue on the horizon seemed to hover like an angel.

"What is that up there in the sky?" he had asked.

Daniel smiled broadly. "That's Our Lady of the Rockies, patron saint of Butte, Montana. Looks like she's floating, doesn't it?"

Lowell's interest in the statue had surprised Daniel. According to the Interfaith Prison Ministry staff at Orofino, during Lowell's years in prison, he had developed a reputation as a hard case. He boxed a bit and learned horsehair hitching—mastering intricate, colorful, geometric designs good for hatbands and bracelets. Mostly he just kept to himself. All of which Daniel thought made him a good match for Butte.

Prisoners about to be released always talked to the associate warden about the transition into a new life after their decades in prison. Daniel knew that from his own training as an interfaith lay minister. He wondered if the warden could possibly have done justice to the experience.

Daniel had tried to use the story of how the ninety-foot statue built in honor of women, especially mothers, had been welded of sheet metal by unemployed miners as a metaphor for overcoming difficult obstacles, a lesson he thought Lowell might appreciate. The description of how a helicopter had hauled the statue in sections to the top of the East Ridge on a windy day in the dead of winter usually impressed even the most cynical. Lowell seemed to listen with one ear.

When Daniel asked Lowell about what prompted his decision to come to Butte, the convict had been straightforward. "No other particular place to go. My mother is in a nursing home back east. My brother doesn't want much to do with me. I can respect that. Most of my friends, aside from my attorney, stopped writing a long time ago. Can't blame them. I don't have much in common with any of them anymore."

Then he had patted his shirt pocket and said, "I got one invitation though." He talked about the many women who had written to him while he was in prison. At first, the country song about him had inspired fan mail, and then the television movie spawned even more. He had heard or seen neither and had no desire to. "I didn't answer most of the letters."

But two years before his release, Lowell had added his name to a list of prisoners who wanted someone to write to them. It would be a good way for him to begin the reentry into society, the interfaith staff had said.

He matter-of-factly described the kinds of letters he had received. The women had their own miseries and wrote a lot about the power of faith and redemption. Most didn't seem too smart. "I wasn't rude about it," Lowell said. "I just didn't write back."

When he started talking about the woman who had invited him to Butte, his tone became more animated. "Kate started writing last year. Her letters were different. She wrote about places where she traveled, and what was going on in the world. She didn't try to convert me, or even ask about why I was in prison to start with," he said.

He showed Daniel a photograph she had sent him and the bracelet he had spent the last three weeks hitching for her. Dressed in a turquoise blouse and blue jeans and leaning on a jackleg fence, she was a handsome woman all right. She wore her dark hair long and pulled over one shoulder. "I designed the bracelet to match that outfit," Lowell said proudly.

Once they pulled off the highway, they made their way to Daniel's house. He showed Lowell to a bedroom that had once belonged to one of his sons who was now married. "There's a bathroom across the hall," Daniel said with a gesture in that direction.

"Let me know if you need something you can't find. Want coffee in the morning?"

Lowell nodded.

Daniel stopped at the door on his way out and said, "I put a Bible there on the chest of drawers. Thought it might be a comfort."

"Look, Mr. Swoboda," Lowell said. "I appreciate all you've done, but I'm not one for religion. Truth is, last Bible somebody gave me, I used most of the pages for cigarette papers."

Daniel nodded slowly and then said, "You still smoke?"

"No, no," Lowell said, waving Daniel off as if his host might be about to hunt down an ashtray.

"See? That Bible did you more good than you realized," Daniel said with a smile and closed the door.

Moments later, laying his head on the pillow of his bed, Daniel parted the curtains to look through the window at Our Lady on the mountain. He took great comfort in being able to see her each night as he fell asleep. He wondered if Lowell would take any notice of it.

Daniel thought about his houseguest, unable to imagine being imprisoned for even a short time. What must it feel like finally to sleep in a room that had no lock on its door, to be able to go outside whenever he wanted for the first time in more than twenty years? More than anything, he wanted Lowell Austin to have faith that his life could take a different path now.

ഇ~൨

The next morning Daniel awoke to the sound of the children next door laughing. Once downstairs, he found Lowell already sitting on the back porch, drinking coffee and watching the kids play. "Did they wake you?"

Austin shook his head with a slight grin. "It's hard sleeping in when you're used to waking up at 6 a.m. every morning for as long as I have."

Daniel had heard about the boredom and mindless routine from other inmates he had counseled. The fact that Lowell wanted to free himself from some part of that routine proved the first sign that the hardness in him might soften.

They sat together on the porch steps, the distant smell of smoke from the latest forest fire mixed with the fresh scent of cut lumber. Lowell took in an exaggerated breath. "Big difference from the smell of nicotine and disinfectant. That's how every prison smells."

Lowell asked if he could have a piece of the kindling that lay in a pile in the bushel basket. He reached into his jeans pocket and pulled out a stainless steel Leatherman tool. "I bought it yesterday at one of the truck stops on the bus route."

Everybody had them these days, Daniel said. They talked about its amazing number of tools all combined into one—knife, pliers, screwdriver, and scissors.

"It's a con's dream come true," Lowell said with a chuckle, "which is why I guess I never saw one in the joint." He opened the knife blade, thin and razor sharp, and began to carve the wood.

"Think I'll have some breakfast," said Daniel. "My wife usually does the cooking, but she's in Kalispell with our new granddaughter until next week. I could probably dig up some cereal."

"I never been a big eater, even before prison," Lowell said. "I'll come inside and have some more coffee though if that's okay."

Lowell sat at the kitchen table, trying to read the sports section upside down. Daniel pushed the paper across the table. "Go ahead and look at it."

Lowell thanked him. "In prison, guys hoard newspapers. Nobody shares anything without some sort of trade—dog-eat-dog kind of thing."

Daniel had not replied then, though he often thought the world outside wasn't much different.

Chance tried not to tailgate as he followed Mr. Swoboda's pickup toward his house on Princeton Street behind the Mountain Man Pawnshop. They had stood talking in the lobby of the police station. Mr. Swoboda, who was clearly upset, did most of the talking. After fifteen minutes, Chance had convinced Mr. Swoboda to let him see Lowell Austin's effects, which they could bring back to the police station, and save the police time. Chance was sure that Agent Perryman would not have preferred this, but then that was what Agent Perryman got for keeping distraught taxpayers waiting.

They stopped at the traffic light near the Great Harvest Bread Store, a favorite of Adrienne's. Chance thought about Mesa's "boy toy" remark, which still rankled. It so limited the relationship he had with Adrienne, but how to explain that to Mesa?

He thought about the first night that he and Adrienne had spent together, Friday evening of the Irish Festival three weeks before. Floating along with the festival music, Irish airs playing from the huge stage on Park Street, they had walked from her gallery to Chance's house. When they stopped to cross at Montana Street, he took her by the elbow, and, once they reached the far curb, he dared to slip her arm through his. They walked slowly in the warm night air without expectation, and for a moment, he felt like he was strolling along in some other time, in a place far away.

By the time they walked the last block, he was holding her hand. Silver Street was quiet. He was thankful the stoops of his neighbors sat vacant. He didn't want to risk that the presence of an audience might embarrass her. He unlocked the door of his duplex and ushered her in.

"Smells like a cedar chest," she said and smiled at him when he had closed the front door.

"A warm cedar chest," he said and opened the side living room window. "I'm sticky with drywall dust." He pulled at the front of his tee shirt and hoped he didn't sound as shy as he suddenly felt. "I think I'll take a shower. Why don't you look around? Won't be a tick, as me old Nan would say."

She grinned at his imitation English accent. Relaxed by her smile, he returned it and said, "Promise you won't leave some poetic note on the kitchen table and then run away?"

She shook her head, and he believed her. Whatever guard she had kept up before was gone. Must have been that Irish music.

"Glasses in the usual place?" she asked and held up the remaining cans of Guinness.

He gestured to the kitchen with his thumb toward the back of the house and then turned toward the hallway and the bathroom. Ten frantic minutes later, he was out of the shower, having thrown on a pair of khaki shorts. He was slipping a white tee shirt over his head when he found her in the kitchen, relieved that she hadn't changed her mind about leaving.

She had been completely candid with him. "I thought I might feel awkward being here, just the two of us." Here she had stuttered, "I haven't been with anyone for a while. I'm not sure ...."

He hadn't let her finish. When he had asked her to come home with him, she had responded with a nod, no questions, no defining, still the uncertainty in her eyes touched him. Taking that risk had meant more than anything else. "Don't think about anything but enjoying the Guinness. A drink's a drink, nothing more."

Eventually he had given her a tour of the apartment and, true, she had decided it should end in the bedroom. They did sleep together, but just that. He had held her, kissed the top of her head. Of course, she came back Saturday night, when indeed everything she might have forgotten or repressed about sex in the previous five years appeared to have come to life again. But boy toy? No way.

The light turned green, and Chance followed Mr. Swoboda down Harrison Avenue. Two turns later, they pulled into his driveway. The two-story brick house looked like a hundred others in Butte. The waning garden still contained a few red geraniums. The lawn had been recently mowed, the porch swept. Austin's death seemed a harsh end to all Mr. Swoboda's kindnesses.

Mr. Swoboda silently led Chance upstairs to the bedroom at the back of the house. School photographs of smiling teenagers, brothers in various stages of growth, lined the wall going up the stairs.

The bedroom contained a single bed, which had been slept in, though the green chenille bedspread had not been turned down. Next to the bed stood an oak chest of drawers, dark with the patina of age.

"Did Austin tell you what his plans were?" Chance asked Mr. Swoboda when they entered the room.

"He wasn't a big talker," Daniel said. "The first morning he was here, I asked him what he planned to do. He wanted to get his driver's license, which we did that Friday afternoon. Passed the written test with no problem. The road test too.

"He told me he had worked in a print shop at Orofino, so I told him I knew a guy at Brownstone Printers. He wanted to see about it, first thing. Seemed like he was thinking about a future here in Butte, but maybe that was all malarkey."

Mr. Swoboda pointed to a black vinyl gym bag at the end of the bed. "That's all he had with him when I met him at the bus station."

Mr. Swoboda sat on the edge of the bed. He picked up a small wooden carving from the windowsill and showed it to Chance. It was a miniature bust of the Virgin Mary. Her features were delicately rendered, the folds of the cloth over her head, her eyes closed in prayer. Running his finger over the marks of the knife on the wood gave Chance an odd feeling, as if the tiny sculpture were an extension of the man. He had shaped this wood, made it his own.

"He carved that from a piece of wood in my backyard that first morning," Daniel said.

Chance could hear the disappointment in Mr. Swoboda's words and tried to comfort him. "I'm sure you did the best you could, Mr. Swoboda."

"I just don't know what I'm going to tell Brother Kressge over at Orofino."

Chance unzipped the bag and used his Bic ballpoint to poke around at its meager contents— extra clothes and a magazine about horsehair hitching, a delicately woven turquoise and black bracelet, a prison ID card, discharge papers— precious little for a man who had been in prison for twenty-five years.

A half-folded letter, its envelope gone, lay on top of the oak chest. Mr. Swoboda and Chance seemed to spot it at the same time. For a minute, Chance thought his old teacher was going to stop him from reading it.

"It might give us some idea about who Austin knew in town. Could lead to information about who killed him."

"Shouldn't we leave this for the police?" Mr. Swoboda said, rubbing his hand over his mouth.

This is what CSI has done to America, Chance thought. We're all forensic experts. "Tell you what," Chance said, "Why don't you call them? Tell Sheriff Solheim you found the letter and to come over."

Swoboda nodded and Chance, careful to touch only the edges of the paper, quickly read through the neat, dark blue-inked letter on light blue stationary. It must be from a woman, or someone pretending to be one.

He was not one to read anyone's private papers, but he felt a sudden urgency to do so. The woman had written how surprised she was by how quickly the last year had gone, and that she could imagine how excited he must be about his release. She would see him soon. Then her signature, "Kate."

Kate? He felt deflated. If this was a woman in Butte, she might as well have signed the letter "Honey Bun."

An estimated ten thousand men had left the Emerald Isle to make their fortunes as miners in Butte in the last century. The scope of the St. Patrick's Day celebration—the biggest in the West—was living proof of their impact. Every other family had a Kate or some other variation of Kathleen or Katherine. He could think of half a dozen women who might fit the bill, and he had a terrible memory for names.

"They're on their way," Mr. Swoboda said when he returned. "Did you read the letter? Was it any help?"

Chance shook his head. "It's from a woman named Kate. He mention her to you?"

Daniel nodded. "He had a snapshot of her."

Chance turned back to the vinyl bag and gave it another once over. No photo. He made another sweep of the bedroom, even looking under the pillow. Nothing. Maybe it was with the wallet.

"He used my phone to call her. I reckon it was the same woman," Daniel said. "I was kind of surprised but in a good way."

"We joked about it. I mean, that it was a woman and he said it had been some time since he had talked to any female besides a dentist who came to the prison. I think he was only half joking.

"I showed him the phone in the hallway. He thought it was the damnedest thing that it didn't have a cord. I think he was a little nervous calling this gal.

"When he came back into the kitchen, he looked like his ship had come in." Daniel smiled. The memory of the conversation seemed to cheer him. "He picked at his shirt and asked where he could get a new one.

"After the drivers' test, I took him to the mall. He seemed optimistic about the job, and that evening he talked on the phone to the woman again. He asked about a nice restaurant that wasn't too expensive. I recommended Lydia's and even offered to lend him a car."

"Do you know what he did on Saturday?" Chance asked, hoping to trace as many of Austin's movements as possible.

"Let's see. He asked about directions to the Club Boxing arena. I lent him that old pickup." Swoboda pointed to a small blue beater truck. "Then he went out in the afternoon and didn't come back until after midnight. On Sunday morning, I invited him to go to church, but he was already dressed and said he had made plans. He never mentioned anything about flying," Swoboda said. "But then, like I said, he wasn't the type to volunteer much. Most newly released men don't.

"I left a little after eight to pick up my mother-in-law for church. That's the last I saw of him. When he didn't come back, I didn't feel it was my place to question where he was."

Mr. Swoboda sighed and then ran his hand over his balding scalp. "I was a bit surprised he didn't call, but then I figured maybe this gal had taken him in. He wasn't on parole, you know. He served his time. I didn't think he'd be inclined to want to answer to me."

He paused for a second, looking around the room. "It's such a shock. I feel like I let him down. They'll be disappointed over in Orofino, that's for sure."

Maybe so, Chance thought. But he also wondered if there were others who thought Austin had finally gotten what he deserved.

ॐ

Mesa walked over to Erin's desk in the newsroom and waited while the young reporter finished a phone call. "Okay," Erin said, "I'll get

Irita. Between the two of us, we should be able to generate a list of possibilities."

Mesa couldn't help being curious about the pieces in the puzzle of the Austin story. And the look on Erin's face made Mesa even more curious. "What's going on?"

Erin looked up with her usual deer-in-the-headlights response to anything Mesa asked. She said, "That was Chance. Apparently, Austin was corresponding with someone in Butte. He's trying to figure out who it is.

"Turns out Daniel Swoboda—you know "Preach" from the high school? He gave Austin a ride to Butte, as part of some prison missionary program," Erin said and clicked her cell phone closed. "Austin wanted to come to Butte because this woman named Kate lives here and has been writing to him in prison. Chance wants to track her down to talk to her."

"How many Kates do you suppose live in Butte?" Erin continued. "Not counting the ones like me. My grandmother still calls me Kate. My first name's Kathleen, even though I officially became Erin when I was in junior high. I'd say twenty percent of the girls in Butte, and that's just the Irish ones."

Mesa had to agree. "Why couldn't her name be Isabel or Dagmar?" Even she knew several Kates in Butte, and she wasn't even a bona fide, full-time Buttian. Kate Callahan, who had sat behind her in homeroom junior year, was assistant director at the Arts Chateau. Katy Drennen, who sat behind Katie Callahan in that same homeroom, now worked up at

the college. And those were just the first two Kates
that came to mind.

"Chance thinks that maybe this Kate woman is
the driver of the maroon SUV," Erin said, her eyes
agleam with the "games afoot" mindset that had
launched Sherlock Holmes.

"So how did Chance find all this out?" Mesa
asked. She was impressed with her brother's
investigative efforts despite the fact that he claimed
to have no real interest in journalism.

"He saw Preach waiting in the police station to
talk to a detective."

Erin's cell rang again, and Mesa gravitated back
to her office, feeling oddly distant. For the first time,
she wasn't writing the story but overseeing it, an
altogether different perspective. Her own experience
as a reporter had taught her that the life of an editor,
while more stable, was boring. You worked the story
secondhand. Tracking the facts, uncovering sources
and piecing together what people want to know was
replaced by the steady workings of the newsroom
and being in charge, whatever that meant.

Then her cell phone rang. "So I hear you were
hanging out with Hardy at the Hoist House last
night," she heard Tara say in a coy tone.

"Don't you have children to raise?" Mesa said,
half kidding. She did not relish revisiting the
previous night's indiscretion, which Tara would no
doubt intuit.

"Two-year-olds take naps, thank God," Tara
said. "You slept with him, didn't you?"

"How did you even hear I went out?" Mesa
asked.

"Mary Connelly, I'm trying to get her into a duplex uptown."

Mesa nodded as she spoke, remembering the nurse at the bar last night. There was no denying Tara.

"So what he's doing back in town?" Tara asked.

"Sounds like his dad is really fading," Mesa said.

"Jeez, that's sad," Tara said. "My dad and Mr. Jacobs started out in the mines together."

Mr. Jacobs had worked for the Anaconda Company underground and then in the pit. When the mine finally closed, miners were faced with a difficult decision. Leave Butte and move the family to where there was work, or let the family stay and work in a mine out of town. Mr. Jacobs had gone to Alaska to work as a welder, making six times what he could in the lower forty-eight.

He lived small and sent every extra nickel home. For five years, he saw his family a week at Christmas and for two weeks in the summer. Meanwhile, Hardy's mother worked as a waitress at the Uptown Café so they could bank all that her husband made. When he came back, they had enough money to buy into the windshield replacement business—steady commerce in the land of pickup trucks and back roads.

"Funny the hold this town has on people," Tara said. "Yukon Glass never used to mean anything to Hardy."

That was true in his younger days. Baseball was going to be his career, until a belly slide into third base while trying to stretch a double had changed everything. "Things change," Mesa said, although she knew Hardy and his father had never been close. All those years apart had created a permanent gulf. By the time his father came back for good, Hardy no longer saw himself as a child. In fact, he had never really grown up at all.

"You tell him you're headed west?" Tara asked.

"Like he really cares," Mesa said.

"Oops, I hear a baby crying," Tara said. "Gotta go."

Mesa had barely hung up when Irita came bustling in from the back office, looking at her watch. "Today's the last Lunch in the Park concert. Come on. I'll take you down there. You can rub elbows with the locals and grab a pasty."

Mesa tried to summon up a sincere response. Historically, pasties—pronounced like "past" and not "paste"—were the mainstay of Cornish miners who referred to the beef, onion and potato pie as a "letter from 'ome." The locals' love for the concoction defied her understanding. Too bland for Mesa's tastes. Still, she knew better than to cast aspersions on one of Butte's culinary specialties, and acquiesced.

Erin joined them and explained Chance's search for the mystery woman to Irita, who began chewing on her left thumbnail. "Women who write to convicts," she said and rolled her eyes. "I guess there's the added plus of not having the guy underfoot. I'll start a mental list on our walk down to the park. You want a pasty?" Irita asked Erin, who nodded enthusiastically, as did Micah, Phade and Cinch when they were asked.

Outside the sky was blue and cloudless, a day made for the tourist guidebooks. "You know any Kates that might qualify?" Mesa asked with muted curiosity.

Irita shrugged, and then said," I'm amazed how much Chance has charmed out of the FBI."

"This Kate with a maroon SUV in a town this size can't be that hard to track down."

"What did you say?" Irita said in a whisper.

Mesa turned to Irita. "This Kate could be the one driving the maroon SUV."

"Oh my God," Irita said stopping in the middle of the sidewalk.

Irita had grabbed at her chest. "What?" Mesa said. "Are you sick?"

"No," Irita said, "just in the throes of another possible moral dilemma."

"What are you talking about?" Mesa said. She had already become accustomed to Irita's flair for the dramatic. Clearly, this reaction was visceral.

"My daughter-in-law, when she was a kid, they called her Kate. She owns a maroon Bronco."

Chapter 14

"That soup's getting cold."

Chance looked up to see Adrienne standing over him.

"For a minute there, I thought you were in a trance," Adrienne said with good humor.

Chance stood up. "Just thinking about you," he said and took her arm. What was it about her that made him such a sap? Romance had never been his strong suit. His ex-wife would attest to that. But something about Adrienne made him feel gallant, when in fact she seemed to need less protection than any woman he had ever met.

Adrienne shook her head and ignored his comment. "Shall we meander down to the park?"

Emma Park, a memorial to the one Anaconda Company mine actually inside the taxable city limits, thanks to clever gerrymandering, covered two city blocks of uptown Butte. Its existence, plain and simple as it was, stood as a sad commentary on the company's idea of reclamation.

A red-roofed white gazebo now stood where the Emma mine head frame once pulled hundreds of miners and ore up and down, twenty-four seven, in

and out of the largest source of manganese in North
America. Despite its once staggering profits, the
mine's yard was now no more than a grass-covered
expanse where small children played and elderly
people sat in lawn chairs to listen to the Community
Orchestra's last lunchtime concert of the summer.
They were playing "A Bicycle Built for Two."

Chance and Adrienne sat on the grassy slope on
the north side of the park. Steam billowed from the
cartons of thick minestrone soup Chance had bought
at the Uptown Cafe. Adrienne licked her lips. She
attacked with a plastic soupspoon, then looked up
and said, "This must be an historic moment. I'm
eating and you're not. What's going on?"

Chance picked up his spoon and began stirring
his soup, "Soup's hot."

"In the three months I've known you, I have
never seen you ponder over a single bite of food.
You even eat the candy suckers at the bank. I've
seen you pick up meat grilling on hot coals and toss
it in your mouth. What's wrong?"

"You ever feel like you know someone so well,
better than they even know themselves sometimes,
and then out of the blue they say something that
totally shocks you?"

Adrienne sipped her soup, and said, "Like when
Devlin told me he wanted a divorce?"

The story of Adrienne's divorce did have its
shocking elements, especially how her ex had
apparently slept with every nurse in their bustling
Los Angeles medical practice. Adrienne said she
knew he was a jerk, just not how big of one.

"More like when somebody whose opinion you value makes a judgment that's so off-base," Chance countered.

"That would be like my sister in Seattle when I told her about you."

Chance looked at her with a frown. "It must be in the air."

Adrienne put her spoon down and said, "Why, who said something to you?"

"Mesa," Chance said, trying to keep a light tone in his voice.

Adrienne sighed and shook her head. "Mine says you'll break my heart. What's yours say?"

Chance hesitated, looking around to avoid being overheard in case Adrienne reacted negatively. "I'm your boy toy."

Adrienne chuckled discreetly, and gave him a little nudge on the thigh.

Chance suddenly felt uneasy. "Well, I'm glad you're not upset."

Adrienne smiled. "I wouldn't want you to think you're not excellent boy-toy material." Then she sighed when Chance did not join in the kidding. "Does it really bother you that much?"

"Kind of like a paper cut. It's not all that big a deal, but it's hard to ignore."

"Her opinion means a lot to you, I know. And it's not that I don't take it seriously, but what can you do? People form their own opinions without the slightest bit of information. Granted, I did tell my sister that I was through with men, so I can see why she was surprised, but she'll get over it."

"Wow, I guess I didn't realize I was swimming upstream," Chance said with an unexpected feeling of warmth.

Adrienne took hold of Chance's hand. "How I feel about you has nothing to do with what other people think."

When Chance still didn't smile, she added, "My sister thinks I should gradually begin to dye my hair so you won't notice."

"No kidding. Mesa mentioned your hair too."

"Would you like me to become a brunette again?"

"Don't be ridiculous. If anybody's going to dye their hair, it'll be me. Is there such a thing as reverse Grecian Formula?"

❧

"I can't believe she'd be involved in anything illegal," Irita said and shook her head. "She's a paralegal and won't even walk against the traffic light."

Which was exactly what Mesa and Irita were doing at that moment. Mesa strode briskly along Mercury Street toward Emma Park to keep up with Irita, who walked as fast as she talked.

"Her name is Kathy, but she used to be called Kate," Mesa repeated to be sure she had heard correctly, "and she does own a maroon SUV."

By now, they were at the edge of the park, headed toward the line in front of the vendor trailer for Pete's Pasties. They walked past the community band, now playing, "In the Good old Summer

Time," complete with a tuba solo. Mesa finally interrupted Irita's ramblings. "Exactly who are we talking about?"

"Kathy—you met at Stodden Park at the Labor Day picnic Monday?"

"With the two kids?" Mesa said, the surprise clear in her voice. Kathy looked like a soccer mom—certainly not like anyone who might be involved in hijacking a plane.

"Actually, she's my step-daughter-in-law. My ex-step-daughter-in-law, to be precise."

"Say again?"

Irita sighed. "It's not as complicated as it sounds. When I was young and foolish, I married a good-looking son-of-a-bitch named Dominic DiNunzio who, besides having a mean streak as wide as the Missouri, had a son from his first marriage. I divorced Dom after he sent me to the hospital twice. But I kept up with the kid."

"So where does Kathy fit in?"

"She married the kid, Phil, although it didn't end well. Five years ago after the state deregulated electricity, the mine closed and he was laid off. Next thing you know, he started in on Kathy the way his father had on me. But she wised up faster. She divorced him, took the kids, and moved back to Bozeman to her mother's. Unfortunately, her mother died last year. So, Kathy and the kids ended up moving back to Butte.

"Since then, I've been a kind of surrogate grandmother. She hasn't got anybody else really. Her father died when she was small, so it's just

Kathy and her brother, the soldier. Remember? You met him too."

Mesa nodded. She had met a lot of people in the past three days, but the polite soldier with the vacant eyes was hard to forget.

"So I help out picking up the kids from school when she needs me to. Take them to the movies when she's ready to throttle one of them. That sort of thing," Irita said, her tone a mixture of concern and confusion.

They were at the front of the pasty line now. The faint aroma of onions and pastry drifted toward them. While Irita ordered pasties for everyone in the office, Mesa stepped away to listen to the band that was now playing a lively rendition of "Seventy-six Trombones."

She scanned the crowd, mostly parents with preschool children, office workers on their lunch hour. Beyond the gazebo along Silver Street, she saw adults from the sheltered workshop getting off a minibus. And on the hillside edge of the park, she saw Chance and Adrienne huddled together. They were deep in conversation. She wondered with a tinge of guilt if Chance was telling Adrienne about their conversation.

Mesa found herself looking around, wondering if anyone noticed the pair. She felt uncomfortable, but Irita didn't seem to see them. She just kept right on talking.

"Kathy works at the new Legal Aid Office on Park Street." They started back up the hill. Irita had opened her pasty. She stopped to rearrange its foil wrapper and take a bite. But her expression was ominous, as if her thoughts were far away.

"But she was with us on Monday at the Labor Day picnic, right?" Mesa asked.

Irita nodded.

Maroon and white were the school colors of the University of Montana Grizzlies, as well as the local Catholic high school. More than a few obsessed Montanans, male and female, liked to show their school spirit by the color of the car they purchased. "A maroon Bronco isn't exactly an exotic vehicle in this part of the country," Mesa said.

They were in front of the *Messenger* office now. Irita looked drained, as if telling the story of Kathy DiNunzio had given her time to realize the difficulty Kathy might be in. "Listen, don't say anything to Chance yet. Let me talk to Kathy first. I can't imagine she would have anything to do with this. She's a bell ringer in the Methodist choir, for God's sake."

"Tell you what," Mesa said, why don't we give Kathy a call, see if she can clear this up right now?" She was tired of taking a backseat to the evolving story. Erin would still write the feature. Mesa would just do a little investigating of her own.

Inside the *Messenger* office, she waited in the reception area while Irita made the call. Mesa nibbled half-heartedly on her pasty—too much pastry and not enough innards for her taste, and tried to focus her thoughts.

They drifted to the night before and Hardy. Something in him had changed. Maybe it was the thirties career crisis—i.e., getting a real job.

Her address book was filled with friends who had avoided what they called the trap of corporate America, or any steady-paying job for that matter. She knew plenty of fishing-boat poets, taxicab-driving playwrights, not to mention voter rights volunteers who lived in dormitory digs because they couldn't afford their own apartment.

Hardy was no different except that his dreams were of the extreme sport genre. Only his body had betrayed him, not social convention. She wanted to tell him to buck up. He could still make good, run the family business, marry one of a host of local babes who would love to have him and his children. Wait. Was this the first glimmer that she might really be over him?

"Kathy's not in the office," Irita said, her voice taut. "She called in sick yesterday and today. I don't like it. I think I'll go over to her place and see what's up."

"I'll go with you," Mesa said. She left Erin and Micah, now sitting at the table in the middle of the newsroom eating their pasties, to hold down the fort. Both of them expressed instant exhilaration, followed by panic. "If you hear from Chance anytime soon," Mesa said, "have him call me."

అ≫

After lunch, Chance and Adrienne walked back up to Park Street where he left her at the Mining City Boxing Club, which ran a training gym on the second floor above Terminal Meats at Park and Dakota. Chance climbed the dimly lit staircase that led up from the sidewalk. Even before he opened the door to go in, he could hear the thwat, thwat of leather gloves finding their mark.

The cave-like interior—a high ceiling with black painted windows— made it impossible to tell it was daylight. Two boxers were sparring in the ring, which was banked on three sides by tiered rows of empty wooden seats. On the fourth side, several other boxers were working out on a speed bag, two others on the heavy bag.

Chance walked over to the far side of the ring to a stocky man with a broad nose and a broader smile. "Hey, Sam, I thought I might find you here. Whose corner you in?"

"Patrick Windy Boy, in the headgear. He's gonna be a good one."

Sam chewed raggedly on a piece of gum and watched the methodical punching of the sparring partners. They were light on their feet and both moved quickly, but their punches did not always land.

"He's driving a haul truck on that seven days on/seven days off shift at the mine. He can't train with my other boys, so I come in on his off days and give him a few pointers.

"Your grandmother need something?" Sam asked while they watched the boxers dancing around the ring.

Like a lot of guys in Club Boxing, Sam Chavez had learned the sweet science in prison. After a stint in the Deer Lodge penitentiary, he had moved to Butte and become Nana's number-one handyman for years, especially after Gramps had died.

Sam could fix anything—the lawnmower, the snow blower, the car. He also fixed the roof, painted the house, and shoveled the snow, often without being asked, or paid. All because Gramps had befriended Sam when he first came to town.

"She's fine," Chance said and felt a warmness toward Sam for asking. "That's not why I wanted to talk to you."

Chance pulled the newspaper photo of Lowell Austin from his shirt pocket. "It's about this guy. Did you happen to see him the other day? I heard he might have come in here."

Sam held the photo in his thick rough hands, nicked, and scarred from years of working outside in a cold and dry climate. He nodded. "He come in here Saturday, I think it was. I figure he was just sprung. Takes a while before you let down your guard."

Sam did not miss much. "Was he looking for somebody?" Chance asked, wondering if Lowell had another contact in Butte besides the mysterious Kate.

The boxing circuit welcomed guys who had done time, even the outcasts who didn't have anything else going for them—of which Butte had more than its fair share. What with the pre-release center and the ne'er-do-wells who were rumored to receive free bus tickets to Butte from the Bozeman or Missoula police, Chance had heard the sheriff say his department had three thousand outstanding warrants in Silver Bow County, which was about ten percent of the population.

"Dougie Kincaid," Sam said and shook his head.

"Strike out," Chance said, his voice deflated. Dougie Kincaid was a Butte rat who in his day had a legitimate knockout punch for the middleweight ranks. Unfortunately, he had used it in a street fight and nearly killed a man in Coeur d'Alene.

Dougie's was a cautionary tale. Welcomed home with open arms once he served his time, Dougie was often seen in the corner of numerous young fighters, at least until this past spring.

In March, he had been caught trying to pawn tools that, as it turned out, had been stolen from several construction sites in the county. Dougie maintained that he was doing a favor for a friend, but the friend was long gone and Dougie was left holding the proverbial stolen property. He was currently serving four months in Deer Lodge at the state penitentiary. "Did he talk to anybody else?" Chance asked.

Sam shook his head. "Wasn't anybody in here except me and Patrick, and Patrick was working on the speed bag. I told this Austin guy about Dougie, and then we talked some. Said he had done some boxing and wanted to stay involved. Dougie could be out soon, I said, and told the guy to come back, that I would introduce him around."

Chance liked the idea that Lowell Austin had gotten to talk to Sam, who would have treated him with some respect. Austin might have begun to think Butte was a decent place.

"Some guys, they come outta prison," Sam said, "They go looking for trouble. But I didn't think that about this guy. I thought I had a good read on him. Course, you can make enemies in prison. Too bad."

Chance took the picture and replaced it in his pocket. "Yep, sounds like maybe somebody come looking for him all right."

Kathy DiNunzio lived on Gold Street in a turn-of-the-century bungalow that had been added onto like most of the houses on the Lower Westside. Three blocks away from Nana Rose's house, it was a neighborhood Mesa could see herself living in. Not that she ever seriously thought about settling in Butte.

Irita rang the doorbell. When no one answered, she opened the door to the enclosed sun porch and began banging on the front door. Thankfully, at two in the afternoon, presumably the rest of the neighborhood was awake.

"Kathy, you home? Let me in," Irita called in between pounding the door. "I know she's in there," Irita said, nodding toward the maroon SUV at the curb and then shaking her head in disbelief. "We're going to get this sorted out and pretty damn quick."

Mesa looked at the late-model vehicle, parked in front of the house in the quiet, residential area. Most of the neighbors were professional people or professors at the college a couple of blocks away. Kathy DiNunzio must be doing all right for herself if she could afford to live in this part of town.

Finally, the door opened, barely. Kathy peeked out. "Oh," she said. "It's you." Then dejectedly, "Come in."

"I was worried about you when I couldn't reach you at your office," Irita said. Her voice echoed in the sun porch, sounding like the loud speaker at K-Mart. "Why aren't you answering your phone? Are you sick?'

Kathy sighed. "You better come in." Mesa wanted to explain her presence, but Irita beat her to it.

"You remember Mesa. I invited her to come along. We're working on a story," she said and looked back at Mesa with a conspiratorial glance.

Kathy wore jeans and a University of Montana sweatshirt with a stain on the front—a far cry from the soccer mom Mesa had met at the Labor Day picnic. She didn't appear to be sick, but the bags under her eyes made it clear she had not been sleeping well.

"What's happened? You don't look good," Irita said. "Are you home alone? Where's Garrett? Has he upset you?"

Kathy shook her head miserably. "He's long gone."

She led them through a cozy, well-kept living room to a narrow den off the kitchen. A fireplace and mantel filled one wall. A half dozen framed photographs sat along the mantel. Family photos, Mesa guessed.

Built-in barrister bookcases stood along the far wall jammed with books, tapes, DVDs, and an empty couple of shelves where the CDs, currently piled on the floor, must belong. Kathy waved half-heartedly at the sofa for them to sit.

Mesa gingerly stepped around the several stacks of CDs. Kathy resumed her place on the floor amongst the piles, taking a handful of CDs from a wall shelf and continuing to sort. "I'm reorganizing," she offered weakly.

Mesa wondered whether Kathy's desire for order grew out of more than a love for domesticity. Mesa knew firsthand that ordering one's surroundings gave comfort when life seemed too overwhelming.

Next to a half-filled cup of coffee, Mesa could see a stack of newspapers on the coffee table. The Tuesday edition lay on top. Mesa's curiosity was piqued when she saw the paper folded to the photo of Lowell Austin. The *Standard* had devoted the lower half of its front page to the plane crash, complete with Austin's last mug shot before leaving prison.

Considering that he had been locked up for two decades, he wasn't a bad-looking guy. With metal-framed spectacles and graying temples, he stared into the camera with a docile expression. Perhaps he knew even then that he would soon be leaving prison. He reminded her of Nana's cardiologist. Kathy matter-of-factly turned the paper over when her guests sat down.

"Bizarre story, isn't it?" Mesa said not about to let Kathy off the hook. She was partly trying to make conversation, but she was keen to discuss the investigation and Kathy's unlikely, but still possible, connection to it.

Kathy looked up but said nothing and began reordering a stack of CDs of female country music singers.

"Lot of irony in that story," Mesa continued. "Guy survives twenty plus years in prison and then dies the week he gets out."

Kathy had moved on to a group of jazz albums—Norah Jones, Diana Krall. "The article doesn't say much about what happened to him," Kathy said. "Do you know how he died? I mean, is your paper covering the story?"

Mesa nodded. "Not every day someone dies in a plane crash in uptown Butte." She said this in a jocular tone, hoping to lighten the moment. But Kathy DiNunzio didn't seem to notice. She put down the CDs and put her hand to her mouth, as if she were unsure what would come out.

Irita reached over and touched Kathy's shoulder. "Do you know something about this man's death?" she asked.

Kathy picked up the paper slowly as if it was a rare book, looked at the picture again, and said, "It says his death is still under investigation. Didn't he die in the crash? What would that mean, 'still under investigation'?"

Mesa looked at Irita, whose rolling eyes suggested that she was skeptical how to proceed. There was no need to upset Kathy. Aside from incurring Irita's wrath, Mesa rarely found that browbeating a source made for a good story. "Apparently, he wasn't killed by the impact of the crash," she said finally.

"How could that be?" Kathy asked, her voice quivering with concern.

"A copy of the autopsy came into the office this morning," Mesa said. "Somebody in the plane stabbed Lowell Austin. It looks like he was murdered." She paused to let this unnerving information sink in. "A witness also saw two men leaving the wreckage."

"Oh, my God," Kathy whispered and sunk back against an ottoman behind her, her hands over her eyes.

Irita couldn't take it anymore. "Kathy, I don't understand why you're so upset about this. What's wrong?"

"It's him," she said finally and tapped Austin's photo. "I knew him."

And then in a low, almost shameful voice, she said, "He came to Butte to see me."

Mesa was shocked. There they had it, straight up. Kathy DiNunzio *was* the Kate from Austin's letter. But the realization of the statement was too weird to be believed. Kathy might as well have said that aliens had kidnapped her.

Time seemed to stop. Irita's eyes widened as if she had just seen a rattlesnake. For a moment, Mesa thought Irita might faint. Finally, her survival instincts kicked in and she spoke.

"How did you know him?" Irita asked in a tone reserved for interrogating witnesses.

Kathy took a deep breath, picked up more CDs, and gently began sorting again. Then the words finally trickled out. "He killed my father."

Chapter 15

Chance crossed Park Street and then cut through the pre-release center parking lot toward the police station, thinking about Dougie Kincaid. People said his troubles had always revolved around money and that with his record he could never get a decent job even in Butte. Once you did your time, you were supposed to be able to start over with a clean slate, but it really didn't seem to work that way.

Now past 3 o'clock, maybe Rollie would be back from Preach's and willing to talk about what else they had found there. Not that the FBI could be expected to share much, even with the sheriff. Inside the police department building, Bernice Hanover sat at her desk behind the glass barrier that separated the public from the inner confines. She always talked to Chance in a slow, sweet way, as if he was still in fifth grade. She had been a close friend of his mother, and came to visit her in the last days, so he didn't mind. She explained that Sheriff Solheim was still with the federal agents at Daniel Swoboda's house.

Chance returned to the street, feeling stymied. Nothing appeared to link Austin to flying or anyone who owned a plane. But how he had ended up in one and why he had been killed there had to be more than coincidental.

Had Lowell Austin figured he would face the same prejudices Dougie Kincaid had? Had stealing the plane been part of some scam that would help build a nest egg to secure his future? Except the plan had gone down the toilet.

Preach had said Austin knew no one in Butte except for the woman. Had she lured Austin into that Cessna? If so, why?

According to Mrs. Penmarron and Kev, two men had abandoned the plane. Had they missed seeing the woman? Or was she an accomplice? And what was their motive for killing him? Had Austin become expendable, or disagreeable, or a liability to their scheme, maybe all three?

Chance decided to return to the *Messenger* to see what, if any, progress Erin had made identifying Lowell's lady friend. If he could find her and she was cooperative, maybe she could lead him to the pilot of the plane.

He supposed a woman could have been the pilot, though the only one he knew in Butte was an upstanding geology professor at the college. She had a German name like Hildegard or Brunhilda. He couldn't quite remember but he did recall she drove a red Suburban.

The professor had a reputation for being a little testy, but unless Edith Penmarron's ability to see at a distance was weaker than she had let on, he did not think a woman had gotten out of that plane.

Chance strolled downhill toward Mercury Street, resisting the urge to make a quick detour past Adrienne's gallery, to see her standing at the counter or talking to a customer. Get a grip, he said to himself with a smile and pressed on down the hill to the office instead.

The call from Layton James of McCall Investigations out of Lincoln, Nebraska, came through half an hour later. Chance was huddled with Erin and Micah in the newsroom, hypothesizing over a list of names of thirty or so women in Butte named Kate who might be worth checking out.

Mr. James explained that he was representing the interests of Consolidated Controls, Inc. in the matter of a stolen Cessna 180. Mr. James's voice was deep and smooth, and all business. "You called Consolidated's main office asking about the plane on Monday?"

Chance explained why he had called. James listened but offered no new information. "I've put in a call to your sheriff. I understand he's already talked with the Moab police."

"Any leads there?" Chance asked, only half expecting an answer.

"Maybe," James said, his voice sounding even more serious.

৽৵

Just listening to the facts surrounding the death of Donovan Birch left Mesa emotionally drained. Kathy described how her mother had lit a candle each night, clutching her children together to pray for the safe return of their father, or rather their father's body.

At first, Kathy thought maybe he would come back. No one talked about the eyewitness who had seen Lowell Austin outdraw Donovan Birch and then shoot him in the back of the head to be sure he was dead. After all, Kathy was only ten.

She told the story in a monotone, methodically sorting CDs and putting them back on the shelf. The details of her father's death reported in the newspaper had made readers stop in the street and gasp, she said without emotion. She pointed to a cardboard box that lay open on the floor next to a stack of greatest hits CDs. It was filled with Idaho *Statesman* clippings.

Mesa began to leaf through the collection of yellowing newspaper articles and was riveted. The story of Lowell Austin took on a completely different tone now compared to the way Cinch and Chance had told it. This was writing that gave readers goose bumps—and justified reporters' ghoulish reputations.

Meanwhile, Kathy talked about Austin as if she were a radio announcer relaying information about one of the CDs she held. "Just before he stood trial, he told one of the detectives where he had buried my father's body. His lawyer convinced Austin it would soften the public's attitude toward him. Not that he would need to worry, as it turned out."

Finally, they had a funeral. Hundreds of people came to show their respect. Many wept openly. Kathy learned these details later, when she read the newspaper articles her mother had saved. All Kathy knew as a ten year old was that her father was never coming home.

"It changed our lives forever," she said. Finally, tears pooled at the corners of her eyes. "The prosecutor wanted us sitting front and center at the trial to remind the jury of what Austin had done, leaving two fatherless children. But my mom wouldn't have it. She went instead, sitting there day after day while the defense lawyer made awful accusations about my dad. I don't think she ever got over losing him."

"So how did this bastard find you?" Irita finally asked. "What did he want?"

Kathy resumed her shuffling of CDs. "He didn't find me," she said. "I found him."

"What?" Irita said, her eyes wild with disbelief. "You contacted him? Have you lost your mind?"

Here, Kathy offered up a grim smile. "Revenge can take many forms." She looked at Irita and Mesa, exchanging glances with both of them as if they were part of her conspiracy. Then, in a voice that sounded more like a small child's, she said, "I wanted to break his heart like he broke mine."

This sounded like some bizarre reality show assignment. Could Kathy really be serious? Mesa and Irita exchanged glances as if the other might have some insight, but neither said a word. They both knew better than to interrupt.

"I was in paralegal school," Kathy continued, reaching for the cup of coffee on the table. "We took a course in the American penal system and prisoners' rights. At the time, Lowell Austin was the farthest notion from my mind. I learned about prisoners and their relationships with women on the outside. Prisoners get married, even lifers. You'd be amazed at all the prison pen-pal organizations that are on the Internet."

Mesa made a mental note to check out the websites. She thought *she* had an attraction to "bad boys." At least none of them was doing time, as far as she knew. Still, she wanted to know more about these women who fell in love with convicts. It might do her good.

"Then about three years ago, around Christmas time, I read D.C. Chandler's obituary." She held up a CD on top of the greatest hits stack. "He wrote 'The Ballad of Lowell Austin.' God, Garrett, and I hated that song. It came out right as the trial started. They even played it on the local radio station."

So Chance wasn't trying to be funny when he said someone had written a country song about Austin. Jesus, Mesa thought, there was no end to what people would do for fame and fortune. "Must have been awful."

Kathy shrugged. "TV movie too. The media liked to portray Austin as the last American outlaw—a folk hero defending a vanishing way of life. From where we sat, it was just plain heartless."

Mesa wanted to fade into the upholstery. She was all too familiar with what mainstream media had become and what lengths it would go to if it meant selling papers or gaining viewers. All the more reason she wanted to work for a counterculture publication like *Pacifica*.

"Anyway, Chandler died of lung cancer, and his obituary mentioned the song. That's when my mind starting spinning, wondering if Austin was as miserable as I wanted him to be in prison. And I started thinking about what I could do to get back at him. Nothing illegal but some kind of payback. I found out what prison Austin was in and eventually I wrote to him.

"I wasn't even sure what I wanted to accomplish—maybe just make him realize what it's like growing up without a father. Maybe give him a chance to show some remorse, which he had never done. Of course, I didn't let on who I was. When he wrote back, I couldn't believe it."

The mere thought of getting a letter from a murderer creeped Mesa out. But maybe knowing the guy was behind barbed wire-topped walls would seem safe. "Weren't you afraid of developing a relationship with a killer?" Mesa asked.

Kathy shook her head. "I was too caught up in 'the plan.' She used her fingers to signify the quotes symbol. Besides I expected his letters, if he could write at all, to be cold and arrogant, which would have made me more determined."

Here she stopped again and shuffled some more CD cases. "Except they were just the opposite. I began to realize writing to me meant a lot to him. That's when I started to think it would be easy to set him up."

Kathy had to be in another league when it came to revenge. Getting even was something Mesa had last thought about on the playground. But mature, healthy adults don't make plans to take revenge, or do they?

She tried to put herself in Kathy's shoes. If someone murders your father in cold blood, what *do* you do? Pretend it didn't happen, be a victim?

Mesa knew how hard it was for her at first after her mother's death, and *she* had died of cancer. Simple questions like "where do your parents live?" became difficult to answer. Part of her just did not want to be reminded of the loss, or have to say the words, "My mother's dead." She could not fathom the pain of knowing your parent had been murdered.

Bringing the killer to justice was supposed to satisfy the victims, but Mesa wondered if it really did. Judges and courts were impersonal. Nothing they could do would bring back the parent or ease the pain of a child's loss.

And when the child grows up, then what? You realize the inequity. Your father's dead and his killer is alive in prison and will get out some day. Maybe it's surprising that Kathy hadn't done more to even the score. Then again, maybe she had.

"But then something strange happened. The more he wrote to me"—she faltered here for a moment. "I know this might sound unthinkable, but—the more I could see he was a human being with feelings. You could tell how lonely he was. He had no one in prison he could genuinely call a friend. No friends or family. No visitors."

Kathy was fully engrossed in telling Austin's story. Mesa pulled out the reporter's notebook she still had tucked in her purse. Just a few notes, she thought.

"He liked art and made jewelry," Kathy continued. "He talked about wanting to live a decent life once he had served his time." She stopped to pick up another stack of CD's. "And somewhere along the way, through all those letters, I stopped hating him."

Clearly, Kathy no longer thought of Austin as the man who had ruined her childhood. Mesa wrote on her pad, "from revenge to redemption?"

"When he wanted to come see me, I did get scared but not of him. I was afraid of having to tell him who I was, peeling back my mask."

"I thought that was what you wanted to do," Irita said, sounding almost irritated.

"I finally decided I would have to tell him right away. But when I heard his voice on the telephone for the first time, even then I knew I wouldn't be able to do it."

Kathy stopped talking and reached for the coffee cup, but it was empty. She began to stand. "I'm going to make some more coffee. You two want any?"

"I'll do it," Irita said and jumped to her feet. "You sit down and don't say another word until I get back. I don't want to miss any of this."

Kathy turned so that her back was to the arm of the sofa. Then she closed her eyes, oblivious to Mesa's presence.

Mesa stood to stretch. She walked over to the mantel and looked at the photos. The largest picture, a family portrait taken some years ago, showed four of them posed on a picnic table. A mother with a husband's arm around her on the table, their feet on the bench, a girl in a sundress and pigtails leaning against her father's legs. A boy with a baseball cap and a grin that exposed two missing front teeth standing next to the mother. She thought of her own family's portrait in Nan's office at the paper, and her heart went out to Kathy, sharing the pain of a parent's death.

In front of the photo on the mantel lay a tarnished key chain with a metal coin insignia of the Idaho Forest Service. Mesa couldn't help thinking of her father, and the medals he had given her as keepsakes.

In matching chrome frames were school photos of the two children Mesa had met on Monday at the picnic. The last photo on the end of the mantel was a picture of Garrett Birch on one knee bookended by the children, one in each arm. They were all smiling. The photos seemed all the more poignant with the memory of the grandfather the children never got to know.

Mesa looked back at Kathy, whose eyes were still closed. Not wanting to disturb her, Mesa tiptoed out and joined Irita in the kitchen.

They whispered conspiratorially. "Talk about truth stranger than fiction," Irita said. "And to think, I had no idea. Poor kid."

"She's in for more heartache," Mesa said. "When the FBI finds out she's the mystery woman, and with a motive to kill Austin, they're going to be all over her like corn on the cob."

"Coyotes on a carcass," Irita corrected. "You're not in Ohio anymore, sweetheart, remember?"

"Whatever," Mesa said and leaned against the kitchen counter while Irita fiddled with the coffeemaker. "What's odd is that she's got me convinced she had nothing to do with Austin's death. She genuinely seems upset about it, like she's surprised somebody killed him."

The phone perched on his shoulder, Chance sat at Nana's desk and listened to what Layton James had to say.

"Brad Simian apparently fell from a mountain bike in Canyonlands sometime late this past Saturday." James sounded like he was reading from a police report.

"He's sustained a serious head injury, cracked ribs, and a broken ankle."

"He's damn lucky to be alive," Chance said. "Canyonlands is rough country." He had ridden there himself on more than one occasion, but he had always been with Hardy, who knew the area like the back of his hand. "Where exactly did it happen?"

Chance could hear the rustling of pages in a notebook. He imagined it was one of those burgundy leather jobs with a loop for a gold Cross ballpoint. "Near a place called Hardscrabble Hill."

That made it White Rim Trail, a hundred miles of the most isolated, red rock country in the Southwest. The locals thought the trail had become an overrated tourist spot, but that didn't mean the ride was a cakewalk. Anybody, from beginner to slick-rock junkie, could get hurt on a mountain bike in Canyonlands, anywhere, anytime.

"Three of his colleagues arrived at the park the day before and began a four-day trip they had planned," James continued, his tone methodical but vexed. "Unexpected business delayed Mr. Simian. To make up for lost time, he flew down in the company plane on Friday. He was trying to catch up to the rest of his party the next day when he was injured."

So this guy was well-heeled thought Chance. President of his own company, flies his own plane, can take off with the boys in the office to go mountain biking. Nice life, except for going endo on the trail.

"I checked with the airport here in Moab. They say that Simian asked them to refuel the plane so it would be ready when he wanted to fly out, but he gave no indication when that would be."

Chance couldn't help but chuckle. The Moab Airport was even smaller than Butte's, nothing but a single asphalt strip and a windsock next to the highway in the middle of red sand desert north of town. Chance had seen longer driveways. Most of its traffic came from general aviation aircraft that flew in for the big mountain bike and jeep off-road races in the spring.

"The Moab sheriff had some suspicions about drug smugglers maybe taking the plane down to Mexico. So we called the FAA, and that's when they alerted us to the situation in your area."

"The FBI is handling the investigation now," Chance said. "I'm sure they will want to talk to your Mr. Simian."

"That could be tough. He's been in a coma since Search and Rescue brought him in Sunday morning."

Chapter 16

"So who took Austin up in the plane?" Irita asked Kathy when they sat down again with fresh coffee.

Kathy had stopped sorting her CD collection and simply sat in the middle of the disarray. "I have no idea."

"Well, when was the last time you saw Austin?" Mesa asked, aware that soon the FBI would be asking all the same questions.

"Saturday night," she said and turned again to the clutter around her, and began to alphabetize CD's by artist as best Mesa could tell.

"He came to dinner. I made lasagna and we talked right here. He sat where you're sitting now," she said and pointed to the couch.

Mesa fought the urge to get up. She felt suddenly uncomfortable with the lingering proximity of someone who had recently died, and so violently. "What did you talk about?" she asked and tried not to sound morbid.

"Butte. Lloyd said he had already met some nice people. He had applied for a job with Brownstone Printing over on Harrison." Then she paused and said, "It wasn't like we had planned some romantic tryst. We were just two adults trying to be kind to one another, for God's sake. What's so hard to understand about that?"

Mesa said nothing, and Kathy lowered her voice. "He left around 9:30 when it was time for me to put the kids to bed."

Mesa tried to imagine what must have been going through Kathy's mind. How could she talk to Austin and not think about her father? "So did you tell him?" Mesa asked.

"Tell him what?" Kathy said, holding a Ray Charles Christmas Collection in her hand.

"Who you were," Mesa said. "Did you have your confrontation?"

Kathy hugged the CD to her and shook her head. "There was a time when I dreamt about the heartbreak I'd make him feel when I told him who I was. But when the time came, that wasn't the way it was. I spent a total of about five hours with Lowell Austin, and in that time, I found some neutral zone. It was a relief to be honest."

Mesa wasn't sure what to think. How could Kathy have betrayed the memory of her father that way? Maybe this was all smoke and mirrors. "You're sure you don't have any ideas about how Austin ended up in that plane on Sunday?"

Kathy was busy again, putting CDs back into the wall case. She shook her head.

Irita took over. "Kathy, someone saw your car at the airport on Monday."

Kathy stopped her shelving and then slowly turned around. "That's not possible. I took the kids up to Georgetown Lake on Sunday. We stayed the night at my friend Connie's parents' cabin."

"You drove up to the lake?" Mesa asked.

"Well, no. We went with Connie's parents in their RV. The kids have been bugging me to ride in it. They drove us to the Labor Day Picnic on Monday, and then took us home."

"What about Garrett?" Irita asked.

"I invited him to come with us, but he wanted to see Tessa. I guess he stayed there overnight. He came with her to the picnic on Monday. I haven't seen him since."

Mesa remembered the blonde at the swings with Garrett. Tessa Revelle. That was her name. She had graduated from Butte High a year before Mesa. "You mean you haven't talked to him now that Austin's dead?"

Kathy put the final handful of CDs back into the bookcase and then looked back around. "Garrett showed up at my house on Saturday evening— barely said two words, dumped his duffle bag, then left again. I haven't seen or heard from him since Monday after the picnic. I don't know that he's in the mood to talk about much of anything."

Mesa was surprised how unsympathetic she seemed toward her brother. He didn't look like he was in such good shape, especially if he was AWOL. "Did he know that you had been writing to Austin?" Mesa asked.

"He called me as soon as he arrived stateside a couple of weeks ago, and I told him that Austin was getting out. That's all. He was shocked I even knew." She gestured with her hands opened in front of her as if to say, "go figure."

"Maybe it's hard for someone else, who hasn't been through what we have, to understand. But the whole time we were growing up, my mother wanted us to remember the good things about my dad's life. That's how you survive—selective memory. Once we moved back to Montana, Garrett and I never once talked about what happened to our father."

Mesa just couldn't understand. She and Chance had become closer after their mother died of cancer. Of course, they were teenagers and old enough to give voice to their emotions. Kathy and Garrett were still in grade school, and their father had died a violent death. Maybe, their trauma was so deep that they'd buried their emotions.

Even now, Kathy seemed oblivious to how others might view what she'd done—enticing Austin to Butte and then he turns up dead. "Kathy, you do realize the authorities are looking for a car just like yours?" Mesa asked. "Might be a good idea to call them before they come looking for you."

"I haven't done anything wrong," Kathy said and then walked to the end of the bookshelves. "At least not by any manmade laws," she muttered. She looked at a shelf of kid's books, picked up a handful, and began sorting them by size. Then she stopped. "I hate the pain of having it all in the papers again. My kids don't know anything about any of this. They're more innocent even than I was."

৶৵

Chance sat at the computer in his grandmother's office. He had helped Irita move it there when she, for all intents and purposes, had begun to manage the paper while Nana was in the hospital. He knew now that it had been a mistake to keep this from Mesa.

Who knew Irita would step up quite like she did? And by the time he began to see she was seriously capable, he had already set in motion the plan to get Mesa to come back to Butte. Maybe, this may have been a slight miscalculation. The truth was he didn't want to face any big changes, especially Nana's decline, without Mesa.

He looked at the clock again. Layton James would be on the 6:30 p.m. flight from Salt Lake, and Chance had offered to pick him up. James knew enough about FBI investigators to welcome any local sources who might offset the FBI's stonewalling and had readily accepted the offer. They both knew the arrangement would be mutually beneficial.

Chance was flipping through the latest edition of the *Messenger* when Mesa walked in. She looked worn. Usually she had this crisp walk, head up, eyes sharp, but not now.

She stopped in the doorway. "I didn't expect to see you. It's way past quitting time."

He took his feet off the desk and stood up.

"Don't get up," Mesa said. "I don't need the computer." She collapsed onto the sofa. "What are you doing here?"

"Just killing time," he said, trying to sound casual. He had decided Adrienne was right. Mesa was going to think whatever she was going to think about his new relationship. He would have to rely on her to get to know Adrienne. Hopefully, that would make the difference. "I'm picking up an insurance investigator on the 6:30 flight from Salt Lake. More info on the plane crash."

Mesa sat up on the edge of the sofa. "Like what?"

"The guy the plane belonged to. Well, he writes it off as a company plane. Anyway, he went biking in Canyonlands over the weekend. But then he flipped his bike and smacked his head bad. In the process of dealing with that accident, his company discovered that the plane had disappeared from the Moab airport."

"There goes the theory about the pilot absconding with the company's payroll," Mesa said. "Simian goes from suspect to victim. Well, don't despair. Here's another tidbit for you," she said. "I found your Kate."

Her tone seemed conciliatory. Chance sat up immediately. "Who is it?"

"Would you believe Kathy DiNunzio? She used to be called Kate when she was a kid."

"Who?" Chance asked. He didn't know any Kate or Kathy with that last name.

"It's Irita's ex-daughter-in-law, and that's not even the big shocker. Ready for it? Her father was one of the two wardens Lowell Austin killed."

"Shut up," Chance said in a whisper. "She lured Austin to Butte?"

Mesa nodded. "But I don't think she had anything to do with killing him. As a matter of fact, I think she feels guilty that he's dead."

Chance listened intently while Mesa explained Kathy DiNunzio's revenge of the heart. "And you think I have strange ideas about relationships," he said with half a grin.

Mesa smiled back. "I just spent the last four hours over there. I think she's sorry she ever encouraged him to come to Butte."

Chance was skeptical. "Maybe she's giving you a big snow job, too."

Mesa shook her head, and explained Kathy's whereabouts on Sunday morning. She was nowhere near the plane crash or the airport, and she has witnesses to prove it.

"And she has no idea who might have wanted to kill Austin?"

"I think she's still in a state of shock about the whole thing. She can't even remember Austin mentioning knowing anybody else in Butte."

"Wait a minute. Weren't there two kids?" Chance asked.

"You are on it. There is a brother. He just came back from a tour in Afghanistan, Army National Guard. Apparently, he has his own troubles. He's AWOL."

"Don't suppose he flies?" Chance asked, suspecting the answer.

Mesa again shook her head. "Drives truck."

They stared across the room at each other. Chance thought about when their mother had died. They were both in high school, but they had still relied heavily on one another. He and Mesa were closer than most brothers and sisters he knew. That was partly why what she had said earlier in the day had bothered him so much—and, he realized at that moment, probably why she was upset that he hadn't told her about Adrienne, at least partly.

Their mother had died at home surrounded by her family, which was hard enough. He couldn't imagine the kind of grief he might have felt if she had been the victim of a horrible crime. "How old were they when all this happened?"

"She was ten. He was eight."

"Wow, that's dark," Chance said. Having to live with the murder of a parent was inconceivable to him. How would your world ever seem right again? "You get her to call the cops?"

"I left Irita with her. She was getting ready to call Solheim when I left."

Chance looked at his watch. "Guess I better head for the airport. Want to come along?"

Mesa sighed and shook her head. "I promised to have dinner with Nan."

"Oh whoops, she invited me over too," he said. "Will you tell her I had to meet this guy?"

Mesa nodded but said nothing.

"I'll get with Erin in the morning about the story," Chance said. "Sounds like we might have a decent feature for the next edition." He took a step toward the door.

Mesa nodded again. "Listen, Chance, about Adrienne."

Chance cleared his throat. He hated these kinds of conversations, especially with Mesa. She could never bring herself to say she was sorry. But he also knew she was always much harder on herself than he could ever be.

"It's not any of my business," she said. "If you butted into my life like that, you know I would give you three kinds of hell." She sounded embarrassed at this last part.

This was the best apology he was going to get, but he still wasn't ready to talk about it. And there were some things he definitely wanted to say, but not now. "I know. See you tomorrow," he said and walked out of the office.

Mesa sat at the oak table in the kitchen picking over what was left of what Nana called "late tea," meaning more than biscuits—otherwise known as cookies—but less than a bona fide supper. This evening it meant scrambled eggs and English muffins.

Mesa had hurried home after Chance left, to find Nana up and about setting the table. That is, until Mesa insisted on taking over.

Now that they were finished eating, Mesa found herself with plenty on her mind—her impending flight to Portland on Friday, but more immediately her argument with Chance. "Have enough to eat?" Mesa asked absent-mindedly.

"More than enough," Nana said and then explained how she had eaten a lovely lunch with Beryl Winstead, a woman in her English Club. They'd eaten Toad in the Hole, though Nana quickly pointed out that the sausages were quite lean and small and the Yorkshire pudding had been made with skim milk, therefore putting this English comfort food quite within her cardiologist's dietary guidelines.

"Nana, you have to take care of yourself now. And that includes watching what you eat." Mesa sounded too much like her own mother, and found the role reversal unsettling.

"Taking care of one's heart also includes lifting one's spirits," her grandmother said in defense of her culinary choices. "It looks as though you might need a bit of that. Have a bad day?"

Mesa rolled her eyes and toyed with her eggs. "Chance and I had words."

"Oh dear," her grandmother said, her voice registering the rarity of such an event. "Whatever about, if I may ask?"

"Adrienne DeBrook."

"Ah, the painter. Lovely, isn't she? What was the scrap about?"

Nana's tone sounded curious, as if she couldn't imagine what the problem could be. This made Mesa even more self-conscious. "I made a remark about their age difference."

Nana took a judiciously timed sip of tea and waited for Mesa to say more.

"Am I the only one who is uncomfortable with Chance being gaga over a woman more than fifteen years older than him?"

"Closer to twenty, I should think," Nana said. She's planning to go to the 25th reunion of her medical school class."

"She's a doctor too?" Mesa said. What a career switch. Mesa found this intriguing, even downright admirable. She sighed. "Okay, I never said she wasn't bright and attractive in her own way."

"And if she and Chance weren't seeing each other, you might even be her friend?" Nana said.

Her voice now had that knowing quality that both irritated and touched Mesa. "Maybe."

"Mesa, how many times have you heard me say you can't help who you love? If I had listened to reason or convention, you wouldn't be here now. I certainly wouldn't have left Cambridge to marry your grandfather, leaving everything and everybody I knew to move to Montana."

"I know," Mesa said. There was no argument here. Her grandmother's courage inspired Mesa every day. Imagine leaving London behind to move to a cattle ranch so you could be with the man you love.

Mesa wasn't sure she had that kind of courage. Maybe that was what bugged her about Adrienne. Apparently, she wasn't worried about what people thought. Maybe it was jealousy of both of them, Adrienne *and* Chance.

"I wonder what happened to Chance this evening," Nana said. "I invited him to come over as well. I enjoy seeing the two of you together."

"I meant to tell you," Mesa said, absently wondering what other pieces to the Lowell Austin puzzle he might be finding. "He had to meet an investigator about the plane crash."

Nana let out a small groan. "I hope we aren't going to dwell on this in the *Messenger* for any longer than necessary."

"It's turning into quite a story," Mesa said and gave her the details of Kathy DiNunzio's account. She made a mental note to call Irita and find out what else she might have learned.

Halfway through the tale, Nana gleefully refilled their teacups. Clearly, the story interested her after all. "I can see the woman's thinking," Nana said. "Make him live with the pain. It's a page out of Dickens, isn't it? *Great Expectations*, remember? Miss Haversham gets left at the altar, no humiliation more public than that. So she spends a lifetime exacting her revenge."

Public humiliation. That was certainly what Kathy's family had endured. Scanning the news articles in the box Kathy had kept, Mesa saw how the defense had tried to cast Donovan Birch as the bad guy, saying he was an aggressive game warden who rubbed hunters the wrong way.

She thought about her own father. Like a lot of military officers, he could be a hard man at times, but he was always fair. But she could see how some of his decisions, when taken out of context, might seem arbitrary.

Whatever the case, she would never have been able to sit still while people criticized him. But how far would she have gone to stop it, or to get even with those who had maligned him? "Aren't we supposed to turn the other cheek?"

"That, my child, is New Testament. Stories of revenge abound in the Old Testament. Righteous indignation fueled God's destruction of Sodom and Gomorrah."

"Maybe so, but in this day and age, most people are content with fantasizing about revenge. They don't go around actually living out their fantasies. That's why reality TV shows are so popular."

"So you don't think this DiNunzio woman had anything to do with getting even with the man who killed her father?" Nana asked in a tone that begged the question.

Mesa had begun clearing the table and stopped in her tracks. Had she misread Kathy's tears? Could there have been a much larger scheme at play, in which she was just acting her part? Mesa put the dinner dishes in the sink and went to call Irita.

Chapter 17

When the passengers from the Salt Lake flight deplaned, Layton James was head and shoulders above others around him. Chance wondered if the investigator had needed two seats on that pint-sized commuter.

It was nearly 7:30 in the evening. The plane had been almost an hour late. Backed up in Salt Lake with the evening commuter traffic, Chance figured. They shook hands. "Bet you're hungry."

"Dang right," James said. "And thirsty too, if you know what I mean."

"A couple of hours in Mormon country will do that to you," Chance joked. "I made a reservation for you at the Copper Baron Hotel just across from the airport, like you asked. There's a restaurant and a bar."

"I want the biggest steak in town," James said and patted his ample midriff, already tightly encased in a dress shirt and tie.

"You got 'er," Chance said. He liked a man with a healthy appetite. "Let's go over to the Lamplighter. It's just five minutes from here and I think you'll like the menu."

Half an hour later, Layton James had settled for a king-sized, 32-ounce slab of prime rib, enough for a family of four, washed down by his first Moose Drool. Chance felt like a wimp eating a measly eight-ounce strip steak. After an initial satisfaction of his hunger with two gargantuan bites of beef, James said with a grin, "Must be the altitude."

Somehow, Chance had the feeling that Layton James ate this way all the time. But the food didn't stop him from talking.

"The guy who runs Moab Aviation, man named Jeppsen, said he gave Simian a Jeep to get into town the night he arrived. Said the keys were hung back on the hook in the office where they belonged the next morning. Made him wonder if whoever brought the car back was local and knew where the keys went."

Chance had met Jeppsen on a trip with Hardy several summers before—a retired geologist who made his living flying aerial tours of Canyonlands and Arches, catering to rich rock hounds.

"He was off in the back of beyond scouting geologic formations early in the morning," James said between bites. "Said the plane was gone before he got back."

So someone who knew Jeppsen's habits could have easily timed their departure to coincide with when the airport was virtually empty. But they would have had to know there was a plane for the taking. That could mean Simian might have shot off his mouth about his plane to someone. "Did Simian hook up with anybody local the night before? Unless the theft was totally random, some townie had to have known he had flown in."

"The sheriff was asking around. But until Simian regains consciousness, who knows? His credit card shows he stayed at a fancy bed and breakfast at the north end of town, but they didn't see him come in with anybody and they didn't see him leave the next day. "

That wasn't surprising. Simian would have left early. Anybody doing serious biking in Moab, even in September, would want to do it before the sun rose too high overhead. The situation had worked right into the thief's hands.

Again, the circumstances pointed to someone local who knew how to make sure no one would see Simian picked up or dropped off. And who knew when the airport might likely be empty. Once Simian had cycled away, the airplane was easy pickings. But the question remained, who did the picking?

Anxious to make an early start with Sheriff Solheim the next morning, Layton James left Chance at the front desk of the Copper Baron. It was already 9 o'clock, so Chance stuck his head into Shoestring Annie's, curious to see if the FBI had stopped in for their nightcap.

It was Comedy Night, and the bar was crowded with the college crowd there for the guffaws. Chance sidled between the tables looking for Perryman and his partner, but no luck. Instead, he saw Hardy

Jacobs standing at one of the bars along the wall, in deep conversation with a sturdy looking guy who looked like he could use a good laugh.

Chance fought his way to the bar for a Moose Drool. By the time he reached Hardy, his friend was moving to the far end of the room. Hardy seemed surprised to see Chance. "What brings you down to the Flat to do your drinking?" he asked.

It was true that Chance rarely ventured this far from uptown unless he was going flying. "Business," he said and rolled his eyes. "Who was your buddy? Hope I didn't scare him off."

"Just some guy I know from working in Big Sky. He lives in Bozeman."

Chance had never reconciled Hardy's decision to winter at the upscale ski resort in the Gallatin Mountains south of Bozeman. Well-to-do out-of-staters, mostly Californians, liked to throw big parties and not invite the locals. Hardy was part of the service class who eked out a living on the mountain while crammed into mobile homes at the bottom. Meanwhile, their clientele lived large in fancy chalets. It just wasn't Hardy's style, being at anybody's beck and call just because they had money.

"So what kind of business?" Hardy asked.

"Just dropped off a guy I been interviewing about the plane crash on Sunday. A couple of FBI agents are staying here too. Wouldn't mind getting a word in with them if I can."

"You still working for the *Messenger*?" Hardy asked. "What happened to remodeling historic buildings full-time?"

"Restoration," Chance corrected him. "That's still the main plan, but I had to help out with the paper until Mesa came back to town. I don't do much writing usually, but this plane crash story has me curious. I'd like to meet the guy who landed that plane. And so would the FBI. Haven't seen any clean-cut, out-of-town suits come in tonight, have you?"

"Not yet," Hardy said. "How do they figure in it?"

Chance took a long swig from his beer and began to explain. Maybe Hardy would have some idea about the Moab connection. "You read about the plane crash?"

"My dad said something about it," Hardy said. His words came slowly, his lips barely opened wide enough to let the words escape. "Gutsy."

Chance smiled. Hardy was never a big talker, but the words he used fit. "You can say that again. Anybody else would have ended that landing with a nose plant."

"I thought the pilot died in the crash," Hardy said.

"Nah," Chance said. "That guy was already dead when the plane hit the ground."

"Gives new meaning to a dead stick landing, that's for sure." Hardy said, his voice half-joking and half-amazed. "What do you think happened?"

Chance shrugged. "Can't tell. All they know for sure is that the dead guy didn't exactly have a lot of friends."

"Somebody local?" Hardy asked.

Chance shook his head again. "An ex-convict just released from prison a couple a days ago," Chance said and noticed Kev Murphy in a crowd at the far end of the long bar, laughing and swilling a beer with a group of guys.

"Whose plane?" Hardy asked.

"Belonged to some business exec from Nebraska, but the plane came from Moab."

"No shit?" Hardy said. He seemed curious now.

Chance nodded. "Looks like somebody just waltzed into Doc Jeppsen's place, picked the keys off the board, and flew away."

"Doc was probably rock hounding. What did the plane's owner have to say?"

"Busted his head riding down White Rim Trail. When the rescue squad picked him up, he didn't have any ID. Nobody knew who he was. Good thing his buddies biked out a day early and came looking for him. That's when the police came looking for the plane and found it missing."

Hardy shook his head and smiled. "Riding alone, no ID. No corner on stupidity. Hurt bad?"

"Well, he's not feeling any pain right now. He's in a coma."

"You're kidding," Hardy said. "You figure he's connected to the dead guy?"

Chance smiled. "Now, Hardy, you're starting to scare me, thinking like a cop."

"Just curious, is all," Hardy chuckled.

"I sure as hell can't figure a connection. The dead guy apparently came to Butte to see a woman here. Far as anyone knows, he came straight from the state prison in Idaho and had never been anywhere near Moab."

"You mean he had a girlfriend in Butte?" Hardy said in disbelief.

"Guess it depends on who you ask," Chance said, thinking about the letter Lowell had kept with him.

"Turns out the woman is the daughter of a man the ex-convict killed."

"Straight up?" Hardy said and whistled faintly. "Man, this sounds like a soap opera." The announcer had reached the mike on stage and was getting ready to introduce the next comedian. "I'm gonna get another beer. Want one?"

Chance made one more sweep of the bar and, seeing neither Perryman nor his partner, shook his head. "I got a date with a lady," he said and made his way to the exit and the parking lot.

ৎ৵৵

"What do you think changed Mesa's mind?" Adrienne asked. She had fashioned a bedroom space in the loft apartment by angling two bamboo screens together in one corner. She and Chance cuddled under a duvet on the futon. No wham-bam, thank-you ma'am for him.

"I'm not sure she has changed her mind," Chance said, resting his chin atop Adrienne's head and stroking her arm. "She's just sorry she said anything."

"My sister came around expediently when I told her you looked mature," Adrienne said with a smile.

When Chance didn't laugh, she continued, "Of course, it is true that when you were starting first grade, I was already in med school."

Chance grinned at the thought of Adrienne, the eager, fresh-faced med student. If he had seen her when he was six, he might just have fallen for her then, too. "Yeah, well, that was twenty-five years ago and now I'm bigger, if not smarter." He turned her face toward him and they kissed again.

"And what else?" Adrienne asked.

Chance liked that she could tell he was preoccupied, not pressing him to make love again like she might otherwise.

He reached for the pint container of huckleberry ice cream next to the bed, half-eaten before they had succumbed to temptations more carnal. "I think part of what's bothering Mesa is that she's uneasy, feeling her way around at the paper. This afternoon she got more involved with the crash story. Maybe that lifted her spirits."

"Involved how?" Adrienne asked and took the teaspoon full of ice cream from him.

"She tracked down the woman Lowell Austin wrote to."

"Good for Mesa," Adrienne said, her tone genuinely enthusiastic. "Anybody you know?"

Chance took the spoon back and shook his head. "But that doesn't stop the story from getting weirder." He described Kathy DiNunzio's revenge plot gone wrong. "I'm still blown away that some soccer mom would go that far."

Adrienne mused for a moment, and then said, "If you lost a parent when you were a child, you might fixate on getting even. You might not ever reach the place where you recognize that serious revenge usually means risking a great deal—which is more or less the conclusion the rest of us reach."

Chance smiled at her, holding her in his gaze.

"What?" she said, beginning to blush.

"You're so clever and smart," he said and fed her a spoonful of ice cream. Chance almost lost his train of thought watching Adrienne slowly lick ice cream from her lips.

"Do you think she had anything to do with Austin's death?" she asked.

"Mesa seems to think the woman is genuinely sorry for what happened to Austin. Supposedly, she and her kids were at Georgetown Lake when the crash took place. So unless she's a pathological liar, I'd say she's off the hook."

"So you're without a suspect again," Adrienne said.

"Maybe not. I talked to this insurance investigator about the plane," Chance said, carefully apportioning the last of the ice cream between them. "It was stolen from an airport in Moab. Belonged to some mountain-biking enthusiast with more money than brains."

"Why do you say that?" she asked, her smile bathing him in warmth. She always had another question.

"He went down into Canyonlands solo and then crashed his bike. Took a day and a half to figure out who he was."

"Somebody could have borrowed his plane while he was gone."

Chance smiled and gave her his last bite of ice cream. "He's one hell of a generous guy if he lent somebody his $100,000 plane."

"So, maybe they didn't ask."

"Well, maybe when he comes out of his coma, he can tell us all about it."

"If he's in a coma, he may not remember anything one way or the other when he does wake up."

"Think so?" Chance said and put the ice cream carton back on the floor. He didn't buy the notion that Simian had lent his plane to anyone. As far as Layton James knew, Simian had hardly talked to anybody in Moab, let alone knew anyone there well enough to hand over the keys to his Cessna.

Out of ice cream, they made love again—grizzly bear love, Chance called it, on account of the huckleberries. They teased each other about who tasted sweeter and fell asleep in each other's arms.

Chance was awakened by the sound of his own voice yelling, "Unlatch the doors, quick, before we hit the ground!"

Then, strangely, he heard Adrienne. "Chance, Chance, it's okay."

Chance turned toward the voice and then realized he was sitting up, with Adrienne next to him stroking his chest, talking softly.

"What was that all about?" she asked.

Chance realized he had been dreaming about crashing his plane. He took a deep breath, hoping to slow his pounding heart. He shook his head and chuckled to himself. "Investigating this crash is taking its toll."

"You were talking about doors," she said with a puzzled look on her face.

"The cabin doors. Fitz used to say if you think you're coming down hard, at the last minute unlatch the doors so they don't jam on impact." He looked at her and shook his head. "Like you could remember to do anything at that point besides pray."

They lay back down and snuggled under the covers. Soon he felt the steady breathing that signaled she had fallen back asleep. He lay there in the dark, wishing he could do the same.

Instead, he kept going over what Layton James had told him about Moab. While Simian couldn't be completely ruled out, he hadn't been the pilot of the plane that flew to Butte. The question remained whether he could be connected to Austin's death and whoever else had been in the plane.

Chance would let the FBI use all their resources to cross-reference Simian's and Austin's lives. Maybe something would come of it, but Chance could do nothing about that one way or the other.

His thoughts drifted to Hardy. He was accustomed to making the rounds of Butte bars when he came home, but what was he doing at Shoestring Annie's on Comedy Night, which he always claimed to hate? The comedians were too lame. And what was he doing driving one of his father's trucks? Chance had seen the Yukon Glass pickup in the parking lot. Like most Montanan guys, Hardy drove a classy pickup and was usually damn proud of it.

He wondered too, if that was who Mesa had hooked up with last night at Mercury Street. Not that he was going to act like it was any of his business. Not after Mesa's apology.

Maybe tomorrow he would talk to Kathy DiNunzio himself. And he would ask Rollie Solheim for another look at the evidence photos of the plane's interior. Something in the photographs of the cockpit of that plane bothered him.

Chapter 18

When Mesa agreed to meet Hardy at Chance's place, she told herself that this would be the last time. She knew Tara was right. While Hardy was always enthusiastic, sex for him was just another form of exercise. "Friends with benefits" was all their relationship would ever be.

At least she was able to get out of Nan's house without the previous night's anxiety. She had found a fleece jacket to wear, and the moon was full. The walk was actually relaxing. She didn't worry about seeing Chance and wasn't surprised to find his apartment dark at eleven o'clock on a Wednesday night.

Hardy arrived a few minutes later. Bearing a six-pack of Bud and a look on his face she had not seen since the night he realized his prospects as a pro baseball player had evaporated, she suddenly wondered if he actually had something besides sex on his mind.

"What's up?" she asked when they had cozied up to one other in front of the fireplace in Chance's living room, curious now that he had made no move to go upstairs to the bedroom.

Hardy stared into the flames for way too long. Finally he said, "You know that feeling when you make a huge mistake and, like, realize there's no frigging way to make up for it?" His voice was low and measured, as if this were some philosophical discussion.

Mesa sat quietly, deciding to assume that this was a rhetorical question.

"Sometimes you make a decision on the spur of the moment," he said between sips of beer, "out of frustration even, but you never mean for it to get out of hand."

Mesa looked at Hardy from the corner of her eye. She couldn't believe what she was hearing. Was he talking about them, their on-again/off-again relationship? More likely, some other failed opportunities in his life, like the snafu in Moab maybe. She realized she wasn't sure, and she really wanted to know.

The light from the fire danced across his cheek, and he looked lost. She felt an overwhelming affection for him. Then he turned and looked at Mesa. "Shouldn't intention count for something?"

Could it be that Hardy actually regretted the way their relationship had gone? Now after all this time, now that she was really ready to move on, did Hardy have something else in mind? "Hardy, what are we talking about?" she said.

He took a long pull off his beer and sighed. "My life's a mess, Mesa, and you know, you're the one person I can think of to tell who might understand."

Mesa pulled her feet under her and put her hand on Hardy's. She still had no idea what he was trying to tell her, but it was obvious he was worried, and she couldn't take the suspense any longer. "Hardy, are you in trouble? Did something happen in Moab?"

Hardy sighed again, the air leaving him in a long, low hiss, like a tire going flat. "I got mad and said some things to my boss I can't take back. Then I did a favor for somebody that didn't work out, and it's coming back on me. Truth is, I can't go back now even if I wanted."

Mesa didn't know what to say. She had known Hardy since they were teenagers, and in that time she had never seen him back down from any situation, no matter how difficult. He was a Butte boy through and through.

He held her hand tight. "If I can just get past the next couple of weeks, I can get back on my feet. Start over. I know I can." He brought her hand to his lips and kissed it. "Then, I'm going to make some changes."

Mesa didn't know what to think. She wasn't sure what, if anything, all this had to do with her. What she knew for sure was that Hardy was actually upset about something, and she wanted to help. "Hardy, whatever happens, you'll get through it. I'll help you." He put his arms around her and hugged her with all his might.

ഗര

Hardy dropped Mesa off at 7:30 the next morning. This time she had decided not to forgo her beauty sleep. Sneaking home at five in the morning to avoid Nana's questions was no longer part of the program. In the end, Mesa had nothing to worry about.

A cheerful "Good morning, dear" accompanied by hot tea and toast was all that met Mesa when she opened the back door into the kitchen. Nana busied herself flipping through the newspaper, trying almost too hard not to seem the least bit inquisitive. Mesa said good morning, grabbed a triangle of toast, and excused herself. "Have to get ready for work," she said and bounded up the stairs with a smile on her face.

She drove Nan's Trail Blazer and arrived at the office at 8:30, surprised to find the newsroom bustling and Chance pacing back and forth in her office.

"I want to go see Kathy DiNunzio. Since she's met you, it might go down easier if you go with me," he said even before she sat down.

"Good morning to you, too," Mesa said. "A little early to be feeling obsessive, isn't it?"

"I went to the sheriff's office this morning to talk to Rollie," Chance said, his hands on his hips. "While I was in the lobby, I looked at the daily police reports. Kev Murphy got beat to a pulp at the Copper Baron last night."

Kevin Murphy's bouts with the bottle were legendary, but Mesa could see Chance wasn't taking it lightly. "This isn't the first time Murphy's—"

"The police report says Kevin was found lying in the middle of Harrison Avenue, attacked by 'assailant unknown.' It's a pure miracle someone didn't run over him. No one in the bar saw anything, and Kev didn't want to file any kind of complaint."

Mesa could tell she had to be careful how she asked the next question. "Chance, you know how annoying Murphy can get when he's had one too many. Guys were probably lined up to give him a smack down."

"Yeah, I know. But I can't help but wonder if this had something to do with that plane crash. Kev saw whoever boarded that plane. Maybe they decided to help him forget."

"Why don't you talk to him?" Mesa said quietly, trying to get Chance to calm down. "Maybe he'll tell you something he wouldn't tell the police." Which was true. Chance usually had that effect on people. He had a way of convincing people to do things others couldn't.

"I'm trying to track him down now. Apparently, they admitted him to the hospital last night, but when I call over there, he's not in his room. He may have taken off. If he calls into work, which he always does, Tyler's going to tell him to call me."

Irita stuck her head in the door. "Am I interrupting? That's a stupid question. Of course I am." She walked in the office, closed the door, and leaned against its handle so that no one else could do the same. "I'm sorry, but . . ." She stopped for a minute and wrung her hands. "Look, I just talked to Kathy and she still hasn't called the sheriff. I don't want to get anybody's ass in a sling, particularly hers. But I especially don't like the idea of the sheriff's office getting the idea that the *Messenger* knows something they don't."

Mesa was surprised to hear this. Kathy had no difficulty telling her story to them. "Why wouldn't she call the police?"

Irita sighed, "She just said she had to think about it. If you ask me, she's worried about Garrett. He still doesn't know anything about her connection to Austin, and I think she's afraid the police are going to want to question him too. What with the AWOL thing, she's afraid he might run from the cops. I thought maybe Chance"—she gave him a pleading glance—"you could talk to her."

Chance looked at Mesa and said, "Just what I had in mind."

৩৶

"I have to be in district court at ten-thirty," Kathy DiNunzio said when she met Mesa and Chance at her front door ten minutes later. She wasn't impolite, but she was in a hurry. While she spoke, she was slipping on the jacket of her day-in-court navy suit.

"This is *my* brother," Mesa said, hoping that attention to the relationship might segue into a conversation about Garrett. "We won't take much time, I promise. Just a few more questions."

Kathy opened the door with a sigh. "Okay," she said, "but you'll have to come in the kitchen while I finish cleaning up."

They followed her through the hallway and stood next to an island counter in the square kitchen while Kathy rinsed breakfast dishes, put cereal boxes away, milk in the fridge. Like most single moms, she found it necessary to do at least two tasks at once, none of which were probably primary in her mind, Mesa suspected.

"I know I need to talk to the police, if that's what Irita sent you here to convince me to do. One of the detectives will be in court today. I'll ask him who is working the case."

"That's good to know," Chance said. "They're definitely looking for whoever Lowell knew in town. Eventually they'll get your phone number from the phone listings from the house where Austin called you. It will put you in a better light if you volunteer the information."

"Did you know him?" Kathy asked, concern filling her voice. "I mean, you called him by his first name like you had met him or talked to him."

Chance shook his head. "I feel like I've gotten to know him in the last few days working on this story. I talked to Preach—Daniel Swoboda—the guy that Lowell was staying with."

Kathy nodded her head encouragingly. Mesa could tell she was hungry for whatever Chance could tell her about Austin.

"He's pretty upset about what happened. Kind of feels like it was his fault."

Kathy wiped her wet hands on a dishcloth and shook her head. "If anybody in Butte is to blame," she said quietly, "it's me. You can tell him that." She walked into the den where she had poured her heart out the previous afternoon, replacing the newspaper on the coffee table. Mesa and Chance were right behind her. She picked up a stuffed bear and a toy truck from the floor and then sank into the sofa. "I was the one he came here to see."

Mesa sat next to Kathy while Chance walked over to the mantel, pausing for a moment to look at the photos before turning around. "Mesa told me about how you wrote to Lowell. You know, he kept your last letter with him. I saw it next to the bed where he slept at the Swoboda's house."

Mesa was surprised to hear Chance talking with such sentiment about the ex-convict. Maybe he felt like Austin was the one victim in this strange story that had no voice. Could he tell Kathy wanted to hear more?

"He must have really cared about you," Chance said, much to Mesa's amazement. She had rarely heard him talk so directly about another man's emotions. Mesa looked at Kathy, wondering if she would break down again.

"It's obvious you're upset about what happened," Chance said, leaning on the mantel's edge with one arm. "But I have to admit, I'm also curious how your brother has reacted to all this."

Kathy's back stiffened and she sat up straight, pushing away from the back of the sofa.

"Did he know Lowell Austin was coming to town?" Chance's tone had changed. "I bet he would have been worried. I would have been anxious if I found out Mesa had been in communication with the man who had killed our father."

Kathy looked at her watch. "My brother has his own problems."

Chance picked up the photo of Kathy with her children and her brother. "Is this him? What's his name?"

"Garrett Birch," she said.

"Did he meet Lowell too?" Chance asked. "What did he say when he saw your father's killer sitting at your dining room table?"

"He never even got past the hall way," Kathy said, her tone defensive. "He just dropped his duffle bag, gave me a quick hug, and said he'd be back later. He didn't even say hello to the kids."

"So he never met Austin," Chance said.

"Not as far as I know," Kathy said.

"Did your brother come back to the house?"

"He came in late. I heard the front door close around 2 a.m."

"So, did you see him Sunday?" Chance asked.

Mesa was surprised at the increasingly intimidating tone in Chance's voice.

Kathy rubbed her hands together, clearly anxious. "I saw him for a few minutes. We were on our way out the door to Georgetown Sunday morning. I invited him to come along but he said he was going to look up an old girlfriend."

"He didn't say anything about going flying?" Chance asked.

"No, not at all. What are you trying to say?" Kathy said. "You think he had something to do with Lowell's death? How could that be possible?"

"Seems like the two of you had ample time to set a plan in motion."

Kathy stood up. "You have no idea what you're talking about. I have no idea how Lowell got in that airplane and as far as I know, Garrett had nothing to do with it either. Now you'd better leave. I have to go."

"Do you have any idea where Garrett is now?" Chance said. "Maybe I should talk to him directly."

"I think he's left town. I told you, he's got his own problems with the Army to sort out."

"Who's the girlfriend? Maybe I'll talk to her."

Mesa could tell Chance wasn't going to let up. She was beginning to feel sorry for Kathy.

"Tessa Revelle. She's an old friend of mine. We used to work together at the Broadway Café before I had kids. She was with Garrett Monday at the Labor Day picnic in Stodden Park. Ask your sister. She met him. He's still trying to adjust to being home, but he certainly didn't act like he'd killed anybody."

Mesa nodded enthusiastically, as if to support Kathy's claims. Whatever scenario Chance was dreaming up, it seemed too complicated to include Garrett Birch. He looked most like a candidate for a PTSD evaluation.

"And since then, you haven't heard from him?"

She shook her head. "Look, I've got to go. I will talk to the detective. Tell Irita, all right?"

❧❧

Mesa buckled her seat belt while Chance started the Land Rover. "What got you so riled up? I told you she didn't have anything to do with Austin's death," she said as Chance made a U-turn on Gold Street and headed back toward the *Messenger* office. "You went after Kathy like she and her brother had some big plan. Where did you get that theory all of a sudden? You really think that Garrett Birch and his sister planned to kill Austin? He can't fly an airplane, and he's practically a transient. According to Irita, he's been back in the country less than a month."

Chance lingered at the stop sign at the corner of Excelsior and Gold. "Those photos on her mantel, the one with her brother and her two kids? That's who I saw talking to Hardy last night at Shoestring Annie's."

Mesa felt her breath catch but she didn't want to let on her anxiety to Chance. Had she totally misjudged Hardy, yet again? Methodically she tried to re-evaluate everything Hardy had said in the past 48 hours, unsure what was important at this point, and what she should say to Chance. "What's that prove? Hardy talks to everybody," was the best she could muster.

Chance nodded slowly. "I started thinking last night about how Hardy showed up out of nowhere on Tuesday."

"He got hurt down in Moab, so he came back to Butte a few months early," Mesa said. That made perfect sense to her, but she added for emphasis, "His dad's been sick."

"So how come he's driving one of his dad's trucks everywhere? I saw it at the Copper Baron. Where's his precious, shiny Dodge Dakota Sport four-wheel Quad cab pickup? You seen it?"

Mesa didn't like the tone in Chance's voice, plus, this insinuation hit home. Hardy was obsessed about the silver pickup when he had bought it four years ago. She had ridden in it to Big Sky with him that Christmas. He called it his entertainment center on wheels, and loved telling people it was so fancy he could live in it. She knew that on occasion he even kept a mattress in the back. "What are you saying? Maybe it's in the shop. Knowing Hardy, he probably doesn't want to pay for his own gas."

"This morning I went back to look at the photos the sheriff's office took of the plane's cabin," Chance said. "I didn't put it together when I first saw them. There were a couple of potato chip bags, a plastic Mountain Dew bottle, and an empty Oberto beef jerky wrapper on the floor."

Mesa felt a chill go down her back—Hardy ate jerky all the time, and if he wasn't drinking beer, it was Mountain Dew. "Come on, Chance, half the guys in Butte are jerky junkies. It's nothing but pure coincidence."

"When I left Shoestring Annie's last night, I saw Garrett Birch standing with a group of guys that included Kevin Murphy. What if Garrett Birch hired Hardy to take Lowell Austin up in that plane? What if Kevin Murphy saw him with Hardy and put it all together? Maybe Hardy and Garrett decided they needed to shut Kevin up. Maybe they stuck around until last call, jumped Kevin, and then left him in the street, hoping he would get run over."

"Hardy couldn't have done something like that," Mesa said. Hardy was a lover, not a fighter. And Chance almost never got so wound up, especially with somebody who was a good friend. "Chance, you know him better than that. Where's your loyalty?"

Chance stared hard at his sister. She knew that look. More than once, he had told her how stupid she could be about guys. A car pulled up behind Chance, so he had to move on. He turned toward Park Street. "How can you be so sure about Hardy?"

"Because," Mesa said, wishing she didn't have to admit it to Chance, "He was with me last night."

Chapter 19

"Tessa Revelle?" Irita said to Erin as they stood with Chance and Mesa in her office conferring about the whereabouts of one of Butte's own. "I know she doesn't work up at the Broadway Café anymore. I think maybe she went back to school."

Chance had looked up Tessa's address in the Butte phone book. All it said was "south of Butte." No one answered the phone when he called. "Up at Tech?" Chance asked.

"Let me call Connor, my brother," Erin offered. "He and Tessa's brother, Bart, used to play hockey together."

Chance followed Erin toward the newsroom but turned toward Mesa just before he left her office. "If you hear from Hardy, tell him I want to talk to him. And if he doesn't want to talk to me, tell him he can talk to Rollie Solheim."

Mesa sunk back into her chair and let out a long, slow breath. Irita came over and leaned on the corner of the desk. "What was that all about? I haven't seen him this serious since your grandmother had her heart attack."

"Kevin Murphy ended up in the hospital last night," Mesa said.

"I heard," Irita said. "Not like it's the first time."

"I know," Mesa said, "but Chance thinks it has to do with this plane business. He has it in his head that Hardy Jacobs and Kathy's brother, Garrett, beat Kevin up. Apparently, Chance saw Garrett talking to Hardy at Shoestring Annie's last night."

"Holy shit," Irita said in a whisper. "I thought Garrett had left town. At least that's what Kathy said."

"Maybe she's trying to protect him," Mesa said. She knew that would be her instinct if she thought Chance were in trouble with the law, which of course she couldn't imagine. "Kathy said Garrett showed up at her house on Saturday night but didn't stick around. She says he never even saw Austin, not that Chance believes her."

"It would certainly be a weird set of circumstances," Irita said. "I don't know Garret that well. He's hard to read. I don't think he ever said more than two words at one time to me. Not that I'd give him a chance, the way I jabber.

"He's always seemed like the somber, brooding type—not mean but always keeping to himself. I wouldn't be surprised if there was a lot of torment underneath. Can't see him wanting to spend ten minutes with Hardy Jacobs though. They're oil and water. How would they even meet?"

"Hardy told Chance they had worked together at Big Sky," Mesa said. "Maybe before Garrett got called up?"

Irita shrugged. "Garrett drove for UPS in Billings before he went off to Kandahar for fun and games. Maybe he delivered to Big Sky?"

Mesa doubted it. The ski resort was more than three hours from Billings. And even though people liked to say that Montana was just one big city connected by really long streets, she seriously doubted UPS looked at it that way. She picked up her cell phone. "Maybe I better ask Hardy myself."

Chance pulled into the parking lot next to the World Museum of Mining, where Tessa Revelle worked three days a week. Erin had needed exactly two phone calls to get the particulars on Tessa. Now that was investigative journalism at work as far as Chance was concerned.

Built on the site of the Orphan Girl Mine, the museum actually spanned several acres designed to replicate an 1880s mining town—the Butte version of a theme park, as yet without the rides. Some of the buildings, the church, and school had actually been saved from Meaderville, when the mostly Italian neighborhood in Butte had been cannibalized to make way for the Berkeley Pit operation.

Chance looked at the mine head-frame, an iron silhouette against the already snow-capped Anaconda Pintler Mountains to the west. A sudden gust of cold wind came up, blowing dust everywhere, a reminder of the long winter to come. He hurried into the museum gift shop.

When he saw Tessa Revelle behind the cash register, he remembered why her name had sounded familiar. She had once graced the arm of Mattie Gronauer, Mr. Hockey Puck, back in their high school days. At least she had had the good sense to dump him quicker than most.

Tessa was a good-looking blonde whose smooth complexion and pink cheeks preserved her youth, though she had graduated from high school a few years behind Chance. She often wore a pouty expression that made her look permanently disappointed. Nevertheless, hers was a welcoming smile when she greeted Chance by name.

"I heard you were back in school," Chance said and picked at a box of tiny bottles near the cash register, each supposedly with a flake of real gold in it.

Tessa smiled and said, "Finally decided to get an accounting degree. It's boring but I'll get a decent job. This is just part-time."

"Kind of quiet," Chance said, looking around at the empty gift shop with a feigned grimace.

Tessa smiled. "My dad helped put this place together when I was a kid. I guess I have a soft place in my heart for it. It's starting to slow down now that Labor Day's past, but sometimes volunteers come in and talk about the old times, which is cool.

Chance stooped to look at a shelf of kids' toys— a miniature miner's lamp, a plastic rock hammer— while Tessa talked. She seemed so gentle. He wondered if she had any idea what Garrett Birch was capable of, if in fact Chance was right about Kathy's brother.

"What brings you to the Museum? Is there something you're looking for?" she asked with a shy smile. "Can I help you find something?"

Chance stood up and shook his head. "To be honest, Tessa, I'm looking for Garrett Birch. I heard he was staying with you."

"I see," Tessa said and nodded, the hint of the pout returning. She turned to a pile of invoices next to the cash register and began to sort them.

"I know this might seem out of the ordinary but I know his sister is worried about him. We were thinking maybe you could help her get in touch with him."

"He doesn't have a cell phone. But I guess you could try calling him at my house, but usually he won't answer the phone. If he's still there."

"Did he say he was leaving?" Chance said, uneasy about the possibility that he might lose the opportunity to talk to Garrett at all.

"He's been talking about leaving for a couple days now, but he was still here this morning." She shrugged. "I didn't know you and Garrett knew each other."

"We don't," Chance admitted. "I just met his sister today, as a matter of fact. She's really worried about him," he added, hoping Tessa might offer some information about Garrett. "The Army called Kathy looking for him. Did you know he was coming to town?"

Tessa shook her head, one eyebrow slightly raised. "He called me Sunday afternoon," she said, "and asked if he could stay at my place for a couple of days." She began to leaf through a box of maps of the mines on the hill and attach price stickers to them while she talked.

"We dated for a while back when his sister and I worked together. He used to drive over from Billings now and then to visit her." She paused, and then added, "I hadn't seen him since he left with the Guard. I was kind of surprised when he wanted to crash at my house, but I don't mind. He's a nice guy."

"Afghanistan must be some experience," Chance said. Had that been where Garrett could have learned how to kill Lowell Austin the way that Adrienne had described?

"He doesn't really talk about it, except he said he needed to be around someone who understood how he can be at times."

"How's that?" Chance asked.

"Sad, mostly," she said kind of absently, as if she were taking stock of Garrett for the first time. "He's been staying in my spare bedroom for the past couple of days. He helped me replace a switch on my furnace, but besides that, I've hardly talked to him."

"When did you meet up with him?" Chance asked.

"On Monday. I picked him up at his sister's house. Then we went over to the Labor Day Picnic to hook up with Kathy and the kids."

"Garrett didn't have his own car?" Chance asked. That meant he could have driven Kathy's SUV on Sunday morning, then somehow got back to the airport on Monday morning and driven it back about the time Jake Brinig had left the airport. His sister would never even have known he used it.

"I didn't ask. He just said he needed a ride so I gave him one."

"So you guys aren't . . .?" Here he motioned with his hands in an awkward sort of way, trying to indicate a stronger connection.

"No, we're friends. That's it," Tessa said, "He's kind of a loner." She chuckled. "Maybe that's why we clicked originally. People say that about me sometimes, living in a cabin out of town by myself."

"Garrett and I got thrown together, you might say. Whenever his sister would have people over, it always seemed like Garrett and I would be the ones without dates." She stopped again, embarrassed perhaps that she had revealed as much as she did. "There's really a good guy behind that long face."

"How do you mean?" Chance said, trying not to sound too eager.

"People mistake him being quiet for not caring about things." She paused, as if searching for words that had once been applied to her, "like he's hard-hearted. That's not true. I know he worries about his sister's kids, being without a father. He says that's part of what made him the way he is."

ৡৣ

Mesa called Yukon Glass and talked to Ronnie Jacobs, who told her his brother had gone out to the parking lot at Wal-Mart. The owner of a gigantic RV wanted someone to check on a crack in its windshield. Hardy had a cell phone, Ronnie added, though what good it did, he didn't know since Hardy intentionally kept it off most of the time. He used it when he wanted to make a call. There was nothing else scheduled for him. They weren't sure when he would be back, but would tell him to call.

Mesa looked at her watch. She could wait and see if he showed up at Pork Chop John's. She decided instead to drive to the big box superstore, which sat all too grandly at the end of a long string of car dealerships, and across from Mountain View Cemetery at the south end of town. Usually the RVs, which Wal-Mart so graciously permitted to park in its lot overnight, clustered near the street.

When Mesa pulled in to the far entrance of the parking lot, she saw Hardy. He was shaking hands with a portly gray-haired man who wore what looked like a pair of suit pants that had been converted into Bermuda shorts and a pair of clean, white tennis shoes. She was in luck. It looked like Hardy was just finishing up.

Mesa parked between two pickups away from the nest of RVs. Walking over to the Yukon Glass pickup, she reminded herself to ask Hardy about his traveling entertainment center, not that he would need it for work. She leaned on the front fender of the truck and tried to look nonchalant until Hardy noticed her. She didn't want to seem overly interested in anything in particular. He came around from the rear and looked surprised to see her.

"Thought you might be ready for lunch," she said quietly. After last night's true confessions, she felt sure she could get him to answer Chance's questions without putting a strain on anybody's friendship.

He looked at his watch and said, "Sure, why not. I got a little bit of time between jobs. Let's go into Wal-Mart to the Subway."

Time between jobs? That wasn't what she had heard from Ronnie. This wasn't like Hardy. If he wanted to blow off work, he would just say so.

While they strolled across the half-empty parking lot, Mesa broached Chance's accusations carefully. "Chance asked me to let you know he wants to talk to you."

Hardy looked over at her and said, "Yeah? Sounds official."

"He wants to talk to you about last night."

"You mean about you and me." His voice sounded slightly surprised.

"No," she said dismissively, "about Kevin Murphy. Somebody jumped him outside Shoestring Annie's last night."

Hardy stopped walking. "What's that to do with me? I was with you. You told him that, right?" He scratched at his ever-present scraggle of a beard. Mesa could see he was uptight. "Murph's going to be okay, right?"

She nodded as they started walking again and cut between a line of shopping carts and a station wagon filled with kids. "You know last night when you said you had made a huge mistake and couldn't go back to Moab?"

He stopped again. "Mesa, what's up? Why all the questions?"

Mesa pressed on. Now, in the light of day, she wanted to know the truth too. At least then, she would know what she could do to help him. "You took that plane from Moab, didn't you? That's what you were talking about last night. Chance saw you talking to Garrett Birch, Hardy. He thinks you took Birch and Austin up in that plane and you had to crash land. Is that what happened?"

She reached out to touch his arm as if to convey her concern. "I know you couldn't kill anybody. But if you took that plane, Jesus, you're in a lot of trouble." Her voice tailed off. She was in no position to judge Hardy for whatever lies he told, but stealing was something else. "Maybe I can help you, but you have to tell me what happened."

Hardy didn't have to say anything. She could see the answers in his face. He had that hung-dog look that always appeared in the waning seconds of a big game that his team had lost, when he knew winning wasn't in their cards. He turned back in the direction they had come, almost walking in front of a van backing out. "I don't know anybody named Garrett Birch. I gotta get going," he said.

Mesa held onto his arm even as he tried to pull away. "It was Garrett, wasn't it? Do you know where he is? I know he might be in a bad space right now, but maybe we can get him to turn himself in."

"I told you, I don't know anybody named Garrett Birch," Hardy said, his usually laid back voice, tinged with irritation.

"I met him at the Labor Day picnic, and I know his sister. He's AWOL from the Army, Hardy. He's got nothing to lose."

Hardy was walking fast now, shaking his head while Mesa talked. "You don't know what you're talking about."

"Okay, how about we can talk to Rollie Solheim. Explain it to him. He knows you and your family. He can help you. I know he can." Mesa was walking fast now, trying to catch up. Who knew what the Sheriff would do, but she had to try to stop Hardy. Her instincts told her that Hardy was on the verge of hopping from the frying pan into the fire. And despite her mixed feelings about him, they went too far back for her to give up on him.

They were almost back to the truck. She had to know what they were dealing with. "Hardy," she said, raising her voice. "Tell me you didn't kill Lowell Austin."

Hardy unlocked the truck door and said in a whisper, "Mesa, I didn't kill anybody. You know me better than that. I made the best I could out of a bad situation, and that's what I'm gonna keep doing." He reached up and touched her cheek, lifting a strand of her hair behind her ear. "I'll be in touch," he said and jumped in the cab of the truck.

He cranked the engine, and Mesa looked around, wondering if anyone had seen or overheard them, as if she might recruit help make Hardy listen to reason. She was exasperated, not sure what to do next. Her eyes settled on the bed of the pickup. Propped on its side against the built-in stainless steel toolbox was a black and green contour backpack she had seen Hardy use countless times. He was going somewhere all right, she realized uneasily, and it wasn't back to work.

Chapter 20

Hardy drove away from Wal-Mart and Mesa, past the airport and away from town. "Women," he said out loud. Whatever you gave them, it was never enough. He cared as much about Mesa as he had for any girl, but sometimes she could be too smart for her own good.

He checked the rearview mirror and then relaxed his back into the seat. He told himself to settle down. All they had to do was get out of town and then the situation would be manageable.

He passed the turnoff to Whitehall and looked at his watch, nearly noon. The sky was blue and cloudless. If he stayed cool, they could be on the road in the next couple of hours. They would drive to Big Sky first, leave the truck at the resort if need be. Then they could catch a ride with somebody going north, maybe up to Calgary.

He looked at the speedometer, careful to stay right at fifty. The last thing he needed was to get stopped for speeding. He thought about the last six days and cursed himself for being so unlucky. The previous Saturday he had just wanted to get out of Moab, now he would be on the run for good.

The shaded, red rock cliffs, blood orange in Moab's early morning light, had suited his mood. At least he had convinced the idiot Simian to take advantage of the cool of first light for the initial leg of the ride to Hardscrabble, where he could meet up with his pals.

He and Simian had met at Eddy McStiff's the night before. The guy talked nonstop about his business, on and on about his plane, and the five-day trip he and his buddies had spent a year planning.

Hardy tried to give the guy some tips like, for starters, how he shouldn't get wasted the night before a strenuous ride, especially in a place where you weren't used to the climate or the altitude.

Simian said he knew what he was doing. He had all his little gadgets, GPS, salt tablets, a Camelback hydration pack—everything but good sense and proper respect for the environment.

In the end, Hardy had struck a deal with Simian to shuttle him to the drop-off point halfway down Horse Thief Trail the next morning. He'd return the Jeep Simian had borrowed from the Moab Airport and stow the extra luggage in his plane.

At the time, it had seemed like nothing more than an easy way to make fifty bucks. But the next morning Simian had talked to Hardy as if he was some flunky—do this, get me that.

Guys like Simian had ruined Moab. The used-to-be-hip mountain-bike subculture was now crowded with every kind of human, and a lot of them were really stupid, not to mention conceited. Money made the problem worse. People who had everything seemed most likely to respect nothing. While Simian wallowed in all his toys, and ordered him around, Hardy started to think about a way to make his irritation easier to bear.

Simian planned to be back in five days, Thursday of the coming week. That left plenty of time for Hardy to fly to Butte, visit his dad, and then fly back by Monday morning, plenty of time before Simian and his crew would finish their White Rim ride.

Hardy's job at Slick Rock Cycling Company was history anyway. After the major falling-out he'd had with his boss about getting a decent commission on the tours Hardy set up, the tour manager job was history. He was sick and tired of being taken advantage of.

As he had driven along the dirt road back to the highway, he tried to concoct a plan where he wouldn't have to fly out on his own. He didn't want to risk taking the plane alone since the guys at Moab Airport might wonder what was going on. Then when he turned onto Route 313 and saw the hitchhiker, everything fell into place.

There was no traffic on the highway. Hardy called out through the Jeep's window and waved. He had seen the soldier at McStiff's the night before. "Hey, man, where you headed so early?"

Hardy drove the Jeep across the highway, swung the passenger door open, and introduced himself. "We met last night at Eddie McStiff's. Wasn't sure you would remember me. You were still drinking when I left."

The soldier nodded. He didn't say much, that was for sure, but Hardy thought he looked the part of the rugged, outdoorsy private plane owner. "On your way out of town already?" he said with a grin, as if he knew Moab didn't have that much to offer if you weren't fascinated with mountain bikes.

"Going down the road," the soldier had answered.

"Which way you headed? I might be able to get you there a little quicker."

The hitchhiker had seemed a little suspicious. "How's that?" he asked.

"Hop in and I'll tell you. Ever ride in a private airplane?" Hardy asked.

"You mean besides the Army's?" the soldier said in a serious tone and climbed up into the Jeep.

"What's your name?" Hardy asked.

"People call me Tree."

"That short for something? Tremont? Gantry?"

"You could say that," Tree said and settled into the seat, staring out the windows at the red rock cliffs.

"Which way you going?" Hardy had asked, wondering why it was taking a hitchhiker, who was getting a free ride, so long to answer.

"Somewhere north will do."

A few minutes later, Hardy parked the Jeep next to the airport's main building, grabbed a couple of nylon stuff bags from the back of the car, and headed into the building.

Tree followed cautiously, his duffle bag on his shoulder. They entered the tiny waiting room, which exhibited no particular signs of life. The lights were on, but nobody was around. Hardy ventured over to a counter, poked his head over it, and called, "Anybody home?"

"Must be dropping somebody off somewhere," he said to Tree. Finally, he put the Jeep's keys back behind the counter, and motioned Tree out through another door and onto the tarmac.

"A guy's paying me to ferry this airplane to Missoula, Montana," Hardy told him. After all, he had done plenty of ferrying jobs before, and he saw no reason to say anything more. "I'm gonna stop for a day or so in Butte. Sound good to you? It's about a five-hour flight over some pretty awesome country."

Tree smiled briefly then shook his head at his good fortune. "Sure, I know some locals in Butte."

"No shit," Hardy laughed, mildly surprised. People with Butte connections were spread far and wide, relatives of miners who had moved on decades ago to find work after the Anaconda Company closed. Tree named off a handful of Butte hockey players, guys Hardy had seen around town or knew by reputation. "Okay then, let's roll."

They walked past a small bi-plane, and then stopped at a sparkling four-seater with red and gold trim. "This is our ride," Hardy said with confidence. It was a Cessna 180, bright and shiny, probably just repainted. He opened the side door of the plane with the keys Simian had given him, stored the gear behind the back seats, and began the preflight. He didn't feel the least bit nervous. If Doc Jeppsen came back from wherever he was, he would assume that Tree owned the plane. Sure as hell Hardy didn't.

Tree had stood outside watching Hardy go through the preflight. Finally, Hardy had to tell him,

"Go on around, and get in. Buckle yourself up. I'm going back inside and check the weather. Once we take off, we'll be in Butte by lunchtime."

When Hardy came back, Tree boarded slowly, and then asked, "Where did you learn to fly a plane?"

Hardy had heard first-time passengers ask these questions before. "You're not nervous, are you? Here, put on these earphones." He pulled out a pack of spearmint chewing gum and offered Tree some. "Now sit back and relax. A buddy of mine back home, his dad taught me. I been flying since I was sixteen."

"You fly much?" Tree asked as they taxied down the single runway.

"Whenever I can get somebody to let me use their plane," Hardy had said with a smile and then they had taxied away.

All along Hardy thought, he had been so clever, playing the other guy. But Tree had called Hardy's bluff at every turn, and now he was in over his head.

Soon the road turned from asphalt to dirt and gravel without a single car on the road since Wal-Mart, as calm as last Sunday morning. Now, as Hardy turned onto Basin Creek Road past an open pasture, he could kick himself for how flippant he had been about the whole setup, never giving a single thought to what could go wrong.

Once they had landed in Butte, Hardy had invited Tree to meet up at the Hoist House Saturday night, nothing fancy just a few drinks. Tree had shown up with a friend. No big deal, right?

Hardy realized now how clueless he had been. It angered him to think how he had let himself get suckered into such a bad hand. He had overplayed his cards all right. He had invited them on a short sightseeing excursion the next morning. "Why not," Tree had said.

Hardy had planned to do a quick run above uptown, show them the Pit and then maybe fly toward the Pintlers. It was early, and he had refueled the plane without anyone noticing. Murph was late as usual, not that Hardy was worried. If Murph had asked any questions, Hardy would simply have told him Tree owned the plane.

He would never really understand what happened between Austin and Tree. Hardy had taken Tree at his word and thought Austin was a friend. Tree had brought Austin to the Hoist House for a drink that night and they had arrived at the airport together the next morning. Obviously, he had been mistaken.

Austin had said something that must have set Tree off. Or why else had the otherwise calm soldier attacked Austin while they were in the air? They had put on their earphones, chatting about the usual kind of thing first-time fliers wanted to hear. Austin had pulled out one of those Leatherman tools, showing it off as if no one had ever seen one before. He had handed it to Tree in the back seat.

Then when they had flown over the Pit, Austin had taken off his seat belt to get a better view out the window. Hardy had been coming back on the throttle as usual to level off.

He had just made the turn west, when the next two minutes changed his life forever. Tree had reached around Austin's neck and before Hardy could say, "What the hell?" Austin began to struggle, pushing for leverage with his legs.

Hardy screamed at them to stop. What happened next, he would never be certain. He had thought about it repeatedly. Maybe Austin's knee had hit the trim tab, because the nose had come down. Hardy had corrected. But then Austin fell forward. Hardy had shouted at Tree to get a hold of Austin, whose weight had pressed the steering controls forward. For a split second, Hardy wondered if the older man had had a coronary.

But he had no time to think about that. He pulled back on the yoke to keep the nose up while frantically trying to shift Austin's body off the extra controls. The ground was coming at them too fast. They had lost too much altitude and the plane was hurtling so close to the rooftops, he could see down the chimneys. There was no way for the plane to gain any altitude. He had to ditch. He pulled back on the throttle, reducing the power to try to land the plane somewhere flat in the precious little air time left before they hit the ground.

The rest was instinct. He didn't have time to think about the traffic on a Sunday morning on Labor Day weekend, or how he would avoid the utility wires along the street, or if the wings would clip a parked car or if the wheels would hit a pothole. Strangely, he had had the presence of mind to crack his door in case it stuck in the crash. And then he had begun to pray.

In less than fifteen seconds, he worked the rudders hard and had set the plane down on Washington Street, practically standing on the toe brakes. He had careened to the left when that wing had clipped something, a street sign maybe, he couldn't be sure. It had all ended with an unbelievable jolt, first from the back wheel that he had steered over a roll of chain-link fence hoping it might create some kind of drag, and then into the side of somebody's house.

Another jolt, this time by a rut in the road, brought Hardy back to the present. He had to pay attention to Tree's directions to find the cabin where he was holed up. It was Two Bit Gulch. He remembered driving up there in high school after football games to keg parties set up on Forest Service land.

A mile later, he saw the sign pointing right. He drove past some good grazing land with a stream on it. Then a couple of houses a fair distance apart came into view on the left. God, Montana was beautiful and he was leaving it all behind.

He was relieved when he saw the log cabin on the right several hundred yards farther up the road, at least until he pulled into its driveway and saw Tree. What had Mesa said his real name was, Garrett Birch? He was standing at the cabin's front window.

Mesa had pulled into the first side road she passed in Two Bit Gulch, surprised how calm she felt. She sat next to a row of mailboxes to collect her thoughts. The Yukon Glass truck had kicked up enough dust on the gravel road to obscure Hardy's vision. There were not that many places to turn off the ranch road that eventually led to the Basin Creek Reservoir. But Mesa could see well down the road, and Hardy had given no indication that he had spotted her. She remembered that the road ran out several miles farther down at the end of the canyon. Finding Hardy's pickup between here and there shouldn't be too hard, but she wanted to think for a minute about what she was going to say when she caught up with him.

She had expected him to head for points east. But when he didn't turn on Highway 2, she remembered Tessa Revelle's address, south of Butte. As she followed him on the route south of town, it occurred to her then that if Chance was right, Hardy might be rendezvousing with Garrett.

Nana had bought her Trail Blazer in the last year, and Hardy wouldn't recognize the SUV from the dozens like it in town. Still, she had stayed sufficiently distant, ready to turn into a ranch entrance or a driveway if he slowed. Besides, what could he do if he did see her? Stop and tell her to go home. She had no reason to be afraid of Hardy. She was sure of that.

Or Garrett Birch, she had decided. Maybe he had killed Lowell Austin. But she suspected that if he had, years of grief, not homicidal rage, had been the reason. One look into his eyes had told her that.

What she didn't know was if Hardy had stolen that plane, had Garrett hired him to help kill Austin? That didn't make sense either. She believed Hardy when he said he hadn't killed anybody. His connection with Garrett was somehow unexpected, Hardy in the wrong place at the wrong time, even if he didn't realize it. And she didn't believe Kathy wasn't involved either. Even if she did invite Austin to Butte, she said she hadn't known her brother was on his way to town.

She felt sure that if Garrett turned himself in, he had a chance in court. A good lawyer could convince a Montana jury of mitigating circumstances. Garrett might serve time, but the sentence would reflect prevailing sympathies in his favor as the son of a murdered man. At least, that was the argument she was going to use.

Chapter 21

Hardy lifted the backpack from the bed of the pickup and walked with a deliberate pace up the steep steps to the concrete slab of porch as if he were used to being on the run. The warm sun accented the smell of pine and sage in the yard. Someone had done a good job fixing up the cabin. It even had a deck attached with a hot tub. Flowerpots overflowed with annuals everywhere, along with half a dozen different feeders for birds. In another set of circumstances, he might have been glad to visit.

Tree opened the door. He didn't smile but simply said, "Did you get everything?" He was all business now.

Hardy nodded and raised the pack, careful to bring what was requested. In the past three days, he had learned plenty about the ex-con Tree had killed, from the newspaper, from Chance and now Mesa. He still wasn't sure how it all connected to Garrett Birch, but that didn't stop him from being a desperate man. Hardy entered the cabin with that in mind.

Inside, the temperature was cool, the cabin small, and cozy. A gust of wind came down the stone chimney in the middle of the main room and the smell of pine ash filled the air. He could see a kitchen had been added onto the right side of the cabin and a couple of bedrooms on the left. It might be a decent place to hole up in if it weren't so close to town.

A computer and printer sat on a desk between the front door and the kitchen. Garrett was printing out several sections of a topo map. "Tessa called me," he said and sat on the chair in front of the computer. "Your pal, Chance, is that his name? He's been asking questions."

Hardy nodded and sighed. He wondered what Chance thought he could accomplish. With both him and his sister asking questions, Hardy began to feel even more anxious about getting on the road. He didn't think either of them would go to the police, but that wouldn't stop them from trying to find out what was up.

"He came to see Tessa," Tree said. He didn't seem angry or likely to fly off the handle again, just cautious. "He was asking her questions when she doesn't know what's happened. She doesn't even get the newspaper. But he's made her suspicious. I put her off by saying I was leaving today. I think she's worried about me being here. We need to rethink our plan. Our head start may be evaporating."

Hardy cracked his knuckles. He liked the plan the way it was. Garrett would write a letter explaining that Hardy had nothing to do with the death of Lowell Austin. He would also describe how Hardy, Garrett, and Simian had met in a bar in Moab and that Simian had agreed to lend Hardy the plane.

Hardy was counting on Simian's injury to leave him confused about what he had done. After all, it was true they had all met at McStiff's. He knew the bartender there, who would vouch for his story.

Hardy might still be liable for what happened to the plane, but at least maybe there would be less chance that he would actually go to jail for grand larceny. To get the letter, all Hardy had to do was help Garrett get out of town. That was the plan, and Hardy wanted to stick to it.

"What's to rethink?" Hardy asked. "Let's get on the road."

"I think we may need a little leverage. Your friend, Chance, is liable to get the FBI to listen to him sooner than later."

"Look," Hardy said. "We don't have time to find any leverage."

Garrett stood up and looked out the window above the computer desk. He reached into a backpack next to the computer and pulled out a pistol, a 44 magnum.

"Where'd you get that?" Hardy swallowed hard, wondering what Birch had in mind.

"It's Tessa's. She keeps it to ward off varmints," Garrett said, a tinge of sarcasm in his voice.

Birch turned to look out the window and Hardy followed after him. A Trail Blazer SUV he didn't recognize pulled into the driveway. For a long moment, they waited for the driver to step out of the car.

"Maybe our leverage has found us," Birch said quietly and put the gun back into the pack.

"She just won't give it up," Hardy muttered and shook his head as he watched Mesa approach the front door of the cabin.

∽≪

Chance snapped the cell phone closed so violently he thought he might have cracked its tiny inner screen. He had clenched his teeth to avoid yelling at Rollie Solheim during the phone conversation. He was still the sheriff, even if the FBI had him hamstrung.

Solheim had confirmed that Kathy DiNunzio had talked to Detective Hennessey, who had accompanied her from the courthouse to meet with Agents Perryman and whatever his name was. The sheriff had sat in on the initial interview. But the FBI was disinclined, that was the word Solheim had used, to act on Chance's theory about DiNunzio's brother or the 'off the record' insinuations possibly implicating Hardy.

"Bear in mind before you make any accusations," Solheim had said, "that, at the moment, we have no fingerprints and no murder weapon. I will take it upon myself to speak to Hardy. And remember, Chance, the FBI are handling this case," Solheim said, "and when they are through interviewing Ms. DiNunzio, to whom they are giving their undivided attention at the moment, I will have them call you.

"If the brother's in the military, they can run his fingerprints with a tap of the keyboard of one of their higher-than-high-speed laptops. For all I know, they already have. If there's a match with the fingerprints in his military file and any prints they pulled from that Cessna, I'm sure they'll be all over Mr. Birch."

"He could be long gone by then," Chance had said, which was when he had raised his voice.

"If he's smart, he'd be long gone already. For all you know, he's halfway to Canada."

Chance shook his head in disbelief as Solheim's words resonated in his ears. The situation at the *Messenger* office was no less frustrating. Irita had just gone to Kathy's house to watch her kids when they returned from school at 2:30. Erin and Micah were frantically trying to finish articles for Mesa to review later in the afternoon. Delilah was interviewing some visiting diva who would be performing at the Mother Lode Theater this evening. Meanwhile, the hotshot editor was nowhere to be found.

Chance pulled a cold French fry from his Pork Chop John's lunch and tried Mesa's cell for at least the tenth time. If she was shacked up in the middle of the afternoon with Hardy, he sure hoped Sheriff Solheim didn't find them together.

The phone rang, and Chance jumped on it. It was Tyler calling to say he had heard from Murph, who was back home at his trailer behind the Copper Baron, sleeping off the painkillers the hospital had given him. He was in no mood to talk to anyone, especially since he had nothing to say.

Whether Murph's reticence was drug-induced or the result of a heightened sense of self-preservation, there was nothing Chance could do, and so he decided to move on. "Something else I wanted to check," he said. "Remember you looked at the fuel register the other day to see who else had flown in?"

"Yeah," Tyler said.

Chance could tell by Tyler's tone of voice that he was more curious about this whole fiasco now that his main mechanic was out of commission.

"Is there any unaccounted fuel usage?"

"You know we don't do that accounting until the end of the month."

"I know, but you could check the fuel records for the days of the month so far."

"What are you getting at?"

"Well, if there's fuel that hasn't been paid for, who would you look to? Somebody local, right?"

"Every once in a while somebody forgets to pay up, and we give them a gentle kick in the butt. Sometimes Kevin or one of the substitute linemen forgets to write down a payment in the register."

"But if no one 'fesses up, it could be that someone who knows where the keys to the truck and the tank are, also filled up that plane."

"What are you getting at, Chance?"

"I checked with Solheim this morning to take a look at what had been left in the Cessna. It was littered with junk including an Oberto beef jerky wrapper. And there was a Mountain Dew bottle left too. Who's that make you think of?"

"Damn," Tyler said. There was a pause in their conversation. Chance suspected Tyler and he were thinking similar thoughts.

On the afternoon that Hardy had soloed, the last of them to do so, Chance and Tyler had sat in the pilot's lounge waiting for their pal to return so the three of them could celebrate.

They had overheard Tyler's dad, their flight instructor, in the office talking to a Forest Service pilot about how the wind had picked up. The Forest Service pilot asked about the solo flight. That's when they heard Fitz say that Hardy Jacobs had the best instincts in the air of anyone he had ever taught. Chance had felt so jealous, and so had Tyler. But they both knew they couldn't argue.

Finally, Tyler spoke. "Well, I guess we both knew Hardy could have landed that plane. We just didn't want to say it out loud."

"I know," Chance said, his heart heavy with his growing concern and frustration for Hardy—the stupid, self-centered bastard—and for his sister if she was with him. "He been around to see you lately?"

"Nope," Tyler said. "I'm beginning to think he doesn't want to be associated with the place."

"Maybe more than we know. Will you check those fuel gauges for me?" Chance asked and held up a finger to Anna Takkinen, who stood at the office door.

"It'll have to be later this afternoon," Tyler said. "Since Kev's gone, I'm handling the lineman chores. The SkyWest flight is due in shortly."

Chance hung up and turned his attention to Anna whose voice was filled with excitement. "There's a fellow from the Canadian Ski Association on the phone up in Calgary. He wants to talk to someone about doing a statewide insert to attract skiers to Alberta, 75,000 copies."

"Holy Shit." Chance couldn't help but smile. A job like that could fill the *Messenger*'s coffers for several months. It was the kind of cushion they needed right now.

"Irita usually handles anything like this," Anna was whispering with anticipation. "She's not here, and neither is your sister. I hate to let the guy go."

Small papers like theirs made the budget by putting together one-time direct-mail jobs to showcase local events, but this was statewide. "How in the hell did he get our name?" Chance asked.

"The usual—he's got relatives here. Line two," Anna said and pointed to the phone on the desk.

Chance looked at his watch. It was past three. He wanted to find Hardy, and then Birch. But he knew golden opportunities didn't come around often, and a "Can you call back" response would be the kiss of death. And it was his "at bat." He picked up the phone and found his usual cheerful voice.

Mesa could tell a woman lived in the cabin as soon as she walked through the door. Lush green plants filled every corner. Hand-crocheted pillows and colorful knitted Afghans covered the sofa and chairs. The presence of two men hadn't changed the atmosphere.

She looked at Garrett and remembered the face of a small boy standing next to his mother in the family photo at his sister's house. "How's the weather?" she said with a slight smile, hoping he would remember their conversation from the park.

Then she turned to Hardy and apologized for following him. "You have to know I wouldn't give up on you, Hardy. I'm not leaving until the three of us talk about turning yourselves in," she said quietly.

The two men looked at each other. Garrett nodded his head to one side as if to say he might consider it. Then he said, "Come into the kitchen where we can sit and talk."

Mesa followed him past a desk where she saw an envelope addressed to "Tessa" on the computer's keyboard. So this *was* where she lived, Mesa thought. The place felt homey and peaceful. She could see why Garrett might want to stay here, although he still had that same weary look on his face. He would need a lot more rest before that changed.

Hardy and Mesa sat at the round dining table in the corner while Garrett stood with his foot on a dining table chair, leaning on his knee and looking out the window periodically. From there, anyone approaching would be easy to spot.

Mesa felt oddly at ease. The kitchen had lots of light, with a large window in the corner and French doors out to the deck along the far wall. On the outside of the window hung a red hummingbird feeder, though the tiny birds had migrated south since the mornings had turned cool. And she knew too much about either of her companions to feel afraid.

Hardy spoke first. "Look, Mesa, I know you mean well, but this is a situation you don't want to get involved in." Then he looked at Garrett for support.

Garrett looked at his watch. "Let her talk. But I have to tell you," he said to Mesa, "we don't have much time. So don't waste your words."

"I know all about your father, Garrett. Kathy told us everything. I can't imagine how awful it must have been, and I can understand why you would want to kill Lowell Austin." She looked up at him while she talked, but she could not hold his gaze. He was intent on watching the road.

"What about his father?" Hardy said.

Mesa looked at him, and began to believe poor Hardy really didn't know what he had gotten into when he invited Garrett Birch to go up in that plane.

"Garrett's father was one of the wardens that Austin shot."

"Mesa, you can't believe I had anything to do with this," Hardy said, half laughing. "I thought all I was doing was giving a soldier a ride."

Mesa turned her attention back to Garrett. "A jury would be sympathetic, especially if you turn yourself in and show some remorse."

"My last experience with the jury system was far from satisfying," Garrett said. His voice was matter-of-fact, as if he were making a consumer complaint. "The death of my father was unbearable, but having his killer escape the death penalty was a slap in the face. The older I got, the sicker it made me." He shook his head and leaned with his hands on the table.

"My father was a decent man doing his job. The defense attorneys tried to blame him for everything. Meanwhile Lowell Austin became a folk hero."

Garrett's voice trembled ever so slightly. "So you'll forgive me if I don't share your faith in the courts."

He stood up and looked out the window where the sky was beginning to cloud up. "Besides, I'm not sorry for what I did." Then he looked at Hardy. "The weather's changing. We better get going."

Hardy hesitated, and then stood while Garrett walked over to the kitchen counter where he picked up some sandwiches he had wrapped up and some of Hardy's favorite jerky. "Pull your truck into the garage. We'll take Mesa's car."

Hardy looked at Mesa. She could see the fear in his eyes. Then he said to Garrett, "What are you going to do?"

"Don't worry," Garrett said, his voice even again. "I'm not going to hurt her. She's just a little temporary insurance."

"That's not a good idea," Hardy said. "I don't want to be driving across country worrying about what she might do."

"We're not driving," Garrett said.

ৎ❦ৎ

Garrett sat in the back seat of the Trail Blazer with Mesa. "As long as you do exactly what I say," he said quietly, "everything will be fine."

Mesa put on her seat belt and watched while Garrett did the same, holding a small blue daypack in his lap. He seemed resigned, she thought. She wasn't sure what he had planned, but she could tell by the look in his eyes, that he didn't expect to let anything get in his way.

Headed back into town, Hardy drove fast while he talked. "This is a lousy idea, Tree. I know a plane might seem like a quicker way out of town, but that's if I can find one. We have no way of knowing what or who will be at the airport."

Garrett shook his head and even smiled a little at Mesa as if he knew she would agree with his thinking. "Hardy, I've been watching you operate for several days now. You got more angles than the Pentagon. You'll figure out something."

Garrett's expression became stern, and he looked into the rearview mirror and caught Hardy's eye. "But we'll have to move fast to stay ahead of the weather."

Mesa turned to look out the window to the southwest, where the sky seemed to have darkened in no time. Chance was always talking about how the weather changed so fast coming across the valley that flying was always a "maybe" proposition. "You can still call this all off," Mesa said, surprised by how calm she felt. "You can still turn yourselves in."

Neither Garrett nor Hardy answered, and ten minutes later, they turned into Aviation Drive. They pulled into the nearly empty Silver Bow Aviation parking lot. Tyler's red Ford pickup was parked at the end of the building. Mesa felt a twinge of anxiety about whether they would encounter Tyler inside. Hardy might be able to handle him, but there was no guarantee. Thank God, Murphy wasn't around. The last thing she wanted was a confrontation.

Garrett held Mesa by the elbow while they followed Hardy inside. "Like they say on TV, just act normal," he said.

Not surprisingly for a Thursday afternoon in mid-September, no planes sat ready on the tarmac for takeoff. Not even a helicopter from the Training school buzzed around in one of its practice patterns.

Hardy called out, but no one answered. He quickly went behind the counter and into the office. Mesa could see him looking at a row of keys on a wooden rack on the wall.

"We'll need a four-seater," Garrett said. He motioned her to join him at the window that overlooked the tarmac, and suddenly Mesa had a sinking feeling. "You can't take me with you," she said. "I won't do you any good."

Hardy joined them. "The trainer's out there, but I can't guarantee how much fuel it's got. Could be close to empty if somebody had a lesson today."

"What about fueling up?" Garrett said and nodded toward the BP fuel truck parked in front of the helicopter school.

"Too big a risk for a face-off with Tyler, the guy who runs this place. Why don't we just take the SUV and make a run for it."

The crunch of gravel startled them. It was Chance in his Land Rover pulling into the parking lot. Mesa looked at Hardy and said, "Turn yourself in, Hardy, while you still can." If she could convince Hardy, maybe Garrett would feel he had no other choice, and he'd give himself up too.

Out the window, she and Hardy could both see Chance, who was talking on the cell phone. Then he looked back at Mesa. "I can't. Garrett and I have a deal, and I need to go through with it."

"Looks like we're out of time on all counts. Let's go," Garrett said, and before she could say anything else, Hardy had opened the door to the tarmac. Mesa felt Garrett's large hand around her bicep, urging her toward the door to the tarmac. The three of them put their heads into the wind and strode toward a row of several tied-down planes. Mesa felt her stomach pitching, her palms getting clammy. She had not ridden in a small plane since Chance had tried to take her up more than two years ago. She had changed her mind before they had even begun to taxi.

Hardy dropped the packs on the ground next to a gray and white plane that had "Silver Bow Flying School" lettered on its fuselage. He opened the door, pulled himself onto the metal footstep, reached into the cabin, and flipped a switch. Flicking the fuel gauge with his finger, he yelled over the wind at Garrett. "She's down to a quarter tank."

"That's enough to get us across the East Ridge, isn't it? It'll have to do," he said.

"What about me?" Hardy said, thumping his chest, his face reddened with anger.

"You can do what you want after you let me out," Garrett said.

Hardy threw the bags onto the far backseat. Then he looked at Mesa and yelled at Garrett, "Let her go. She hates small planes. We don't need her now."

At that moment, Mesa wanted to throw her arms around Hardy, but his expression looked foreboding again. She turned to see Chance running toward them.

Garrett moved Mesa forward. "Get into the plane now if you don't want anything to happen to your brother." His voice had lost its reassuring calm. He reached for the blue pack on the front seat. "Start up the engine," he said to Hardy. "I'll get rid of him."

Chapter 22

Chance could not believe his eyes—Mesa willingly stepping into that small aircraft, with Hardy going through some kind of preflight routine, and Garrett Birch headed this way. "What do you think you're doing?" Chance yelled as a dust devil swirled around them.

"We finally meet," Garrett said. "I've heard a lot about you from Hardy and your sister."

"Fine, so now you can kidnap her?" Chance said. "If you think that's going to help your situation, you're crazier than I thought."

"She came voluntarily," Garrett said. "She's got guts. She keeps trying to make a case for us to turn ourselves in, but that's not going to happen. I'm just taking her along for a little insurance. I won't hurt her as long as you cooperate."

"The wind's come up," Chance said. "A storm front must be blowing in. Hardy will tell you this is no time to go flying. But if that's what you want, take me, not Mesa," Chance said. "I'll be of more use to you than her." He took a step forward as if to get around Garrett.

The stockier man reeled him in with his left arm and said, "I understand you're just trying to protect your sister, but don't be stupid. Get back inside the office now and stay there until we're gone." He reached inside the backpack and pulled out the 44 Magnum. "If I see you, or anyone else, try to stop our takeoff or intercept this plane once we're in the air, your sister will pay the price. If you're smart, you'll keep quiet. I promise to release her once I get where I'm going. You have my word, but don't cross me."

These last four words he said slowly, and Chance found himself holding his breath. The sounds of the plane's revving engine drowned out anything else they could say. Still holding his hand inside the backpack, Garrett retreated, motioning Chance to return to the terminal.

Chance turned away, angry and frustrated. The trainer was a Cessna 172, in good shape for a fifteen-year-old plane. But a thousand things could still go wrong, especially if you were flying with a gun at your head.

He didn't know what to make of Birch. He had expected the grim, ruthless avenger. Instead, he seemed resigned to what was happening and weary—determined to get away maybe, but bone tired.

Chance looked back once more as the plane began to taxi and then checked his watch. It was just past five o'clock. He could see Mesa's face at the back window of the plane's cabin. She pressed her hand to the Plexiglas and then the plane turned, taxiing toward the south end of the runway.

Chance opened the door to go back inside the lobby when something caught his eye. Through the window of the reception area, he could see into the parking lot. Sheriff Solheim was getting out of his black police cruiser, accompanied by the two FBI agents, Perryman heading for the door first. "Now you bastards want to show up," Chance said under his breath.

৩৵৶

"Put your headphones on," Hardy yelled at Mesa from between the front seats, and pointed to the floor. She reached down and picked up what looked like a new set of black vinyl earmuffs with a slender, wire mouthpiece and sponge mike. Then Garrett stuck his head around his seat and handed her a stick of gum.

"Have some Juicy Fruit." She could hear his voice now clearly through the headphones. "It helps keep your mouth from getting so dry."

They sounded like they were talking into a tin can. The roar inside the cabin had been distracting. Now with the headphones, she could hear herself think. Not that that was a good idea, given her penchant for panic attacks when enclosed in small places.

Back against the seat with her belt fastened, she felt her breathing quicken. The seat next to her was piled high with gear, the backpacks, and a down jacket. Headrests on the front seatbacks blocked her view of the cockpit, and any sense of human comfort. She felt like she was inside a shoebox. Her throat began to tighten.

Only the plane's windows gave her some relief. She was thankful the sun was passing in and out of the clouds. At least the cabin wasn't stuffy. The one time she had flown with Chance in his little two-seater, he had cracked a window so she could feel the reassuring flow of air on her face. No such luck now.

As they approached takeoff, she thought about seeing her brother back track. She knew he felt helpless, which was never good. Powerless, his frustration would build, making him prone to do or say something stupid. He wouldn't let go of his curiosity about what had happened to the plane and Austin, and look where it had led. She knew he would blame himself.

She felt the vibration of the plane's engine, and as the Cessna's speed increased for takeoff, she told herself she was in good hands. Hardy was never more suited to anything in life than flying a plane.

"We have less than an hour of fuel," she could hear him saying to Garrett. "I don't know where you think you can go."

"Where there aren't any roads," Garrett said.

Great, thought Mesa. When more than half the state had a population of less than six people per square mile, there were plenty of choices. She watched as the plane left the bounds of earth, the ground below becoming a series of rooftops that turned into squares of green and brown as they gained altitude. She chewed her gum ferociously, craning her neck enough toward the front to see that

Garrett had spread a topographical map on his lap.
"Head east," she heard him say.

Hardy banked the plane to the right. Mesa began
thinking about Lowell Austin and wondered what
had gone through his mind in the moments after
takeoff on his final plane ride. She could see the
steeple of St. John's a block from where the plane
had crashed, and she wondered what exactly had
triggered Garrett's attack.

She could see how getting Austin into an
airplane had been a good idea. From her back seat
view, it was apparent how vulnerable Austin had
been. He couldn't get away, and he would have
trouble fighting back.

Apparently, the flight path had triggered Hardy's
curiosity too. "Why did you hit him when we were
right over the town, for Christ's sake?" she could
hear Hardy asking.

"That's what I don't get," Hardy said. "Why not
wait until I landed the plane somewhere. Were you
trying to kill us all?"

Hardy was talking about Austin's death as if it
was a poorly played hockey match, Mesa thought.
She felt anxious making Garrett talk about it at all.

"I didn't plan it," Garrett said, muttering into the
map. "I spent most of my adolescence fantasizing
about ways to avenge my father's death. But when I
finally came face to face with the chance, I felt
numb.

"I've seen plenty of useless loss of life in
Afghanistan. Children, old people, soldiers giving
out candy." Garrett stopped for a minute, and then
said, "I wanted to confront him, that's true, but I

didn't intend to kill him. If he had kept his mouth shut, he might still be alive."

"What did he say?" Mesa asked.

"Too much," Garrett said. "I'm not sure I would have even recognized him if he hadn't bragged about doing a stretch in the Idaho penitentiary at the Hoist House."

"So you didn't know anything about your sister inviting him to Butte," Mesa asked. "You didn't see him at her house?" The irony of it all, Mesa thought. You could make the argument that Austin's death was justifiable in some karmic way. It wasn't like Kathy DiNunzio or Garrett Birch had conspired to cause his death. Yet their actions, even Austin's own, had converged to cause it.

"Nope," Garrett said. "I knew Kathy had company. When I walked up to the house, I could see the light in the dining room, people sitting around the table. That's why I didn't go in. I wasn't in the mood. You know what I mean. I just dropped my stuff and went for a walk up toward the practice football field up at Tech. Sat down on a bench. Nice view from there."

"Let me get this straight," Mesa said, beginning to finally understand. "Hardy invited you to ride in a plane you didn't know was stolen."

"I borrowed it," Hardy said, correcting her.

"You guys got to Butte Saturday afternoon," Mesa continued.

"We went over to that bar in the Copper Baron and eventually hitched a ride uptown," Garrett said.

"Some alum from the college gave us a ride," Hardy chimed in.

"So when did you finally meet Austin?" Mesa asked.

"He was getting into his truck when I walked back to the house. He asked me if I was Kathy's brother. I thought he was just some guy she knew. He ended up giving me a ride up to the Hoist House to meet Hardy. So I asked if he wanted to have a beer."

"This doesn't seem possible," Mesa said. "It's like fate."

"Maybe. I don't much believe in that stuff," Garrett said. "He talked himself into a grave. When he told me my sister had written to him in prison, and invited him to come to Butte, I got this uneasy feeling. Then Hardy showed up and Austin introduced himself, I couldn't believe it."

"Why didn't you confront him then?" Mesa asked, still reeling from the odds that something like this could happen.

"I don't know. Suddenly I didn't feel like there was any hurry. I wanted to see how he would act, if prison had changed him. I knew I could take him down whenever I wanted. And because I could, I didn't."

"So when I invited you guys to take a ride in the plane," Hardy asked, sounding as curious as Mesa "you didn't have a plan to kill him?"

"Nope, but after I left the Hoist House, I went back to my sister's and slept like a baby for the first time since I got back to the States."

"She wanted to break his heart, you know," Mesa said. She wanted Garrett to understand what his sister had done. "She wrote to him to entice him to come here, then she was going to confront him, but by the time he showed up, the desire for revenge was gone. Austin never knew who she was."

"Me either," Garrett said quietly. "I just told him to call me Tree."

"I still don't get how you did it," Hardy said. "He was fiddling with that Leatherman one minute and the next thing I know he was all over the controls, and we were in a nose dive."

The tone of Garrett's reply was unmistakable. "His fate was in his own hands by that point. He passed me the Leatherman with that thin knife blade already out. We had an ex-grunt in our unit who used to read all these magazines about weapons and mercenaries. One night when we were sitting around waiting for who knew what, the guy started showing everybody this stealth shit like how to kill somebody without the victim making much noise. We used to practice on cantaloupes."

Garrett was quiet again. Across the East Ridge, in the distance Mesa could see Delmoe Lake, where their parents used to take them high in the mountains to swim at least once a summer. Garrett's quiet determination had calmed her fears for her own safety but she couldn't help thinking about the mistake Garrett was making.

He was taking his chances heading into the back country, thinking to lay low while the authorities concentrated their search along the Interstates and the more populated urban areas. More likely, he would die of hypothermia or fall and break a leg in the rugged terrain. Either way, Mother Nature would do the feds' work for them.

"How much air time do we have?" Garrett asked.

"In this wind, maybe another fifteen minutes.

"Keep going," Garrett said, and pointed to a place on the map.

"There are no roads all right," Hardy said, "but no water either unless you head toward Whitetail Reservoir."

Garrett nodded. "Find a flat place to put 'er down."

೮೦ல

Chance cursed himself for following Irita's office protocol for once, and telling Erin where he was going. When Solheim called the *Messenger* to talk to Chance about Hardy, Erin had done her best as always and passed on the information. He prayed Birch had not looked back and seen Solheim's police cruiser.

When Chance explained Birch's threat, Roy Perryman promptly went into overdrive. Solheim spread out the topo map on the desk in the pilot lounge and showed Perryman the area in the direction Hardy had flown. "Tyler says the trainer maybe had 45 minutes of fuel left. Depending on the turbulence, he could probably get over to Belgrade before he needed to gas up."

Perryman took a pen and traced a crescent arc an equal distance through Belgrade, Montana—north toward Townsend and Canyon Ferry, south toward the Gallatin National Forest and Yellowstone. "Get the Salt Lake office on the phone," he said to his assistant. "Tell them we have a hostage situation. Alert all local airfields."

Chance leaned on the wall next to Solheim. "They're not going to land in another populated area. Dozens of small airstrips have been built all through this part of the state. Forest service strips for fire camps, ranches with their own strips, small-town strips where there's nobody around—just a self-service pump that takes a credit card. Hell, I've seen Forest Service pilots land on frontage roads and taxi into a regular gas station. Maybe that's what Hardy's got in mind."

Rollie gave Chance one of his patented "watch your mouth" looks. Chance jammed his hands into his pockets and walked over to the window near the hangar, his frustration level teetering on overload. To keep from lashing into Perryman, Chance stared into the surrounding skies, and made a promise to himself.

The FBI had all kinds of resources at their fingertips, but he had no faith that they could match the mixture of resolve and regret he had seen in Garrett Birch's eyes. If Mesa got out of this one, he would make it up to her, he swore.

He felt a hand on his shoulder. It was Rollie's. "Look, I'm sorry I couldn't get these guys to move any faster." Chance shrugged.

"Any ideas where else they might be headed?"

"Hardy can land a plane anywhere. We've all been witness to that, even Birch. That's what I would take advantage of in his shoes. They could land somewhere near the Interstate and Birch could hitchhike north. The Canadian border is only 250 miles away. Just because they headed east out of Butte doesn't mean they couldn't change directions once they were out of sight of the airport."

Mesa knew the dense foliage of the Deer Lodge National Forest below them, ponderosa pines and granite boulders in every direction. Only twenty minutes from Butte, national forest land accounted for every acre, a small part of the more than nineteen million mostly empty acres of federal land in the state.

Where Garrett Birch was going, she couldn't imagine. But she was struck by the irony of his tactics. He was taking to the wilderness just like Lowell Austin had done. He had spent a year and a half in the backcountry eluding authorities, reaching the FBI's ten most wanted list, and adding to his folk legend as a mountain man turned renegade.

"Mesa, are you buckled up?" Hardy asked. "I'm putting her down on this two track just north of the reservoir.

Mesa looked below at the opening of a relatively unobstructed flat stretch with a narrow dirt road. Hardy banked the plane to the right and began a descent before she could decide to be scared. The wheels of the plane hit the bumpy trail, and she held her breath as the plane stopped just short of where the path disappeared into the trees.

It was actually a beautiful meadow covered with dry grass waving gently in the wind. Garrett had begun giving directions to Hardy.

"Here's the letter. It's addressed to your sheriff. The other one with the stamp is for my sister. Will you mail it for me?" he asked. Hardy nodded and put the letters in the pocket of his fleece vest.

Mesa took off her seat belt to lean forward, and get the wind on her face. She tried to plead with Garrett one last time. "I don't understand this," she yelled to him. "You know the FBI will come after you. You're pulling the same stunt Austin did after he killed your father."

Garrett responded with a grumble. "I guess that's what the papers will say. You can tell them it wasn't intentional. I just can't go back to my old life. I used to think that the day I killed Lowell Austin, I would be free. I thought getting revenge would fix whatever had felt broken in me since the day my dad died. But nothing's changed, not yet anyway. Now, all that seems to feel tolerable is this. Space, lots and lots of it." And he gestured toward the mountains.

"I don't know how far I'll get with these maps," he said and then reached inside his jacket pocket and showed her a worn gold compass case, "but I have this. It belonged to my dad. I'll have a lot of time alone to think about what to do. Maybe that's what I need. Who knows, I might turn myself in someday. If I do, I'll look you up."

He pulled off his headphones, opened the door, and stepped out onto the hard pack. Hardy pulled the passenger seat forward so that Garrett could reach the backpack and coat in back. With the engine still idling, as soon as Garrett pulled the gear out and closed the door, the plane began a slow turn back the way it came.

"We have just enough fuel to get back to Butte," Hardy said. "Hopefully, we can beat the weather," he said, looking at the fast-moving clouds. "Buckle yourself back in."

They had reached the bottom of the meadow, and Hardy turned the plane again so they could take off into the wind. As they began their takeoff, Mesa looked out her window. Garrett Birch had mounted the pack on his back and was walking toward the reservoir.

If he maximized his survival skills and stuck to the backcountry, he might actually make it through Montana's five hundred mile, amorphous border into Canada. Making minimal contact in Montana's small towns, the mentally deteriorating Unabomber had lived at the edge of the national forest, avoiding authorities for decades. And Garrett wasn't crazy.

As they flew by, Garrett lifted a hand and waved, as if they were good neighbors. A ray of sunlight hit the window and a tear welled up in the corner of Mesa's eye. She told herself it was the intense brightness and that's all it was.

Chapter 23

Chance leaned on the corner of the desk in the pilot's lounge, drinking coffee and checking the sky between sips. Deep gray, storm clouds filled the sky to the south and the wind had picked up. The rest of the valley was overcast, but the clouds were high. It was nearly six o'clock.

The FBI and Solheim had returned to the police station. One of Hennessey's guys, who had taken a statement from Chance, had just left. Suddenly aware of the silence, an unfamiliar feeling of loneliness engulfed him.

Twenty minutes before, the radio had crackled, and Chance had jumped out of his skin. It was a local freight plane out of Billings calling in its approach. But for a moment, Chance thought it was Hardy.

He couldn't explain why, but he had this feeling they were coming back. As soon as the detective left, Chance had called Adrienne and told her everything. He could hear the worry in her voice, but she had reassured him. "Stay there," she said. "The radio is their first line of communication. Your voice will mean a lot." And so she had given him the go-ahead he needed to maintain the watch.

Tyler came in through the hangar. Dressed in Carhartt coveralls permeated with the smell of airplane fuel, he had been refueling one of the helicopters when the police arrived. He walked over to Chance, handing him a pair of binoculars. "Hardy may be a player most of the time, but he would never let anything happen to your sister. You know that, right?"

Chance sighed and agreed, putting the glasses to his eyes. Hardy wasn't dumb. If anything, he had a frustrated intellect that had never found an outlet. When he felt like he was being taken advantage of, that was what usually led to his recklessness. Like stealing someone's plane. "I know it. He'll be there for her when she needs him."

Then the radio began to crackle, and they both jumped a foot. "Mayday, Mayday. This is Cessna 734 Zulu Tango inbound through Gunsight."

Chance whirled the binoculars to the north end of the valley at a spot in the mountains that resembled the vee-shaped notch on a gun barrel. Coming over Gunsight was a natural way to line up with the Butte Airport, which rested smack in the middle of Summit Valley.

"Losing altitude, running on fumes." Hardy was talking fast. "Tyler, are you there? I'm in trouble. We may not make the airport. Rustle up the fire brigade."

Chance reached the radio first, grabbing and almost dropping the hand mike. "Advise on passengers."

"Just me and Mesa in good shape so far. The engine is starting to sputter. Christ, I'm gonna have to bring her down right now."

❧

Hardy had come due west across the East Ridge, trying to conserve fuel, crossing at Elk Park. The winds had begun to buffet them as they followed Interstate 15 back into Butte. Mesa had done her best to focus on the terrain ahead, trying not to panic. She'd said her ABC's backwards each time her anxiety began to overwhelm her, a trick a therapist at Damascus had taught her. She began to think she was home free when she saw the lights of the city through the pass.

They had just flown over the top of the massive open mining pit, a surreal view. From the air, the giant blue and white shovels and the haul trucks filled with molybdenum ore looked like a child's toys left in an enormous sandbox.

Then she heard Hardy radioing the airport. The sound of Chance's voice on the other end brought a sense of relief. They would soon be on the ground safe.

And then the engine began to sputter. Another cough and then, just like that, nothing but a deafening silence. For a moment, Mesa thought the plane was standing still.

Then she realized the engine had stalled. They were going to drop from the sky. She felt her lungs turn to stone. She couldn't breathe. She wanted to tear off her seat belt and run—run as far and as fast as she could. She began reaching around the cabin, her arms flailing until she realized there was no place to go.

Then she heard Hardy's voice. Maybe he had been talking all the time, but in her panic, she had heard nothing. Without the roar of the engine now, the sound of his voice pulled her in.

"I'm coming in dead-stick" she heard Hardy say. He sounded amazingly calm.

"Roger that," Chance said. "Bring her down easy." Then to Tyler, "Call the Fire Department."

Mesa could not bear to look at the ground. She closed her eyes and thought of Chance, tall and strong, coming to get her, even though his voice sounded like it was coming through a tin can a long way away. She could feel the plane banking to the right like the hawks she always watched at the cemetery when she went to visit her mother's grave.

She heard Hardy's voice again. "We're coming down on Continental," he said quietly.

If Hardy could be so calm, then maybe they wouldn't die. And so she found herself bargaining for life. She closed her eyes tighter and prayed. "Dear God, please don't let me die. If I get out of this plane alive, I swear, I swear I won't—I'll never leave Butte again."

She could see the chain-linked fence of the mine's property bordered by Continental Drive, a four-lane street that circled the east side of the city. The plane was gliding silently down, the terraced edges of the mine pit beneath.

On the north end of Continental sat a section of empty property, almost as big as a city block, opened up when houses had been demolished as part of the Anaconda Company's pit mine operation. If they could avoid traffic, which would surely try to avoid them, maybe they had a chance, even if they missed the road.

Mesa could hear Hardy muttering to himself, "Easy baby, easy." It sounded almost sexual. "Come on, come on," he coaxed. "You can do—oh...shit!"

A scream stuck in Mesa's throat, dry as trail dust, and she buried her head in her hands.

Chapter 24

When the Cessna hit the ground, they bounced so hard Mesa felt her teeth puncture her bottom lip, quickly followed by the salty warm taste of blood. She welcomed the pain, a distraction from the disaster unfolding before her. The plane bounced again and then swirled and skidded. In the awful silence, the one sound she heard clearly was Hardy pumping like a thirsty man on the foot controls.

She kept waiting for the final impact, but it never came. When the plane finally stopped and Mesa opened her eyes, they were nose up, the Belmont head frame at the intersection of Continental and Mercury Street in front of them, its decorative red lights illuminating just at that moment.

She could not tell how much time had passed. But later she would say that the length of the flight from Elk Park pass to a safe landing was her definition of eternity.

Hardy did not move for some time. She could hear sirens in the distance. "Hardy," she said. "Are you all right?"

"He said, 'There's always an easy way and a hard way.' That's all he said."

"That's all who said?" Mesa asked, wondering if Hardy was in shock.

"Austin. I was complaining about a headwind being so strong. That's what he said. That's when Garrett killed him."

❧

Tyler held the binoculars, so he had gotten the best view of Hardy's emergency landing, at least the beginning of it. Once the plane was out of sight, Chance had wrestled with what to do. He knew a stalled engine didn't kill pilots. Panic did. He wanted to stay in contact with Hardy on the radio, but the urge to get to the plane was overwhelming.

After what seemed like time without end, they heard Hardy who sounded half in shock on the radio with his gallows humor. "Cessna 734 Zulu Tango requests instructions for taxiing."

They ran to Chance's Land Rover and then did some low level flying themselves. They covered the six miles from the airport to the Belmont mine in less than ten minutes, honking their way through three traffic lights.

By the time the Land Rover pulled up, a fireman was helping Mesa out of the plane. Chance ran to her and they hugged and cried and laughed. Chance even hugged Hardy before he had to limp off with Sheriff Solheim, who had taken him into custody.

Chance and Tyler surveyed the landing site with sullied admiration. Once again, Hardy, the sketchy bastard, had succeeded where probably no one else could.

The plane had hit the road and then skidded into the adjacent, vacant field, one wing shearing off a recently planted chokecherry sapling. But Hardy had masterfully kept the plane from sliding farther into the grassland, where a heap of rusty mining equipment could have stopped them cold and hard. Instead, he managed to turn the plane back up the hill where it careened ninety degrees when the left landing gear hit a ditch. In the end, the plane had not even been damaged.

"Surviving two crash landings in one week," Tyler said. "That's some kind of record, don't you think?"

"Mesa's back in one piece," Chance said. "That's the only kind of flying I care about."

The storm broke as Chance drove Mesa to St. James. While she spent the next two hours getting the once-over in the ER, sixty-mile-an-hour winds, hammering rain, and marble-sized hail downed trees and utility lines all over Butte, and created minor flooding in the very part of Continental Drive where Hardy had landed the plane. Chance could not bring him himself to think what Hardy would have done with that plane if the storm had hit an hour earlier.

Other than her swollen lip, and bruises on her shoulder and across her chest from the seat belt, Mesa was unharmed. Chance had taken her home to Nan, where he stayed with her well into the evening.

Adrienne had warned him to watch for signs of shock. Nan had taken all the excitement with relative calm, making a pot of tea with plenty of milk and sugar and insisting that Mesa drink several cups.

Despite Nana's faith in the recuperative powers of milky tea, Chance spiked the last cup with brandy. Mesa had gone to bed and slept, without so much as a whimper, let alone a nightmare, until well past the departure time for her flight to Portland on Friday morning.

Once she was fully awake, she had called Derek. Prepared for a barrage of questions, he was in a meeting with the publisher and could not be interrupted. She left a rambling message on his voice mail. He would be upset, but she knew *Pacifica* would have no trouble finding other candidates.

Afterward she called Irita, who had already gotten the scoop the night before from Chance. "He damn well knew better than to let me hear it from anybody else," she said, then paused for a minute and said in a tentative voice, "Does this mean you're taking your first, official sick day?"

Mesa smiled and winced as her sore lip cracked. "I guess so. And Irita, about the Portland job," Mesa said. "I deep-sixed that whole plan, okay?"

"Whatever you say, boss" Irita said. "Guess I better dust off Erin's story and your photo for the editorial page this week."

"Right. And that Portland conversation?" Mesa said. "We never had it, so not a word, to Chance or my grandmother, ever, okay?"

"I'm going to my grave with it," Irita said. "You take 'er easy and I'll see you on Monday."

This time Mesa had the feeling Irita would keep her word.

But instead of going into the office on Monday, Mesa paid Kathy DiNunzio another visit. She wanted to hand-deliver Garrett's letter, which Hardy had given her just before he had been taken into police custody.

Kathy opened the letter, and Mesa turned to go. But Kathy, her eyes filled with tears, asked her to stay. Mesa made coffee, and they spent most of the morning talking about Garrett and Mesa's last conversation.

In the letter, Garrett wrote that he didn't want his sister to think that he blamed her in any way for bringing Lowell Austin to Butte. He knew they both had their reasons for doing what they had done, even though neither might ever understand. The important thing was that she know he still loved her, and that he promised she and the kids would hear from him again one day.

Mesa had begun writing a story about Austin and Donovan Birch. She had spent most of Friday afternoon reading the file of faded news clippings Kathy had given her. It was through one of them that Mesa began to understand what Hardy had said.

According to the defendant's testimony, Donovan Birch had threatened Austin, saying "There's an easy way and a hard way, makes no difference to me." The warden was spoiling for a fight, Austin claimed.

When a reporter interviewed Mrs. Birch about that testimony, she maintained that in her fifteen years of marriage, she had never heard her husband use such a phrase. Mesa concluded that the expression had been one of Lowell's instead. Those indifferent words repeated by Austin, and remembered over a lifetime of loss had triggered Garrett's deadly reckoning.

Mesa finished her story by midnight. "A Legacy of Revenge" would run as her first feature in the *Mining City Messenger*. She thought about sending a copy to Derek to discuss when he was ready to speak to her again.

That weekend, Butte awakened to snow on the East Ridge. The first snowfall always generated an air of anticipation, especially when it came early which would mean plenty of game headed to lower altitude just in time for hunting season. The valley saw a flake or two, but the weather report had predicted six to ten inches at higher elevations for the next few days.

Each morning when Mesa walked to work, she would glance toward the mountains and think about Garrett Birch. The search for him was more than a week old, but the snow would slow it down. She had no way of knowing if his survival instincts were as good in the mountains as they had been in Afghanistan. In the spring, shed hunters looking for antlers often came across human remains. She could only hope this would not be how Garrett would end up.

She and Chance had gone together to see Hardy, who was now a guest in the Silver Bow county jail awaiting extradition to Utah. He would face grand larceny charges for the theft of the Cessna. Sheriff Solheim had conferred with Layton James. If Hardy agreed to plead guilty and make restitution, he had a chance to be paroled without serving any time, but that would mean he would have to stay in Utah.

Hardy had changed, that was certain. Mesa couldn't be sure exactly what had done it—seeing what had happened to Garrett Birch, or surviving another plane crash. Either way, Hardy seemed older and wiser.

On Sunday morning, Nana went to church with Philip Northey. Mesa begged off. Instead, she drove out to Mount Moriah cemetery, which had once been the edge of town but now rested quietly between uptown and the flat.

For some time, she sat on the concrete curbing around the Ducharme family plot where her mother and her grandfather were buried. She watched the black and white magpies hopping from gravestone to gravestone, and a Red-tailed Hawk circling above.

The cloudless, cobalt skies were the ideal advertisement for Big Sky country. Even though it was barely sixty degrees, the bright sunshine warmed Mesa. The wind was gusting, and she removed several pinecones that had fallen onto the burial plot. Finally, she began walking back to the car. It was then she saw Chance cycling toward her up the cemetery path, his red and white cycling shirt dazzling in the sunlight.

When he reached her, he took off his helmet and wiped the sweat from his brow. "Adrienne saw the Blazer parked outside the cemetery gate and wondered if maybe you were here." He got off his bike and walked alongside her. "I think we should talk about the *Messenger*."

"Is this where you tell me you're pulling out of the newspaper business altogether?" Mesa said, teasing him.

"Nothing like that," he said, his voice serious. "Just the opposite. I know you coming back to Butte was mostly because of the pressure I put on you. That was my mistake, and a big one. If you want to go back to your old job, I'll understand. I'll work with Irita and Nan and we'll get along. It won't be the same without you, but it will have to be good enough."

He paused a minute and toyed with the buckle on his helmet. She could see he felt awkward, but she said nothing.

"Mesa, when I saw you fly off in that plane the other day, not knowing what would happen, I promised myself that if you made it back, I'd make it up to you. That's what I'm trying to do."

They had turned at the cemetery office, and Mesa could see Adrienne leaning on her bike against the wrought-iron entrance gate. "What about your budding restoration business that Irita keeps telling me about?"

"It will just have to bloom a little later, that's all." He made this last declaration with an upbeat tone.

Mesa smiled and picked up her pace. "You know, Chance, that plane ride had an impact on me too. A lot of people crossed my mind after that engine died—people who really matter to me, the promises we've made, what's really important. I would never want us to drift apart like Kathy and Garrett did."

Adrienne had spotted them now and was putting her helmet back on. Mesa lifted both hands and gave an enthusiastic wave. "I said I'd come back and help, and I mean to keep my word." She put her arm through his, and gave it a quick squeeze. "You may come to regret it, but I'm here to stay."

Acknowledgements

It may not take a village to write a book but it feels like it takes a similar kind of support to see one to publication. The first person to give me the confidence to call myself a writer was Liz Trupin-Pulli, my one time agent who I met at the still fabulous Antioch Writers' Workshop. She invested time and effort in me and did her best to place my work in an increasingly turbulent publishing world. Without her encouragement, I would not have continued to write.

Likewise I must acknowledge my writerly buddies coast to coast (women, you know who you are). You read drafts and offered critiques, cheerleaded, and commiserated, and never once did any of you shake your head or say, "Give it up." Many of you still struggle to write, when so often keeping body and soul together is a full time endeavor. I honor the creative spirit in each of you as it certainly inspires me.

In Butte, Sheriff John Walsh; Coroner Lee LeBreche; and Butte Weekly Publisher, Norlene Holt, provided me with factual information and helped 'keep it real.' Also, thanks to pilots Hugh Dresser and David Daughtery who generously flew me around the twenty plus mountain ranges of Southwestern Montana and never snapped at me once when I asked questions like, "If you had to bring this plane down right now, where would you put it?"

ABOUT THE AUTHOR

A transplant from Kentucky (Derby Town, USA), Marian began visiting the west on camping and skiing vacations where she found the wide-open spaces a respite from her harried career as a college administrator. Once her daughter was grown, Marian and her husband finally made the big move to Montana. Now, she wakes up each morning to meditate on a view of the mountainside, and spends her days immersed in the writerly life, regularly reminding herself that while writing might be for sissies, getting published is not. Trout fishing on the Big Hole River is her favorite place to be.

Visit with the author on Facebook at Mining City Mysteries.

You can also read her blog at www.miningcitymysteries.com.